A DOLLY MYSTERY

DOROTHY DUNNETT

Rum Affair

Farrago

This edition published in 2023 by Farrago,
an imprint of Duckworth Books Ltd
1 Golden Court, Richmond, TW9 1EU, United Kingdom

www.farragobooks.com

First published in the UK by Cassell & Co. Ltd in 1968 as *Dolly and the
Singing Bird*; and in the US by Houghton Mifflin as *The Photographic Soprano*

Print ISBN: 9781788424110
eISBN: 9781788424127

Cover design and illustration by Nathan Burton

Have you read them all?

Treat yourself again to the first Dolly novels –

Tropical Issue
Make-up artist Rita Geddes travels to Madeira in search of who killed her mentor Kim-Jim, and needs all her nerve to succeed.

Rum Affair
Tina Rossi, a famous coloratura soprano, has come to Edinburgh to sing – but finds a dead body, and her lover Kenneth gone missing.

Ibiza Surprise
When Sarah Cassells, recently trained as a chef, hears of her father's violent death on Ibiza, she refuses to believe it's suicide.

Turn to the end of this book for a full list of the series, plus – on the last page – the chance to receive **further background material**.

1

Men with bifocal glasses: I spit.

I have surprised you, no doubt. I have a name for hard work and magnificent singing; and very little for temperament. But now, all that is changed – since Johnson came into my life.

That August, I had two concerts to give at the Edinburgh Festival – you may have heard me. I had been singing in Holland and Germany and was travelling incognito: my manager Michael's idea.

So in London I had no welcome at the airport, no bouquet, no private lounge, no free champagne and coffee and no small English change for the telephone. Also Michael's idea: I found I was travelling under his name: Mrs Twiss.

While he is a brilliant manager and répétiteur, sometimes Michael can bounce back disturbing echoes of the Tottenham Court Road. I mentioned on the plane that I felt certain reservations towards the name Twiss as a chic incognito. I removed my dark glasses. The air hostess went pink and hung up my Balenciaga. Five people asked for my autograph. Michael would have gone pink also, except that he was airsick, as ever. We arrived in Edinburgh, not a second too soon.

There, to begin with, all was perfectly normal. I was met by the director of the Festival with wired roses and heather; there were more flowers at my hotel and eighteen invitations, as well as my maid, my secretary and my solicitor with some papers concerning a lawsuit for me to read over and sign. I rehearsed, I rested, I had my hair set with my platinum hairpiece and was interviewed by the press.

Michael had told them what to ask. They asked some other irrelevant questions. They asked if I intended never to marry. They asked if it was true that I could sing G sharp in alt.

I replied that should the right man come along, I should certainly give up my singing for love. I said that if someone would recite the whole of 'Tam o' Shanter', I should sing G sharp in alt.

Someone did, and so did I, fortunately right in the centre: the press conference ended with tremendous rapport and the publicity footage in the evening paper pleased even Michael my manager. Also the pictures were quite delightful. I am, after all, the only really photogenic coloratura soprano alive. My only problem, just about then, was in staying alive.

The first concert went well. Thalberg, who had come from Munich to conduct for me, was sober both at rehearsal and performance, and was so far disturbed by my following that he took his teeth out before coming on stage and required to be helped from the podium. But there was still no doubt who received the larger ovation. Wearing the Bonwit Teller dress I cannot sit down in, I was recalled eleven times to the platform, while the good folk of Edinburgh drummed their Hush Puppies on the concert hall floor.

I find Edinburgh braces the throat. I had never sung Donna Elvira better, with the registers perfectly blended since that week's work with Michael at Düsseldorf. In the artists' dressing room Thalberg kissed my hand, first replacing his teeth. He then chaffingly used an insulting expression and I made a fitting reply. It is a cut-throat business, like any other. He then left to join his friend in the North British station hotel; and I left, to keep an assignation with a clean-living lover called Kenneth.

I am not, of course, promiscuous. With the work I have to do, this would be impossible. Occasionally, between touring and filming and recording, one meets a partner of like mind, but only occasionally. It is hard to pick out from the proposals and the mere propositions the men who like Tina Rossi for what she is, and not for what she can earn.

Kenneth Holmes and I had met the previous year in Nevada, where Michael and I had flown for a rest during a long and strenuous American tour. Kenneth was the hearty, ball-playing kind, with style, good looks and brashness ridiculous in a highly trained engineer. He was working in the States under an exchange scheme, and had been given an expensive laboratory, which he had to himself.

I was resting. I wished peace, relaxation, security; and he gave me all these. Afterwards, he continued to send me notes and small gifts. Then he left for London, and later for a place called Rum in Scotland, I heard.

From Talloires, which is our official base, Michael makes up my diary months and years in advance. But it was Christmas this year when he negotiated, at my request, two appearances for me at Edinburgh, to be followed by ten days of rest. And in my handbag now, as I changed in my hotel and shook off Michael Twiss and my maid and slipped out of a side door in the darkness, was a note saying simply, *22B Rose Street tonight love love love Kenneth*.

Rose Street is a small lane of pubs and warehouses and boutiques and minor mews openings which lies behind the main street of Edinburgh. It took me five minutes to reach it, slipping head down past the knots of lingering revellers and the suggestive voices in doorways. In dark glasses, headscarf and raincoat, I was surely unrecognisable.

Silly, of course. You would expect this of a fifteen-year-old, stealing out of the dormitory; not of Tina Rossi the Polish-Italian nightingale. But I could not do, airily, what Thalberg does. I would not subject my career to the risk.

I was hurrying, the last little bit. I remembered so well the set of his shoulders and collarbone, his fingernails, and the rough brown hair his Bronx barber reduced to a plush. I found the entrance to No. 22 and ran upstairs, and across a small wooden bridge to a conversion with a bay tree on either of its steps and a door painted yellow – 22B. The flat of a school friend, Kenneth once said. The only place for a rendezvous if you want peace and privacy...

I took out the key which came along with the note, and opened the non-drip primrose door.

It was warm inside, with a smell of sweet peas and pipe smoke and hot soup which was exactly Kenneth's thoughtful but not extravagant identity on a sharp August night. The flat was small, over-lit and vividly decorated, in the kind of thing popular about ten years ago, say in Kensington. I walked slowly past the green Morris wallpaper and looked at the six satin steel doorknobs, and called softly, 'Kenneth!'

No reply.

'Kenneth? Where are you?'

Still no answer. Sleeping, probably. I began opening doors.

A bedroom, untenanted. Another bedroom, with towels, soap and a wardrobe full of clothes, none of which I recognized as Kenneth's, although the bedcover was rumpled as if someone had packed or unpacked there, and the pipe smoke was very strong. Puzzled, I wandered on.

A bathroom, with the basin wet and still warm, and a grubby towel hanging. A kitchen, minuscule, with an electric cooker bearing a panful of canned soup. The can, empty, and a can-opener. The cooker was switched off, although the soup was still warm. What then was the buzzing sound? I located it; a refrigerator with the door not quite closed. Inside were two raw steaks in paper, a packet of chips and a bottle of champagne, barely chilled. I shut the door guiltily, and moved on.

The last door led into the sitting-room. The chairs were all ebonised and upholstered in burlap and lurex, and the pot-plants could have done with a watering. In the hearth, a wood and coal fire burned brightly yellow and red, although coal had spilled on the swept tiles and recently smoked itself dead. Before the fire on a small table was a tray set for two, with champagne glasses standing ready. The chairs on either side of the table were empty. The room was empty. Kenneth was not there.

I did not at first quite believe it. The flat felt tenanted. The wood of a chair cracked. Coal shifted, distantly, in the grate. I went back, quickly, through all the rooms I had already visited, and opened a cupboard or two in addition. I called, then; and even unlatched the yellow front door and studied the street. There was a couple kissing in one of the doorways, and a man lighting a cigarette on the kerb glanced up momentarily, but of Kenneth there was no sign at all. I shut the door and came slowly back.

I considered. Kenneth had, perhaps, not yet arrived. Or, he'd gone out for some cigarettes. Or a friend had called and whisked him off for a drink. Or the owner of the flat had returned. The possible answers were many.

In the bathroom, the grubby towel fell off the rail with a slither, and I jumped, like a fool. Then I pulled off my raincoat and headscarf and, letting them drop on the floor, I sat down in front of that splendid fire and applied some common sense to the problem.

It was then that I noticed the little card on the mantelpiece. It was quite an ordinary card, a pasteboard die-stamped visiting card, with *Dr Kenneth Holmes* and his London address printed on it. I got up and took it down and turned the thing over. On the back, in Kenneth's characteristic big writing, were three solitary words. *Darling, I'm sorry.*

Darling, I was sorry too; and I ripped his goddamned pasteboard in pieces to prove it. But in a little while, when I recovered my temper, I also came to my senses. The deliberate farewell without explanation was not in Kenneth Holmes's nature. Kenneth is, I suppose, the most painfully honest individual I have ever encountered. The argument we had before he would seduce me I shall never forget.

So he left suddenly. So he did not wish to compromise me. At the same time, nothing would give Kenneth more agony than the thought of my arriving tonight and finding him gone, with such a cursory message. Surely, somewhere, if I looked, I would find a clue to his sudden departure? Or another message, perhaps, somewhere else in the flat? I got up, took a deep breath, and began systematically to look.

Nerves are not one of my weaknesses, but I did not enjoy that search. Muffled by plastic foam underlay, my footsteps made no sound. Only, sometimes, in a room I had just passed, a floorboard would creak, or a door swing in some draught. For all its modern furnishing, the house was quite old. But although I did not like it, I searched that flat thoroughly, and I had my hand on the last door, on the wardrobe door in the hall, when the doorbell at my ear suddenly rang.

It was after midnight. In the empty flat, where all the lights still burned in the tenantless rooms, and the fire smouldered low, the noise shrilled with alarm. After a moment's silence, it rang again, and went on insistently ringing. At the same moment, under my hand, the door of the hall wardrobe moved of its own accord, pushing against my hand, my arm, my shoulder and finally falling wide open, while from its depths something dark and heavy and silent suddenly moved.

And I stood there and just watched it topple towards me: the person of a slow, cold-eyed, powerful man who followed me on to the carpet, arms flailing, his brute weight flattening even my trained, resilient lungs.

I fell with his hair brushing my face, and the scrape of his unshaven chin on my cheek; and anger swallowed my fright.

I shoved hard. I held him off and drew breath to shout to the men who stood on the far side of that yellow front door, whose voices I could hear and under whose hand the bell was ringing, ringing above us both still.

I remember all that. And I remember the moment when I looked at my own clenched hand holding off his, and realized that his fingers were limp, his wrist cold, his limbs rubber. When I realized that my cold-eyed attacker was dead.

He lay on the carpet staring upwards from those pale open eyes while the doorbell rang and rang, and the round, black hole in his shirt showed how he had died. In Kenneth's flat, from which Kenneth had fled. Outside the door, a voice said, distantly, 'I don't like the look of it, sir, if the lady's in there alone.' And then, raising itself, it said, 'Hallo! Will you kindly open up in there? It's a matter of urgency. This is a police officer speaking.'

Instinct is a marvellous thing, I dare say; but I prefer to use my good sense. You, perhaps, with a strange man lying dead at your feet would have welcomed the police with an exhibition of nervous relief. I, on the other hand, kept my head.

I won't pretend I had recovered. But I could isolate the two essentials. If I were to pursue the course I set myself, the name of Tina Rossi must not be involved in either scandal or killing. And Kenneth Holmes must, if possible, be protected from persecution and scandal as well. So I stood over the dead man, and drew a long steadying breath and shouted at half pitch, 'Hallo! I'm sorry, I must have dropped off to sleep. Will you wait a little while, please?'

And while the same voice on the other side of the door was saying, relieved, 'Yes, of course, madam. Sorry to disturb you. Take your time,' I had the body gripped by one arm and a leg and was dragging it back to the wardrobe. I locked the door and dropped the key in my bag.

Then I put my dark glasses on, patted my hair, took one last look at the cupboard and, marching to the yellow front door, jerked it ajar. 'Sorry to keep you waiting so long,' I remarked.

There were three men on that doorstep between the two bay trees, and two of them, thank God, were genuine policemen. Of the third I had a first impression only of a pair of bifocal glasses, their half moons bright in the light, and a smile of boundless vacuity. The senior officer said, 'I hope you'll excuse us troubling you, but it's a matter of robbery with violence, and we're making a door to door inquiry. Would you mind if we entered?'

They came in, stumping past the hall wardrobe and into the sitting-room. The fire was almost out, and in front of it, the table with the two empty champagne glasses made one think of underfinanced operetta. I said, 'Please sit down. Just how can I help you?' Dear God, dear God who looks after coloratura sopranos, they hadn't recognized me. I could be Miss Smith from Blackheath, visiting my brother-in-law. I listened hard, while the sergeant intoned.

It was simple enough. Three flats in the nearby square had been broken into this evening, and Mr Bifocals, who rented one of them, had disturbed the thief and given chase, helped by the law. The fugitive had disappeared into Rose Street and could have entered two or three possible houses. This flat was one. Had I seen anyone, asked the police sergeant briskly. And would I object if they had a wee look, in case someone had come in unbeknownst? I was not, he inquired bluffly, the tenant? He was told that a Mr Chigwell normally lived here, although he sometimes lent it to friends… He was tactful in the extreme.

I had been seen to enter, obviously, by the neighbours. Perhaps Kenneth had even been seen to depart. The question was, when had he left? Before or after the beastly figure in the wardrobe had arrived? It occurred to me that, unshaven as he was, the man who lay bundled behind that locked door hadn't looked like a layabout.

Could the thief have committed the murder, in a panic, then shoved the dead man in the wardrobe and left? But no one had left. The sergeant was saying so, comfortably. 'It seems pretty clear from the inquiries we've made, that if the chap came into one of these houses, he's still there. These front door locks would present no problem to him. But you've heard nothing, Miss?'

I shook my head.

'And you're alone in the flat? Might I ask when you came?'

I told him. He knew, obviously, already. A street of busybodies.

'And I'm told that the gentleman Mr Chigwell sometimes lends the flat to, left a little before that?'

There was a question in the voice. The champagne glasses, of course. 'He's my brother-in-law,' I said. 'We were to meet here for a drink, but I found a note saying he'd been called out. I waited a bit in case he came back.'

I held my breath but he didn't pursue that. He was only concerned with the man he was chasing, after all. I gave him the name and Edinburgh hotel address of a fictitious Miss Smith of Blackheath and then stood like a dummy while he shut up his notebook and announced that he was now going to search the flat.

'But there's no one in it,' I said. 'I would have heard them. I'm absolutely sure.'

'Well now,' said the sergeant. He had a bass-baritone voice of a kind I particularly dislike. 'You were asleep for a bit, didn't you say? And he'd make much less noise than a doorbell. You can be quite sure of that.'

'It won't take long,' said the other policeman brightly. He was a tenor. 'And you'll feel a lot safer, I guarantee, afterwards.'

I could hear my voice rise a little. 'But I'm not staying here anyway. I meant to leave long before this.' I followed the sergeant into a bedroom. 'Look, do you need me any more now? It's late. I'd like to go off.' They had moved into the kitchen.

Someone took me by the arm and I jumped. A pair of bifocal glasses, topped by two black eyebrows, shone into my face. 'They'll only look under a few beds and then go off,' said my third visitor kindly. 'Routine, you know. Why not let me make you a cup of tea while they do it, and then I'll find you a taxi?' And, while I drew breath to answer, he had the effrontery to press my hand. The bifocals flashed.

'You dropped this, Madame Tina,' he murmured. And closed my fingers, gently, over the pieces of Kenneth Holmes's card.

2

My mind, I think, was perfectly blank while I sat there in front of the almost-dead fire staring at the champagne glasses and listening to the hiss of Bifocals filling the kettle in Mr Chigwell's neat kitchen, and the soft sounds of the policemen moving all through the flat. Bedroom. Bedroom. Bathroom. Now there was only the hall. In the kitchen, I heard the rattle of cups. Since he had given me Kenneth's torn-up card Bifocals had spoken to neither policeman: why? He knew I was Tina Rossi, it seemed. It was to be expected. I am famous. He now knew, for the fragments were all too easy to read, with whom I had an assignation for tonight. Still, he showed no haste to expose me.

I didn't know whether my money or my virtue was in jeopardy, and I didn't, immediately, care. I could deal with bifocal gentlemen if I must. I couldn't deal with the law.

And the law were now in the hall. Every nerve in my body heard that wardrobe door rattle and pause.

'Miss Smith!' It was the sergeant. 'D'you know why this door is locked?'

I got up and went through. The hall wardrobe stood firmly locked as I had left it, the key in my bag. 'No. I haven't locked it,' I lied. 'Mr Chigwell must keep it shut.'

The sergeant rattled the door again. 'It's a sort of cloakroom, isn't it? Funny place to keep locked.'

'Keeps his golf clubs in it, I expect,' advised a mild voice from the kitchen. The bifocals appeared, pot of tea nursed in its hands, and leaned against one of the doorposts. 'Amazing who'll walk off with a golf club when you lend your flat to a pal. It's like books. Some chaps have no conscience.'

The policeman rattled the handle again. 'All the same, it's a roomy place: just the spot a fellow would hide in.'

'It is, of course.' Bifocals, laying down the teapot, advanced and peered at the lock. The two policemen peered at the lock. I could not look. Almost anything now was going to give it away. A trickle of blood on the carpet: a blow on the door that would dislodge the body inside... The smell of blood, even... Except that there had been almost no blood. The sergeant said, 'It'd be an easy lock to force, that,' and fetched a piece of wire out of one pocket. The telephone rang.

It rang insistently, as irritating in its way as the doorbell had been, and as incongruously welcome. It rang steadily until the sergeant, listening, suddenly said, 'That might be for me, Miss,' and got to his feet just as I fled through to the sitting-room with another thought in mind: Kenneth. It might be Kenneth, with God knew what story to tell, and the police listening, here in the flat. I got to it first, and said, 'Hallo?'

It wasn't Kenneth. It was a policeman, to say that they thought they had apprehended the thief. In two minutes, before my heart had stopped thudding, the two policemen were trading courteous farewells and admonitions. Bifocals, returned to nursing the teapot, inquired whether I should find it offensive if he remained to share a small cup of tea, assuming the law would allow him to identify the miscreant later.

The law gave him the necessary dispensation, and so did I. The door shut behind the two departing police officers and in five minutes Bifocals and I were sitting like china cats, one on each side of a rebuilt and roaring fire, drinking strong Indian tea, a pursuit that may seem to possess no particular appeal unless you have been through what I had been through in the last hour and a half. I studied my undesired champion.

He was difficult to place. Not, my God, a man about town, with that green knitted pullover and those socks and the pipe sticking out of one pocket. But a man who went to a really good barber about three weeks less often than he should, and who could afford a rented flat in the Square, and the kind of cash and camera and cufflinks a thief thought worth having. A member of the professions, perhaps: but which among these would rent a flat in Edinburgh in August in solitary state? A university don, perhaps, who took a pride in following the European festivals? A medical man? Some inquisitive, music-loving rector from a Surrey vicarage, with more money than sense? He was older than I was, but not old. The agile eyebrows were black, and the shining puff of jet-black hair showed no grey as yet. He might as well have had no eyes or mouth, so dominating were the spectacles. 'Thirty-eight,' he remarked.

I jumped.

'Painter. London. On holiday. Got your records. Who's in the cupboard? Boyfriend? Body?'

I had to trust him. I hadn't any choice. 'Body,' I said.

Johnson, his name was. It didn't ring any bells: not then. He listened without comment to my whole story, and seemed to find nothing anti-social in my desire not to be found by the tabloids alone in a love-nest with a corpse. 'No, no,' he said. 'Another cup...? It could ruin your winter programme. No, no. An anonymous phone call to the police once you are well out of town. That will do it, if the interests of justice are concerning you. Dr Holmes is, you believe, the murderer?'

I couldn't afford to snap, but I came rather near it. 'Dr Holmes, I am quite certain, is not the murderer. On the contrary. He is a thoroughly responsible Government engineer of some repute.'

'Oh. And who then was the corpse?'

'I don't know.'

'And if my burglar didn't kill him and neither did your Dr Holmes, who was the murderer? Or did he kill himself, maybe?'

I stood up. 'I hadn't thought of that. He could have; he was shot in the chest. If he did, there'd be a gun in the cupboard.' I opened my bag and stopped, key in hand. 'But why on earth kill himself in a wardrobe?'

'Tidy habits,' said Johnson. 'Come on. Show me your body.'

He was a remarkably *casual* little man. Together, we went into the hall. I gave him the key. Bifocals flashing, he unlocked and swung open the hall wardrobe door.

It was empty.

I remember, on stage, going to a cupboard where there should have been a prop bottle, and the shelves were all bare. There was the same feeling of cues abysmally missed, of interfering hands and unreliable minds. I said, 'But he was lying there. All folded up, on the floor. I just flung him in anyhow and jammed the door shut and locked it. The key's never been out of my bag.'

'Well, see for yourself,' said Johnson. 'Clubs, bats, brollies and rows of tatty old coats. Wait a bit. I saw a torch in the kitchen. Maybe he rolled when the bobbies were bashing the panel.' And he went off, chirpily. I don't think he ever believed in that corpse.

But I did. I had had it fall on me. And believe me, it was well and truly dead. I looked closer into the cupboard.

It was very dark. The clothes rail with its dozens of hangers ran across the cupboard from left to right, and the recesses of the wardrobe behind were stuffed with sporting gear and a variety of shoes. There was a pair of shoes, too, near at hand, which seemed to have the socks still crumpled inside them.

Then I realized that they had not only socks but feet and legs in them, and trousers above. Swaying gently from his hanger above me, his stiffening shoulders square in a coat, hung the cold, staring face of my dead man, the bullet-hole black in his chest.

I shrieked, then; and from among the coats something jumped out and struck me a hard blow on the neck that sent me flying down to the carpet. But the man who fell stumbling over me this time, kicked free, darted over the hall, and, wrenching open the yellow front door, fled out into the dark silent street was not a corpse. It was a little, spare man in a jersey and slacks with big, powerful hands and a single gold tooth that flashed as he drew in his breath. The person whom I had locked in with his victim before he could dispose of the corpse. The murderer, who had been in the flat with me all evening, of course.

'What happened?' said Johnson, standing over me. He peered out of the open door, then closed it and came back. I explained. 'Well, at least we've now got a corpse,' Johnson said. 'I wonder where Chigwell went for his hangers. All the hooks come out of mine.'

'You must ask him,' I said.

Johnson just stood there, studying the corpse without even helping me up. 'Not in this world,' he said, cheerfully. 'I've just found a photograph in the bedroom. That's Chigwell: your corpse on the hanger. He's the chap who lent Holmes the flat.'

We had another cup of tea, but it had got rather stewed, and it was Johnson who finally thought of the champagne. 'Holmes won't mind, will he?' he asked. 'After all, it's his reputation we're protecting.'

I gazed at him steadily. My dress, chosen for Kenneth, was plain but good: three layers of chiffon in coffee and white, slit from neck to waist at the back. While he was in the kitchen I had shaken out my hair, which was coming down anyway, and repowdered my nose and done a small thing or two. I also put back the yellow diamond I had slipped off when the policeman arrived. Even tired and untidy I am beautiful; but I like to make the effort, as well.

'You really mean you won't report all this as you should? It could mean trouble,' I said.

The cork had popped a moment before, but he didn't seem to notice, and the foam ran all down his hand before he got some liquid into the glasses. 'You know, it takes a bit of believing that you sing as well as all this,' he said. 'Cheers. No, I don't mind. Someone'll notice, if it's only the charwoman, and they'll get on your little man's track; but I'll tip them off by telephone, to make sure... You're certain there *was* a little man?' And as I frowned: 'All right. I'm sure hallucinations are not in your field. In any case' – he rose from mopping up champers – 'you said your friend Holmes was an engineer?'

I nodded.

'Queer things happen to engineers,' said Johnson. 'For example, why should this table be bugged?'

'*What?*'

'This table,' said Johnson mildly. 'It's got a microphone under it. I wonder if that's why your friend left so suddenly? Saw it and knew he was under surveillance?'

I bent down. There was something wired under the table, but someone had found it before us. The wiring was broken, thank heaven. None of Johnson's conversation or mine would be on record.

'Did you know Chigwell had planned to be in the flat?' Johnson said.

'No.' Neither had Kenneth. Chigwell's presence must have been quite unexpected. Chigwell had been going to move out. But Kenneth left first. And before Chigwell could leave, he was murdered.

'I wonder...' said Johnson, his second glass in his hand.

'I wonder...' said I, at exactly the same moment. 'I wonder if they thought Chigwell was Kenneth? But why should anyone want to kill Kenneth?'

'Dunno,' said Johnson. He was, I saw, decidedly squiffed. 'Engineers. Scientists. Iron Curtain after them every day.'

I lifted my third glass. 'I suppose so.' I was bored with the topic. And Johnson was the type who would hog your last bottle. I was watching him hard.

To be candid, my recollection of the following half-hour is not perfectly clear.

At three in the morning, having finished the champagne, we put out the lights, and leaving Mr Chigwell hanging in his wardrobe, drew the yellow front door gently behind us. We kissed, Johnson and I, at the side door of my hotel, because it seemed the polite thing to do, and I slipped up to my room while his bifocals were still all steamed over.

I promised him, as I remember, my next album of records. Ah, silly, innocent youth.

Next day there were more photographs, an interview for a Sunday magazine, lunch with a countess, a tour of the Castle, and a rehearsal for the evening programme with Thalberg, who had had a tiff with his secretary and kept taking the tempo too fast.

There was nothing in the morning paper about a dead man in a wardrobe in Rose Street; and nothing in the evening paper either. I gave away the chiffon dress, wore a dressed-up piece from my wig box, and tried, without success, Kenneth's London telephone number.

There was another rehearsal, this time at the proper tempo: Michael fixed this. Musicians respected Michael for his Andrew

Sinclair trousers and for an instinct for music that amounted almost to genius: his accent almost never slipped now. In between, I discovered from the AA that Rum is a small island off the Scottish west coast which can be reached by a hired boat from Mallaig, and that it takes practically all day to reach Mallaig from Edinburgh.

I waited, and just before the evening performance, after drinks with the Festival Committee, I rang up the Scottish Nature Conservancy laboratories on Rum. Dr Holmes was there, but was not receiving calls on the phone.

That was my biggest moment of relief. My fear had been that, afraid of involving me, or of some unknown persecutor, Kenneth might have vanished: taken himself somewhere out of my reach. Rum was bad enough, heaven knew; and how I should reach him there without the whole communications network being aware of it, I didn't yet know. But recalling that corpse hanging alone in a wardrobe in Kenneth's borrowed flatlet in Rose Street, I was going to have a bloody good try.

The matter concerned me, but did not affect my singing, although Michael said I overlooked one of his precious *rallentandos* in the *Alcina*. I told Michael, as we prepared to go on to the Lord Provost's supper party, that he would have to cancel this year's *Messiah*. I simply couldn't face all that fuss over the *recitativi secchi* again. He talked soothingly and helped Janine to put my hair properly up. Oh, Michael was useful. One could not deny that.

One cannot eat much, of course, before a performance, and when we arrived at the supper party it was after eleven and I was therefore very hungry. I saw however as the introductions were made that the cold buffet appeared delicious, set among a perfect bower of flowers. These looked charming even after the City Parks and Gardens Department had removed the gladioli, which give me hay fever. I started, after the first flush of bailies, with a plate of cold salmon. I am fortunate in that I need rarely diet. That night, for example, I was wearing white broadtail, with a clip and earrings in baguette diamonds made for me by a little man in Stockholm who works for N.K. Very few singers can wear tailored fur. By nineteen or twenty the expanding voice has stretched the rib cage, the diaphragm, the muscles of neck and shoulders and bosoms. There is an overhang: an undertow. Except with Tina Rossi.

I finished the cold salmon. With the turkey came a solo violinist, a producer, two critics, a broadcaster, an actress and a few of the Corps Diplomatique.

Among these were old acquaintances: an ambassador and his wife up from London to support their small but well-meaning opera company. She was wearing, no doubt for the first time in Edinburgh, a dress photographed in May when she attended the London Polio Ball. A mistake.

With the Ambassador was Johnson. I could not be deceived. The black hair, the caterpillar eyebrows, the damned housefly bifocals. He had even the same knitted green pullover on. 'May I introduce,' said the Ambassador, 'an old family friend, Mr Johnson? Johnson, this is…'

'She's *very* like someone I spent last night with,' said Johnson, with thought. 'Name of Smith.'

The Ambassador sighed. 'Now is not the time to play jokes. Johnson, it is not everybody I introduce to Tina Rossi, and why do you have to be dressed in this non-trendy suit? It is not, for example, cold.' His English was very good.

'I'm the Higgins type,' Johnson said. He hitched a trouser leg up. 'Look, too. Folksy socks.'

'You are impossible,' said the Ambassador. 'Madame Rossi, I apologize for my friend. I will leave him to pursue these eccentricities on his own. Should he become intolerable do not hesitate to abandon him entirely.' Bowing, he and his wife left us together.

'Thought you'd be here,' said Johnson. He hauled out his pipe, looked round at all the black and white ties, and put it regretfully back. 'Found your Kenneth Holmes yet?'

'No,' I said. I was feeling regretful too. I might have known that in cash or kind I should have to pay sometime for last night's assistance.

'Wouldn't tell me if you had, anyway,' said Johnson. 'But if I were you, I'd get on to him pretty damned quick and tell him that he left you alone in the flat with the police and a dead man last night, and if anyone traces you, there's going to be a lot of explanations necessary from someone some time soon. Even if he didn't kill him.'

'I told you he didn't. You saw the killer yourself.'

'No, I didn't. Heard you call out, that's all. But even if your Kenneth didn't murder his flat-owning pal Chigwell, he might suspect who did, and why. I phoned the police, by the way. Are you doing anything tonight?'

Just like that. *I phoned the police.* I kept my voice even. 'What did you say?'

'Are you doing anything tonight?'

'No, damn it. What did you say to—' I broke off. The Ambassador had returned, smiling. He put a manicured hand on Johnson's undistinguished shoulder.

'Ah, I knew it. He is persuading you to go to the jazz club. Let me advise you to go. I do this for posterity, I tell you, and not from my affection for this undoubted moron. The world demands a Johnson portrait of Madame Tina Rossi.'

And then I realized who Johnson was. *A painter from London.* My God.

And I had just accepted an invitation to attend a late night revue at the Lyceum with a sunburnt gentleman with yellow hair, a shipbuilding yard and a divorced wife in Nassau. Michael would go crazy.

'You'd rather not,' said Johnson helpfully as I hesitated. 'Another time. Next year.'

'I'd love to,' I said, and I meant it. 'It's just that I've already been asked by someone on the Festival Committee, and accepted. But tomorrow...?'

He shook his bespectacled head. 'The Scottish Sabbath. Two concerts, then I've got to be off. I'm racing on Tuesday. Schizophrenic culture-patterns, Madame. Bed to Bizet to boozet and bach to bed again.'

Considering the time of year, it was an unlikely story. 'Where do you race, dear man?' inquired the Ambassador.

'On the sea. In a boat,' said Johnson with lucidity. 'From Gourock to Tobermory this time, as a matter of fact. Off the Scottish west coast, you know. Picking up the nice little islands. Like Rum.'

'Johnson,' I said. 'Mr Johnson. May I come to the jazz club with you tonight?'

The Ambassador grinned and moved off. 'With pleasure,' said Johnson. 'But what about the gentleman from the Festival Committee?'

'I have a very bad headache,' I said. 'Mr Hennessy will understand.'

'In view of the Koh-i-noors hanging under your ears, he won't be surprised,' said Johnson irritatingly. 'Did you say Stanley Hennessy?'

'It was Stanley Hennessy who invited me out, yes,' I said. 'Do you know him?'

The bifocals glistened. 'Everyone knows Stanley Hennessy,' said Johnson. 'Builds oil tankers. He's racing on Tuesday too. In a yacht like the *Queen Mary*. He's worth going out with, as well. Bed to Bizet to boozet and bach to…'

'I got it the first time,' I said. 'What did you tell the police?'

'When? Oh. Said we'd seen a fellow run out of the flat and gave them the Rossi Identikit. Small, thin, big nose and wart on the cheekbone: that's it, isn't it? They might as well improve their minds looking for him instead of bothering anybody else. Then when they find the late Mr Chigwell, they'll really have something to think about.'

'Did they find your burglar?' I asked. 'The one who stole your camera?'

'No. All the better,' said Johnson. 'I'll collect the insurance, and wart-face the blame, and you will come on a little holiday with me on *Dolly* to keep my mouth shut. Will you?'

'Yes.'

'And let me paint you?'

'Yes.'

'Clothed?'

'Even that.'

'Stanley Hennessy will be very, very angry,' said Johnson. He did not appear to be upset at the thought.

'So will Michael Twiss,' said I.

*

Next day Michael, of course, was apoplectic. As far as ethics went, he would't care if I slept with a Dr Barnardo's ball boy, so long as it didn't affect my career. My career, which had brought Michael his Reliant Scimitar and his alpaca overcoat and his Nivada Grenchen steel watch, was a religion with Michael. He and Eddie Ugboma. All through breakfast, he sat on the edge of my bed and complained, while I sold him a cruise on Johnson's yacht *Dolly*.

'I'd never have let you go off, if I hadn't thought you were with Hennessy. What he'll think…'

'It's all right, Michael. Really. He sent me six dozen pink roses this morning and all kinds of manly condolences over my headache. He'll never find out I went with Johnson instead.'

'And what sort of tub is it, anyway; and who the hell's heard of Johnson? You'll ruin your voice. I got you that trip in the Aegean last year; what's the point of souring all that with a tinpot canoe-tour of the peasantry?'

'She's thirty-four tons.'

'Look, the *Christina*'s one thousand eight hundred.'

'She's a gaff-rigged auxiliary ketch which can be handled by three at a pinch. Johnson owns her.'

'He does?' I knew that would help. 'What does he do, anyway? Apart from making potty remarks?'

'He makes me laugh,' I said lightly. It had been a rather good, if decorous, evening. The club had produced mainstream jazz and a respectable meal, and Johnson had come up with a chaperone: a big golden Guards officer named Rupert Glasscock, who was also the mate of Johnson's gaff ketch, the *Dolly*. We danced a Hully Gully. And then, since nobody recognized me, Johnson performed a frenzied Watusi. It was like before and after with Flit. I smiled incautiously now, and Michael snapped back. 'Well, you can call the whole bloody thing off. The tub's probably not even leak-proof.'

'She can go anywhere. She's racing.'

He thought he'd got it now. '*Bluebottle* there?'

'No, it's more a *Britannia* thing. It's a sort of Club cruise in company, open to all classes of boat, with a handicap. They start off at Gourock on Tuesday and get back to Tobermory, Mull, a week or so later, checking in their sailing times at various islands en route.' God knew if I'd got that off right, but it sounded good. 'Look, they're not all proles, Michael. You've got to be pretty well heeled to own a yacht between ten and fifty odd tons. You haven't heard yet what Johnson does for a living.'

Michael was unappeased. 'Let me guess. He's a soloist with the Bournemouth Symphony Orchestra.'

I had kept the straight left till the last. 'He's *the* Johnson. The Academician. He's the portrait man, Michael. And he's going to paint me sailing on *Dolly*.'

And that did it, of course.

The clash between Johnson and Hennessy took place next day, and was the last event in the sporting calendar before I left Edinburgh. It was inevitable, even though my defection to jazz remained, miraculously, unexposed. In fact, it came about by sheer chance, when Stanley Hennessy took me out for lunch and found Johnson and his friend Captain Glasscock at a neighbouring table.

To begin with, it rated no more than an exchange of cool nods, and we got down to the menu. But all too soon, the subject of yachts floated into the arena: Hennessy's sunburn waxed with enthusiasm and his stiff yellow hair curled and crackled with vim as he described the joys of the sea.

There was no point in concealing my plans. Over the pâté I confessed I was sailing on *Dolly*, and over the trout my sunburnt friend pulled all the switches he knew to persuade me to sail off on the Hennessy yawl *Symphonetta* instead. *Symphonetta* had just made a killing at Cowes. *Symphonetta*, it appeared, was in the Clyde and willing to abandon the nasty old race and leave for any part of the world at my whim.

It was tempting; but Hennessy was not, he would be the first to concede, a court painter of world renown. With real regret, I refused.

Then, as I sat, in blonde tweed from Bergdorf Goodman and the champagne diamond I earned from *La Gioconda*, peaceably eating my lamb noisettes, I was irritated to find Hennessy rising, with the briefest apology, and departing to lean over the unoffending table of Skipper Johnson and his mate Mr World. He greeted them chattily and said, in the voice that built oil tankers, 'I hear you're in for the

Royal Highland cruise. I've been telling Madame Rossi she'll find *Dolly* quite a nice little boat.'

'Thank you. You're just cruising around this year, Stanley?' said Johnson. The Archbishop of Canterbury addressing Cardinal Spellman. It was the same sort of tone.

Hennessy said, 'To be honest, I got a bit bored with winning the thing. Thought I'd let all you others in for a stab. But I'm tempted to alter my mind.'

The bifocals glinted under the pink-shaded lights. 'You mustn't think about us. We'll all have a jolly good sail; and we'll do our damndest to give you a race. Won't we, Rupert?'

Rupert agreed, in time, and Hennessy, his voice sharpened a little, said chaffingly, 'Oh, come now. I've said *Dolly*'s a nice little boat, but you won't pretend she's a match for *Symphonetta*. Gave her a birthday present this year: complete new set of sails – jib, stays'l, main, mizzen, the lot; and a hell of a lot of new gadgets you've never heard of, you bunch of caravan owners. You'll never *see Symphonetta*, far less make better time.'

His manner was jocular, though his words were not. Johnson merely grinned, but Rupert said, with equally furious levity, 'What d'you bet?'

'Five thousand quid,' said Hennessy.

And Rupert said, 'Done!'

The retort of a child. As Hennessy returned and sat down, I remarked, 'Why do that? He'll never pay if you win.'

He was not displeased that I had overheard. 'Oh, these young Guardsmen are rolling in loot. I know *Dolly*. She's been here before with her bloody circus act: glass-eyed Rembrandt and a boatload of models. They'll make a cock-up of the whole thing before the race is a couple of days old, you mark my words, and you'll be glad to cross over to old Hennessy's boat.'

And bach to bed again: I suppose.

3

The Royal Highland Club headquarters at Rhu was full on Monday evening when I arrived from Edinburgh in my chauffeur-driven Humber Imperial, with my luggage and one or two cases of Michael's. Here, I was to stay overnight. For the next six to seven days, as everyone knew, I was to sail with Johnson on his yacht *Dolly*, where I was to be painted in oils.

The send-off from Edinburgh had been memorable: Michael had done a good job. It was a pity that the sea made him sick. He would join me instead at Tobermory, where the Club race would end, and where we had booked rooms in the biggest hotel.

On the other hand, it wasn't a pity at all that Michael would not be on board when I got to Rum to see Kenneth. Michael disliked Kenneth and had done his utmost to part us. Happily, he had never discovered that, although I wrote to Kenneth in London, the letters were actually forwarded to Rum. If Michael had known about Rum, I should never have been singing at this year's Edinburgh Festival. On thinking that over, it struck me that Michael was acquiring altogether too much grip on my life.

In any case, the press and television coverage had been good, and in the evening papers there was quite a lot about Johnson, as well as the usual rags-to-riches blurb on my life. Michael was skilful at keeping the story alive. People resent success: but not when it happens to one of themselves.

Johnson's background was landed gentry: his people were well known in Surrey. After public school and university he had joined the Royal Navy, thank God: I was apprehensive a trifle about my future on *Dolly*. But for the last fifteen years he had

23

been known for one thing: his celebrity portraits. From being a good technician and a sympathetic artist, he had become probably the best known portrait artist there is. By now, of course, the hallmark of having arrived is a portrait by Johnson. Long before then, he could choose his commissions from a list as long as the phone book.

He was unmarried. Who needs a wife with a boatload of models?

I had wondered, as Michael made all the arrangements, whether I was being quite wise. But I was too well known, and Johnson was too well known, to do this in secret. Do it with a fanfare of publicity, and let the press have their interviews at the times and places we wanted, and we had control of the thing. Let it be discovered by some underpaid local correspondent and all hope of privacy had gone.

I had wondered, too, whether I should have made the attempt to reach Rum alone. But how to shake off Michael, when I had no tale to tell but the truth? Michael would never allow me to meet Kenneth, or to travel alone. And even if I had no Michael to contend with, I might still be recognized, and what of the news stories then?

When you are well known there is no certain way to do these things. This, with its chance at least of a private encounter with Kenneth, offered the best hope. And I was, at the same time, keeping an ally in Johnson and having painted a portrait which would be invaluable in my career. I said nothing to Johnson about Kenneth's presence on Rum. The fewer I had to trust now, the better. Until I knew what part in all this Kenneth had played.

At the Clubhouse, my room and Rupert the mate were found without difficulty. Johnson, it seemed, was in the bar. Large, giggly and golden, Rupert steered me in there to find him.

For dining with Johnson, I was wearing a Princess Galitzine trouser suit in Bangkok quilted silk with a little bow on the bottom. Rupert wore a white Navy sweater under a blazer from Rugby. Johnson, when we located him, was dressed in immaculate dungarees and talking to a thin man in a pixie cap and a tarry sweater four inches above the knee. Rupert said, 'Oh Christ,' under his breath;

and conveying me up to the bar called, 'Hallo, Ogden. Hallo, Skipper.' He eyed Johnson's attire.

'What's packed it in? The engine? The cooker? The heads?'

'None of them. So far,' said Johnson; and turned, solemnly welcoming.

Rupert said, 'Good; I'll stay then,' and unbuttoned his blazer. 'Madame Rossi, what'll you drink?'

It was not the Aegean. The queue for the one-armed bandits, hunting for sixpences inside their jerseys, did not appear to be *Financial Times* readers. Neither did the two small rotund persons, one male, one female, who now passed within an arm's length of me, both wearing gum boots, big jumpers and thick knitted hats, with their arms full of tonics.

To these last two, Rupert waved. *'Binkie,'* he remarked in explanation. 'My God: that wee wife isn't tanned, she's jolly well cured.' He relayed our orders and continued to Johnson, 'Then why dungarees?'

'To keep me pretty for dinner.' Unzipping the dungarees carefully, Johnson simultaneously introduced the thin man beside him. Inside the dungarees was the same green pullover and brown flabby suit that Johnson wore while in Edinburgh. Underneath his companion's pixie hat was a long, melancholy face with a chin like the end of a dogbone. This was Cecil Ogden, owner-skipper of a cutter called *Seawolf,* who would be racing against us tomorrow, 'if we can fish up his port navigation light in time. The string broke,' said Johnson, explaining.

Rupert, it seemed, had to smother emotion. 'Did it? Did you have it tied on with string, Cecil?'

'I had a lot of string,' said the man called Cecil Ogden, without a trace of a smile. His voice was English, and cultured, with no regional accent I could trace.

'Ogden built *Seawolf* himself single-handed from nothing practically but a half-rotten keelplate. A jolly good show, actually. He's still building it, aren't you, Cecil? A few bits to do. But he entered for the Club cruise last year and did pretty well.'

Two patches of red appeared above the long ribs of Ogden's jawbone and cheeks. 'She was caulked in wet weather,' he said sulkily. 'The planks always spring when they dry out. The bloody *Britannia* leaks in dry weather.'

'I'm sure you're right,' said a new, genial voice. 'But I don't expect she'd find herself pooped through the seams from the wake of the Greenock car ferry.'

It was Hennessy. He kissed my hand, all neat, corrugated head and dimple and European suave gallantry: why did I feel like Ginger Rogers? Ogden said, 'I don't have three paid seamen to do the bloody work for me. Maybe that's why I don't win races and stick my bloody neck out where it's not wanted.'

He put down his glass. 'Thanks for the drink, Johnson. I'll have to go. Since I do my own sailing, I've one or two things to look after.'

He nodded briefly to Johnson, remembering at the last moment to include me, and strode off, slightly wide at the knees. Watching him go: 'Where's the girl?' inquired Hennessy.

'Laying in stores at Helensburgh, and conning the nearest affluent young man into driving her here with them,' said Johnson, ordering Hennessy a drink. Ogden, it appeared, was subsidized by his sorrowing family to live up there on the Clyde, building and rebuilding his yacht with the help of the pittance which was all they dared allow him, and all the help he could scrounge.

'Including a girl? How domestic!'

Hennessy smiled back at me, but Rupert said, 'Oh, there's always been a girl. He's the helpless type who attracts them. But he's damned lucky this time. He's got Victoria.'

'A plum,' said Johnson, his bifocals stationary. 'Rupert is a friend of the family.'

'Don't be an ass.' Rupert, predictably, was carmine again. 'She did the season, and I saw her now and then after. It's a bit of too much, actually, Cecil commandeering her. There's a limit to what you should ask anyone to do; and Victoria never thinks of herself.'

He stopped. I said, 'Is she the only hand on *Seawolf*?' It seemed very Bohemian for these Calvinist parts.

'Oh, they'll manage.' Rupert was confident. 'She's Bermudan, and pretty easy to run.'

'Well, good luck to them,' Hennessy remarked. 'I don't expect her miseries will endure very long. On past form, the boat'll begin coming to bits when the starting gun fires.'

'Yes. But you heard what he said.' It was Johnson who chided. 'They have plenty of string.'

Dinner at the Royal Highland Cruising Club is a civilized meal, and Johnson and Rupert provided agreeable company. I found I was recognized after all; and at intervals between the soup and the coffee I signed a great many menus.

The last menu was Johnson's. I received it, surprised, and opened it ready for autograph. Above the smoked salmon was a quick ballpoint portrait of myself in the Galitzine suit, with the nose shortened just that fraction I have always promised myself. It was ravishing. A perfect likeness. I remarked on it.

'Yours, if you like that sort of thing,' said Johnson. I thanked him warmly, and we both gazed after the drawing which, lifted by a passing acquaintance, had begun to travel from table to table. It reached Hennessy who, rising, called, 'Nice bit of work, Johnson. Care to auction it for my committee on Oxfam?'

There was a stir of interest, and I concealed my annoyance. It was my drawing. On the other hand, I must think of my public.

It was auctioned for two hundred guineas, the closing bid being Hennessy's. His hand, while I signed it for him, rested adhesively on my silk-covered shoulder and he smelled discreetly like the Nice branch of Hermès. He invited me to visit the *Symphonetta* at our first shore-going checkpoint to see the drawing framed in his cabin. The thought of being framed in Mr Hennessy's cabin lingered with me through the rest of my dinner.

Johnson himself seemed quite unaffected by the incident, although he remarked, with some innocent pleasure, that it was the first time he had delineated a lady with her head in the smoked haddock and her bosoms in the cheese. I remembered that he could command two hundred guineas at a time for one thumbnail sketch, and that a finished painting, if as good as that, could be used for publicity for years instead of having my nose shortened. Over the liqueurs, when Rupert had excused himself to complete his work for the next day, I said to Johnson, 'Now, let's talk about Johnson.'

'Let's,' he said immediately. I have never met anyone with such a nondescript face: except for the hair and the eyebrows it seemed positively manufactured of glass. I tidied my hair, fleetingly, in his bifocals. 'I like Bach, whisky, striped underpants, Montego Bay, shooting and Peruvian brandy,' said Johnson. 'Also beautiful ladies of character. Hasn't it occurred to you that they will try to kill you as well, now? Assuming your friend Holmes isn't the murderer?'

My *Rigoletto* of last year had brought me a ruby along with the silk from Bangkok, and I had had it made up in the Burlington Arcade: it made an unusual ring. I twisted it. 'No, I hadn't thought of that,' I said slowly; and it was the truth.

'You're the only one who could identify him,' said Johnson. '*If* he was the murderer.'

I let go the ring. 'He must have been.' It was too ridiculous. 'Look, some tatty little sneak-thief caught raiding a flat and letting fire with a gun isn't going to have the nerve or the money to hunt down and kill someone who may or may not have seen him. He's going to be far too damned busy getting out of the country.'

'Granted. But are we dealing with some tatty little sneak-thief?' said Johnson. 'You saw the bugged table. Your friend Holmes had gone, and he wasn't the juvenile lead in "Mrs Dale's Diary." So you say. How do you know he hasn't been kidnapped?'

'Because I've checked, and he hasn't,' I snapped back, with a smile. If there was a lip-reader among the admirals, we were sunk.

The beetle brows rose over the enormous bifocals. 'So it did occur to you,' said Johnson. 'Then what did your friend say about the late Mr Chigwell?'

I got up. 'I'll tell you when he comes to the phone.'

He stood too. 'So you haven't spoken to him?'

I could feel my teeth clench. Then, my back to the room, I spoke quickly and softly. 'Listen. You're partly right. Kenneth is a scientist, and his work is important. That's why the table was bugged. But it's nothing to do with the murder. It's because of me.

They don't like international attachments. He's not supposed to be seeing me, even.'

'They must be frightfully pleased then, that you're on board *Dolly* with me… Shall we go out?' inquired Johnson.

I led the way, rather thoughtfully. For the fact was, after all that publicity, it must be all too clear to Kenneth's bosses as well as to Kenneth that I was making for Rum… *if* they knew that I was the person he was expecting in Rose Street that night. And if they knew that, and the late Mr Chigwell came to light any time in the next three or four days, they had the perfect excuse for detaining me. On the other hand…

'On the other hand,' said Johnson, exactly as if I had spoken aloud. 'Our first theory may be right. Chigwell might have been killed by someone who thought he was Dr Holmes. And having found out his mistake, our little friend with the warts may be at the other end of the country just now, trailing the good Kenneth Holmes.' The bifocals flashed at me. 'But you say you can warn him. So that must be all right.'

All right, hell. If somebody was trailing Kenneth Holmes with intent to murder, that somebody was here, on the west coast of Scotland, going the way I was going, to Rum.

I said goodnight to Johnson soon after, at the door of my room where he found considerable interest, it seemed, in gazing over my shoulder at my night attire, laid out on the bed, with my big, gold-fitted toilet case beside it. The trunk and the four travelling cases were standing still locked.

'Uh, tell me,' said Johnson. 'Have you ever gone sailing before? On anything less than three thousand tons, for example?'

'*Is* there anything less than three thousand tons?' I replied. I was irritated. I added, remembering the portrait, 'I'm sorry; but are you trying to say that the *Dolly* is too small for my luggage?'

'No, no. She isn't too small.' He thought. 'But she'll sink like a lift.'

Ten minutes later, all my cases were open and had been cannibalized into a small heap of unappetising woollies, some mine and some Johnson's. I was to put these in the smallest of my cases and leave it outside my door at eight o'clock sharp. Breakfast would be at 8.15, after which Rupert would row me to *Dolly*. At 9.30 we should set sail down the Clyde estuary for Gourock, and after an early lunch, the race would begin.

I listened; I answered; I bade him goodnight; I saw him into the corridor; I returned and took, in due course, to my bed, having made my sole (as yet) gesture of explicit contempt.

I did not give myself the trouble of locking the door.

Next morning the sun was shining, but I had seen the sun shining in Scotland before. I dressed to my satisfaction, and had three calls to my bedroom before I was quite ready, at eight forty-five, to saunter downstairs.

The hall of the Yacht Club was full of pixie caps, turtle necks, stained denims and an inorganic culture of toggles. I was wearing my thin kid trouser suit in almond pink, with matching boots and knitted silk jersey. My hair was in a French pleat, and my dark cat's glasses were bought in Miami. I wore a little scent by Patou, and on my right hand was a large uncut emerald.

As I descended the stairs, the noise abated; and Johnson, stepping forward, escorted me into breakfast in a silence almost complete. The bifocals shone with the most profound admiration. 'The soft kill. Delicious,' he said, 'and you're not to worry. There's some Thawpit on board.'

I was not worried, although a little surprised to find after breakfast that instead of Rupert, the girl Victoria had been detailed to row me to *Dolly*. She was, of course, the sole shipmate and crew of Cecil Ogden, the lugubrious remittance-man of yesterday's encounter at the bar.

We were introduced, Victoria and I, on the jetty. I looked for a hockey player and I found one: a centre-forward, small, bony and agile. The central zone of the face, revealed by the inner selvedges of long, hanging, mud-coloured hair, displayed large cow-like eyes under thick eyebrows, and a mouth much too big. She wore denims and a faded striped sweater and talked in a high, clear cordon bleu voice about the last thing I did for Stokowski. But she did not, at least, ask for my autograph.

Seawolf's dinghy I did not altogether appreciate. It was a light wooden, flat-bowed shell, known as a pram; and I, for one, was no baby. Victoria all too clearly knew I was about to get wet: she tucked oilskins, still talking, over my trouser suit as soon as I was seated, cast off, and took up the oars. Her arms were bare, and so were her feet. A little water at the bottom of the pram slopped over one of my kid boots. Between tugs, 'Thank God there'll be someone on *Dolly* with the glands to stand up to Johnson,' she said vaguely. 'He's done you an epic scene already, I bet, about the right clothes to take.'

'He has. I had a selected caseful of warm waterproof things fixed to go on board first thing this morning.' I paused. The strip of face between the almost united curtains of hair was mildly expectant. 'However, to be on the safe side, I bribed the Club porter to row out three more cases before Mr Johnson was up.'

I was rewarded by a large toothy smile. 'I knew you'd be super,' said Victoria. 'I adore Johnson: he's so slow and so frightfully switched on; he gets his own way with everything, and of course Rupert worships him and now Lenny the Crew: if you visit *Dolly* it's like coping with the Memphis Jug Band… The *épater la bourgeoisie* thing is marvellous, if you can bear to go on with it. But anyway you'll love every second. They all do. The racing bit doesn't matter much, although some of them make rather a thing of it. But the islands are absolute heaven. Do you know the Hebrides?'

I did not. I was prepared to suffer the Hebrides until I came to the one that was called Rum. The others might sink, plop, as of that moment. I shook my head.

'Oh, but how super! You'll adore them. I like them when it's *very, very* wet. It is, often. I walk about in my bare feet and the mud goes squidge. Do you know we're going to pass Staffa?'

I knew. Staffa, which has an underground sea cavern and a rock formation superior to the Giant's Causeway: I knew. I was sick of Staffa. It was beside Iona, the third call; that was all I was interested in. Then Barra and Rodel in the Outer Hebrides. Then the island of Skye; and then Rum. After Rum, *Dolly* could sink; assuming my portrait was finished. As Victoria prattled on about Staffa, I looked round.

The sea sparkled. On either side of the Gare Loch the hills were green, and above, the sky was a filmy, spacious pale blue. Just ahead of us, as Victoria, twisting round, picked her way towards the lanes between moorings, were the first of the yachts. Some were quiet, with bare poles, but most were bustling with people. There was chat, and the noise of generators and engines turning over, and the grating sound of ropes in pulley-blocks as sails were hoisted; all made thin and harmless by the unconfined water and air. As we began to pass them, Victoria did a very passable if libellous commentary about each.

Only twenty, I gathered, of the Club's eighty odd members had entered for this particular race: in any case for reasons of safety (safety?) the smallest were barred. For the rest, there was handicapping of a fairly cursory sort over the two halves of the circuit: before the day's sail to the Crinan Canal which would give us access to the west coast proper, and again on Thursday, when we restarted from the far end of the canal. Everyone was forced to clock in at a checkpoint on each place to be visited, and only the actual sailing time between islands would count in the end. If the weather was bad, there was no reason, explained Victoria comfortingly, why one shouldn't lie up in harbour until it improved: in fact everyone usually did. But if there was a good wind, for example, you might find yourself sailing night and day to make use of it. It depended.

'It seems an odd way of spending a holiday,' I remarked as we rowed past all these frantic small boats occupied, according to Victoria, by vacationing judges, doctors and chartered accountants, accompanied by their wives, friends and occasionally nieces. 'But you and Mr Ogden are awfully keen?'

'Cecil is. Cecil's marvellous,' said Victoria. Her head screwed permanently over her shoulder, she was digging alternately with this oar and that, avoiding boats big and little. 'That's *Weevli*. That's *Ballyrow*: they've got a super new record-player; you'll hear it at Crinan; and there's *Blue Kitten*: I'm afraid he practises piping. But *Nina*'s absolutely dreamy: he plays the Hawaiian guitar; he has a cousin in a Group. Crinan's mad: they all get together and get sloshed. You'll love it.' She turned round, her way being momentarily clear, and added, referring, I soon realized, to Ogden: 'He built

Seawolf practically himself. How many men could do that? With his own hands. On nothing, just about: his people are creeps and he's got a thing about asking for help. You know. But people know the boat is his life, and they appreciate that, around here. He knows all the locals and the anchorages, and people are jolly good and help when they can. They know he's genuine.' Suddenly, she tossed her hair back and before it was blown straight back over her face by the wind I saw a thin, bony, rather sad face, like a medical missionary who once addressed us at the Home. Victoria said, 'He feels a bit spare at times: who wouldn't, with the hard work and the loneliness. But he's a rather epic type, really… This one's *Binkie*.' She indicated the boat we were just about to pass, of a rather disgusting shade of dark red.

'What does *Binkie* do?' I asked gloomily. Johnson. And Ogden. And Hennessy. My God. This particular racehorse of the seas was smaller than most of the others, and was engaged in washing up its breakfast dishes on three inches of deck. As I spoke, a small round person in a knitted cap lifted and emptied the washing-up bowl, to a screaming of seagulls and a man's voice crying, 'Nan! Nan! Did ye feel for the teaspoon?'

It was the man and wife seen last night in the bar, their arms full of bottles of tonic. 'Bob and Nancy Buchanan. He runs a garage in Falkirk,' said Victoria, rapidly, and hailed them. 'Hallo! This is Madame Rossi: I'm taking her out to the *Dolly*. Well, are you cosy, Bob? How's the Wee Stinker?'

The face of the man Buchanan split into an affectionate grin. 'Fine. Grand, absolutely. You can hang your socks on her and they're dry in ten minutes.'

'They've got a new stove,' explained Victoria. '*Binkie*'s got everything, haven't you Bob? Wee Stinker's their stove, and their engine's called Buttercup: an absolutely stunning great object by Kelvin. And they both eat out of dog dishes: a perfectly super idea because they can't tip even when you go about, and keep hot and everything. You've no idea the wrinkles they have.'

The woman had joined the man. Both their faces were mahogany with weather and flattery. The man Bob said, 'Well, you know.

A tidy ship is an efficient ship. And an efficient ship is a happy ship. We keep the Good Book handy and do what we can.'

The woman Nancy hit him on the arm. 'Bob, Madame Rossi will be wondering. That's just the name we give the *CCC Sailing Directions*; don't heed him.' She suddenly knelt. During all this, Victoria was attaching the entire dinghy to *Binkie* with one calloused hand on their gangway. We bobbed up and down but she showed no signs of discomfort. The woman Buchanan addressed me at close quarters.

'I'm not meaning to be cheeky, but Bob and me and the others at the Clubhouse think your coming with us is great. And in a good working boat: *Dolly*'s been up here a few times before, and she's a good boat with good people in her. We get the carriage trade slumming up here from Formentor and Alghero with their wigs and their fancy men and their beagles doing the bathroom at every lock gate west of Cairnbaan, but it takes a real lady to try her luck in the Minch. Not that I've anything against dumb animals: I'm a vegetarian and a member of the RSPCA and I've never worn an animal's fur in my life, but it's the principle... Are you a good sailor, Madame Rossi?'

'I don't know yet. I hope so,' I said. I was fascinated.

She clicked her small, blackened teeth. 'Tell Johnson to give you a pill. And remember, we're vegetarian but we're not a dry ship. If yon debutante's dream Rupert's forgotten the booze, there's enough here lying snug in the bilges to see us both right.'

I thought of it; and I was still thinking of it when, having made our suitable farewells, we left the Buchanans and arrived at last at Johnson's yacht *Dolly*.

She was bigger than I had feared. She was a long white boat, with two tall masts, brass rails and a polished wood companionway. At the top of this, two heads emerged in welcome. One was Rupert Glasscock's, tousled and blond, above glittering chrome yellow oilskins. The other belonged to a small, middle-aged man with large ears and an old navy yachting cap whom Rupert, blowing kisses to both of us, introduced as Lenny Milligan from Golders Green, ex-Royal Navy, ex-Royal Yacht, ex-a very fancy job with a millionaire's steam yacht in Monte. 'Signed on for a season to slum it in

Britain,' said Rupert as Victoria flung up the painter and planted a prehensile bare foot on *Dolly*'s gangway, ready to board.

'Good show,' said Victoria absently, turning to lend me a hand. 'It won't take him a season to find out there's nothing wrong with British yachting but lousy old British weather.'

'Lousy weather and herberts like Cecil,' said Rupert, helping us aboard and down into a large and well-cushioned cockpit. 'You're dotty, darling. You know that you're dotty. Your soul-mate's an incurable nut. He got *Seawolf* from Santa in a polythene bag with a tube of soluble gum. He did. I swear it.'

'You're just jealous, my Rupert.' Victoria was unperturbed. 'My God, new bedspreads.' She withdrew her head from the aft cabin. 'I wish I had Johnson's income tax to live off, that's all I can say. How'd you like it?'

This to me: I didn't answer. I was still looking.

This, I was glad to find, was quite a suitable boat for Tina Rossi. To luxury yachts, of course, I was no stranger. But the small kind one sees at Monte and St Jean and Gibraltar – I have observed them. This was different. She had aft a double cabin, with bathroom and shower, which would be mine. Through the cockpit, one descended into the saloon, by way of various amenities, including good lockers. The saloon, with bedcouches and hammocks, would sleep four, but was shared, I was told, by Johnson and Glasscock. Beyond was the galley and Lenny's quarters, with a central passage leading through to the forward cabin which had its own hatchway, and thence to the fo'c'sle.

The steering was done by wheel or by tiller from the cockpit, from which one could reach winches on either side deck for working the sheets. Round the wheel was a mass of dials to do with the big Mercedes Benz 60 BHP 6-cylinder diesel engine (said Rupert), which was located under the cockpit. There were seats fitted on either side, and Victoria and I reclined there, until Rupert ceased demonstrating. Eventually, 'Gear, eh?' he inquired.

'Very,' said I. I had seen my four cases out of the corner of my eye. 'By the way, I've brought you a little champagne. Where do you keep it?'

'With the caviar,' said Rupert. 'In the bilges. My God, have you really, Madame Rossi? It's a privilege to sail with you. Here,

35

quick, before the skipper louses it up. If *Symphonetta* beats us into Tobermory I'll need it more than he does.'

'Will she beat you?' I asked. I had seen *Symphonetta* not far away among three or four of her own kind. She was coloured black, tall and stately and shining with brasswork and paint. Three nimble figures in snowy white oilskins had just taken off her sail suit and were preparing to get her mainsail pulled up.

'Poor bastards,' said Milligan. They were the first words he had spoken, but he made himself clear. 'Would've bedded down on that boat last night with nothing but some crimpy crisps and a shandy between them if the Buchanans hadn't stood them a beer or two each in the bar.'

'They are Hennessy's paid crew?' I inquired. It seemed an unfair advantage.

Victoria shook her head. 'In Scotland, he has students mostly. They're loopy on sailing, and there aren't many boats like *Symphonetta* up here. He leaves his paid hands at Cowes, and economises with a few bob and free smokes for the boys. Talking of which, what's the current bit about some crazy, lush bet? Rupert, you're bonkers. And a bit of a twit to expect Johnson to knock up *Dolly* winning the race against Hennessy for you.'

'He won't need to knock up *Dolly*,' Rupert was beginning in peeved astonishment when the snarl of an outboard interrupted him, and there was Johnson, eyebrows rampant and black hair sifted up by the gathering breeze. 'Victoria, superchick, Cecil's got a short in his starting motor and if you don't get over fast, he'll either be kippered or out of the race. Lenny, the engine. Madame Rossi, you're going to be cold. Rupert, your troubles are solved. I'm going to lend you my worry-beads.'

In ten minutes we were under way. To Kenneth, and Rum.

4

I had never raced in a small boat before. I did not expect to be seasick. I did not expect, on the other hand, to enjoy it particularly. It could be said, in that way, to have exceeded all my expectations.

To begin with, almost before I had changed, the mainsail was raised, causing a great many draughts, and we had cast off our mooring and were under way down the Clyde Estuary to Gourock, where the starting-gun was firing already, at half-hourly intervals, for the departure of each class in the race.

Next there was a great rattling and the mizzen sail went up, causing me to arrive suddenly on the left wall of my cabin en suite with my four cases. It was clear now why Johnson appeared so unconcerned on finding them aboard after all. I was to play pontoon with them for the cruise.

When I hooked back my door, Johnson was alone at the tiller, perched above my head with his feet on the cockpit cushions, the face glassed-in this time by polaroid bifocals, in black. He was whistling. The rattling, the flapping and the calling had all stopped and *Dolly* was sliding along on one glossy white flank, her sunny canvases masking the sea. Around us the hills were bright green, and the blue water was spiked with sails, coloured and white, tilting slightly at odds, like unrehearsed bows in a *tutti*.

I sat down with my back to the saloon wall and my feet on Johnson's Moroccan wool cushions, and suddenly from below there was a flood of soft music and Lenny appeared at my elbow with a mug of steam-flustered coffee and a ham sandwich, just cut. Johnson took one too and put it on deck, resting the tiller under his elbow. He did not turn his head much, but the dark glasses inclined towards the sails, the bow, the headland, the distant ribbon of small towns and at me. Continuing to contemplate me, 'This,' said Johnson agreeably, 'is just the commercial. The flip side'll slay you.'

At the time, I was mildly amused.

The morning passed. I had my first experience of changing direction. On advice, I first retired to my cabin. Then Johnson observed, mildly, 'Ready about, gentlemen,' and put the tiller down, and the boat came erect, sails flapping, while the bow began a big swing to the right. For a moment *Dolly* hesitated, and then the wind caught and filled her sails from the new side and turning, she heeled flat out on her right flank. While Lenny scampered about crouching on the foredeck and Rupert in the cockpit had his hands full of whipping white ropes, the two wooden booms holding the sails had swept across, as Johnson prophesied with some confidence that they would.

He and Rupert had ducked. I had no need, being pinned in my cabin by my four cases. It was Rupert who helped me up. 'Bit inconvenient, don't you find?' he said kindly. 'You could always leave them on shore at Ardrishaig, and pick them up later... Oo, I say! That's a bit hasty.'

He was gazing at my biggest case, which I had just swung into the cockpit and thence overboard.

'Why? It's unpacked,' I replied. It was true. The contents of one I had managed to squeeze into my locker.

'But my God, it's crocodile, isn't it?' said Rupert, ululation, despite himself, in his voice.

It was. But, of course, it was also insured. I shrugged. 'The other three perhaps *Symphonetta* might be persuaded to take for me.'

Rupert caught Johnson's eye and started to laugh. 'Persuade! Christ, Hennessy's bearings'll seize. Madame Rossi, you're marvellous.'

'Tina,' I corrected him. Better be done with it.

'Rupert,' said Rupert.

'Johnson,' said Johnson, smartly. 'Rupert, I don't awfully want to go about again immediately, but I shall have to if you don't let the mainsail out at the double.'

I crossed the cockpit and knelt, looking out to sea, on the cushions beside him. I was wearing Pucci trousers and Ma Griffe. 'Johnson?' I said. 'Just so? Like one's gardener, or one's clerk?'

'Or one's president or one's floor polish,' said Johnson, watching the mainsheet reel out. 'It's my first name as well. Parents palsied, mentally and physically, by the happy event.'

'Johnson Johnson?' I really did not believe it.

'You'll get used to it,' he replied.

The start of the race I am sure was exciting, but lunch (out of a tin, as Rupert said with disgust) consisted of partridge stuffed with Perigord truffles, preceded by a good Amontillado, and the Sauterne which followed put an end to my interest in nautical things. Assured that we had crossed the starting line, in the end, in reasonably good order, I retired to my cabin and slept.

I came out of sleep a long time later, very slowly. It was warm. I was lying on my back, being rocked softly from side to side, as if in a cradle. There was a sound of lapping water, like notes of music, *pizzicato*, with small agitated runs between. There was, all about and above, a stirring, a bumping, a minuscule groaning. I rolled over and out of the cabin and into the cockpit. We were becalmed.

We were all becalmed. Between green coast and distant green coast; from the far hills of Arran and the nearer hills of Cowal and Argyll to the Renfrewshire coast and the sandy beaches of the Cumbraes, the estuary lay deep as a mirror, scattered with the goosewings of yachts. Here were the red sails of *Binkie,* the patched striped spinnaker of *Seawolf,* the vast china-blue genoa, like some minatory, chiffon-draped Turandot, of *Symphonetta,* languishing with the larger sisters behind. We were all made equal by the absolute calm, and there was nothing to do.

'Hullo,' said Johnson's voice. Rupert, at the tiller, was stripped to the waist and lying face down on the decking beside it, three-quarters asleep. Lenny, I could see forward, his back propped by the coachhouse while he made buggy-winkles. (That is what he said later.) Johnson, I now located, as he spoke, above my head on the roof of my cabin. He was half hidden by a small canvas, held erect on a strange device like a piano rack, which projected upwards from above my cabin door. On the deck beside him was a palette carrying paint and two pots of liquid, and beside him was a pile of white hogshair brushes. He was wearing his usual bifocal glasses and an open-necked shirt, and I noted that at least there was hair on his chest, unless it was a wig. I have known, since I began filming, wigs of every variety.

'Hullo,' said Johnson. 'Happy days at the races. Christian, lock up the water.'

'Lock up the water if you like,' said Rupert's voice, muffled. 'So long as you don't lock up anything else.'

'I got the last hint,' said Johnson. 'But I still won't ask a man to drink and drive. Lenny, an iced beer for Madame Rossi.'

'Not unless everyone joins me,' I said definitely. Rupert stirred.

'Rupert on iced beer is a sex maniac,' said Johnson.

'I like sex maniacs,' said I.

'In that case,' said Johnson, briskly, 'we'll all have one. Lenny…?'

And suddenly it happened that while I lay drinking my beer, he was painting me. He was talking about *Dolly;* and about what he called the therapy of small-boating.

Through the rough white stuff of the canvas, I could see large scrabbled areas of tone taking shape. 'No one sails then because they just like it?' I asked. He had not asked me to keep still, and I did not.

'Oh, you'll find plenty of people attached to the sea for its own sake: ex-Navy types, or characters with shipping or shipbuilding interests; or people who are just good at it; rowing Blues and middle-aged peers whose grandfathers sailed their steam yachts in Oban Regatta. There's the Farex-and-potty brigade, who want to toughen their toddlers, and small, decent blokes, like the Buchanans, who enjoy mastering the thing and risking a bit of smallscale adventure as they go. Of course –' he uncapped a fat tube of raw sienna and squeezed a heap on the polished mahogany '– plenty of others sail as you've sailed, to have a ball socially; entertaining co-respondents or clients, or dancing on deck all night to a record-player, or horsing up a burn with a splash-net like one of the locals…'

'Johnson doesn't approve,' said Rupert, turning over to toast his stomach and chest. The smell of warm turpentine lingered inside the cockpit.

'Not at all,' said Johnson. His glasses flashed up and down. 'Why be immoral in a flat in a fug, when you can do it at sea and be healthy?'

All the canvas was covered, and I could no longer see what he was doing. 'Rupert,' I said, 'why does Johnson go to sea?'

Rupert Glasscock turned his big heifer's head to contemplate Johnson, and Johnson looked back through his bifocals. 'Because he hasn't got a flat,' said Rupert after some thought, and failed to prevent a brush loaded with vermilion from completing a crude cartoon on his spine.

Then there was a call from Lenny and both Rupert and Johnson jumped to their feet. Far across the blue, glassy water there was a smudge, like a finger mark in wet paint. In a second the palette, the brushes were stowed, the canvas was flung, with apology, into my cabin, and all three men were busy with ropes. There was wind, I deduced, on the way.

After a while I got up and went into my cabin, where Johnson's painting lay, right side up, on the bunk.

Thinly suffused with sweet colour; flat and soft as a painting on silk, my own face lay mistily there. Made-up for Gilda, I looked like that.

I was entranced. Handling it lightly by the edges, I picked the wet canvas up, and stared at the arrangement of earth and soil and mineral pigments which the mind behind those bifocal glasses had transformed into my face. Beneath my feet, the deck tilted as the sails far above me, touched with wind, started to pull. My door swung open and sunlight filled all the cabin, bringing with it the smell of leaves, and flowers, and the salt tang of the sea. Dazzling with sun, the fresh-laundered curtains over my porthole filmed and fluttered against the blue sea beyond, and the sea itself glittered, coarse blue and white in the hearty young wind.

Dolly leaned over with sudden decision, and something tipped, with a clack, from the other end of my bed. I laid the painting down, wedging it flat with my jewel case, and went to retrieve and secure what had fallen.

It was a coat hanger.

I hadn't left a coat hanger there. I had it in my hand, vaguely wondering whose it was, when suddenly, without question, I knew. That powerful hanger, with the riveted hook, the hook which had never come out despite the dead weight it carried, was none of mine or Johnson's ownership.

It was the hanger on which the dead body of Chigwell had been suspended, by his own large and well-fitting overcoat, in the wardrobe in Rose Street that night.

Johnson, when I called him, did not come at once. When the incredible nautical crisis, whatever it was, had been resolved and he finally entered, I had pulled myself together; although I could not bring myself, yet, to pick up the thing from where I had dropped it again, on his plushy blue rug by the bunk. Johnson's eye, travelling past both it and me, lit upon his painting, still jammed on the bed, and saying, 'Oh, that. Thanks,' he picked it up and disappeared, carrying it to the slotted overhead fitment where he kept his unfinished work in the saloon. I heard him come back to the tiller.

By that time I was out in the cockpit. 'It wasn't that. *Will you leave the bloody boat and listen, you fool?*' I spat at his moony bifocals. He handed the tiller to Rupert and followed me into my cabin.

Johnson did not share my distaste. As I told him what had happened he sat with the thing in his hands, turning it over and over. 'There was no hanger like this on the boat,' he said. 'It's certainly Chigwell's.'

'But how could it be?' I do not smoke. There are times when I wish that I did. 'The police know you were involved. But if they've found the body, they wouldn't do this. Neither would Kenneth. And apart from the police and Kenneth, the only person who could connect either of us with Chigwell's body is—'

'The murderer,' said Johnson. He was silent, his hands quiet on the wood. 'Not the nicest of thoughts, is it? We had him saving his skin, or else intent on pursuing your friend Dr Holmes. It seems he's not doing either. He's following you.'

'Could he be on board?' I asked. It was a sensible question. I tried to sound sensible asking it.

'No,' said Johnson. 'There's no doubt about that. But it would have been easy to put the hanger aboard while we were sitting in the thick of the traffic at Rhu. It's been there all day, I expect, but you haven't noticed it. Probably Lenny picked it up and shoved it on to your bunk, thinking it yours... That's *how* it was done. *Why* it was done is another matter. I think—' he hesitated.

'What?' Now we had facts, or near possibilities, I felt suddenly better. Dead men cannot swim.

'I think you should go back and get police protection. Hang the scandal. A two-day tabloid headline is better than losing your life.'

'No.'

'Look,' said Johnson patiently. 'I'm sure your friend Holmes would be the first to agree. After all, he's none too safe either, is he? I should think the chief of security would do his nut if he thought Holmes's life was in danger.'

'No,' I repeated. 'You say the man who planted the hanger isn't on *Dolly*. Right. That's more than you can say of any piece of ground in this kingdom. I'm staying on *Dolly*.'

It looked pigheaded, no doubt. Almost I confessed about my plan to meet Kenneth on Rum. But not quite. Not yet. Not until I knew from Kenneth what had been happening. For Johnson or no Johnson, the kind of work Kenneth was doing was no topic for loose conversation. There were research laboratories on Rum: Nature Conservancy laboratories, pursuing all kinds of eclectic problems to do with ecology and red deer.

There were other laboratories, too. And in South Rona, not far to the north, was the base of the atomic submarine *Lysander*, just now undergoing some of her instrument trials. If Kenneth was on Rum, he was not there for tagging red deer.

There was a long silence. Then, unexpectedly, Johnson said, 'Right. What you need is a stiff whisky. Give me five minutes to check course and you shall have it. Next, tonight we're due in at Ardrishaig, and just north of Ardrishaig is Lochgair where friends of mine have a bloody great liner called *Evergreen*, with the most powerful radio receiver on the west coast of Scotland. After we check in, I'll motor *Dolly* up to Lochgair and we'll telephone everyone we can think of for news of any scandals in Rose Street. For all we know, by this time, the police might have found the body and murderer both. In any case, you won't set foot ashore, and you ought to be safe. Done?'

'Done,' I agreed. A surprising man, Johnson. It took a bit of believing that he could paint too, as well as all this.

I am a stubborn woman: have been all my life. Someone was trying to frighten me. Someone, too, was doing his level best to prevent me from connecting with Kenneth. The someone didn't know Tina Rossi; that was all.

5

We arrived at Ardrishaig at night, after a brisk sail during which we had no contact with the outside world whatever. There, Rupert checked in; discovered to his alarm that both *Symphonetta* and *Binkie* had arrived ahead of us on corrected as well as actual time, and came aboard having sunk, I should judge, about four double whiskies. Then Lenny started the engine and we swung away from the yellow street lamps, the flashing light and dark strip of the breakwater, and the red and green lights of other yachts like ourselves, moving slowly about waiting to enter the sea-lock and find a berth in the basin of the Crinan Canal for the night.

Except that we wouldn't stay, that night, in the canal, where any passing stranger might step aboard. There are no locks on a cockpit. Tonight, free to use our engine, since we were no longer racing, we should move north to Lochgair, and anchor there beside Johnson's imposing friend *Evergreen* until morning, when we should rejoin the rest of the club as they chugged through the canal. Then on Thursday, the open sea again, and surely, comparative safety?

I had assumed that we should be alone in making that hour's extra journey north to Lochgair. Certainly Stanley Hennessy, triumphant in *Symphonetta*, was already safe in the basin, although I could see no sign of the Buchanans in *Binkie*. I watched, the wind in my hair, as the small lights diminished and the waterfall sound of the lock was lost in the hammer of *Dolly*'s powerful engine.

The sound of our engine concealed at first the hiccoughing eruption of another diesel quite near us. Then, unexpectedly, the pea-green, ill-painted quarter of *Seawolf* loomed up behind us, the mainsail taped to the boom like a comic umbrella. Rupert rushed to the gunwales to hail her. 'Cecil! VICTORIA! Follow Daddy, my sweetie! Who wants a Ber-loody Mary on *Evergreen*?'

They understood. Victoria waved in assent, and *Seawolf* picked up and moved into line just behind us. Rupert sat down firmly beside me. Johnson, his hands bent, was lighting a pipe. *Dolly*'s sailsuit, glimmering in semi-darkness, was neat as a pipecleaner, and her sheets coiled on deck were like optical puzzles. I inquired who *Evergreen*'s owners might be. Rupert took my hand casually to help him reply.

It was not what I had expected. 'The name is Bird. Retired showbusiness, darling. May knits and Billy plays poker, and they have a sing-song after dinner and a few drinks, and tell smoking concert stories – *vulgar* smoking stories. Rather good ones, in fact.' He squeezed my hand.

'Their Bloody Marys must be spectacular,' I said. The emerald was bruising my fingers. I withdrew them, attracting a flash of bifocals.

'Don't worry: it's all show,' said Johnson kindly. His pipe glowed a soothing red in the soft windy dark against the smooth gloss of Loch Fyne. 'Put a bookmark in, Rupert; and I'll go and be sick.'

I could believe I was getting to like Johnson, at times.

Compared with Ardrishaig, the bay of Lochgair was quite dark, save for a pricking of lights from the hotel half hidden behind foreshore and trees, and the moving beams of cars slipping to and from Inveraray. Around us, as the engine cut and the anchor chain rattled down, were little white roadhouses, floating on the calm sea like indestructible plastic toys – the motor yachts, the luxury arm of the fleet.

The largest – eighty tons; eighty-four feet overall, with twin-screw oil engines each 6-cylinder and 250 BHP (said Rupert) was *Evergreen*. From her decks, a nightmare of striped awnings, Sekers curtains and potted geraniums, came a shouted invitation to drinks. I slipped below quickly to change. The black kangaroo dress with the copper chain belt, I thought; and small copper boots. *Seawolf,* who had had water in her carburetor, arrived in the anchorage just as I fixed my eyelashes on.

The first I knew of it was when I slammed my chin in the eyeshadow and my three cases crashed at my heels. Something had hit *Dolly*'s side with a hideous thud. There followed something like the quartet from *Trovatore*, with Victoria's shrill drawl distinguished among other, masculine voices, heated and also resigned. I repaired the scars in my make-up and, rubbing my back, marched up on deck.

Feebly lit in the sparkling concourse, *Seawolf* was there on our beam, swiftly retreating under the aegis of an almighty shove by *Dolly*'s owner and crew. *Seawolf*'s engine was off, although not far behind her one could see several large boats with which she would shortly collide. Ogden, who had patently seen them too, was now clambering into his pram with a towline. He fixed this, shoved in rowlocks, took up his oars; then with *Seawolf*'s lashed sternpost looming in front of him started to pull her away. He rowed, slowly at first; and then like a charnel-house in a wind-machine as *Seawolf*, responding, began to change course, and finally veered out of the danger zone after him.

'Gawd,' said Lenny reverently. He, Johnson and Rupert, argumentatively sober, stood on *Dolly*'s deck watching.

'What's happened?' I asked. 'Why doesn't he start *Seawolf*'s motor?' They were going to enjoy answering.

'Because the engine's jammed full ahead,' said Johnson, his expression completely covered with glass. 'He can't go slow or reverse: very fussing. That's why he hit us. And the wind's gone, so sailing's no good. Poor Cecil. He'll have to tow *Seawolf* clear of us all to get room to drop anchor... Oh, God be praised. I know what's going to happen.'

We all strained our eyes. 'The tow-rope's going to break?' suggested Rupert.

The tow-rope broke. Ogden performed a back somersault inside the dinghy. Ogden's yacht, still sailing backwards, overtook Ogden's dinghy, caught it a smart blow on the beam and flipped it aside, upside down. She then sailed slowly on, backwards, while Ogden, somersaulting briskly into the water, rose bubbling beside the fast-dispersing shapes of his oars.

Rupert squeaked. 'Shut up. There's another reel,' said Johnson.

There was. Victoria, finding herself alone on a powerless yacht backing rapidly out into the shoals of Lochgair, rushed to the cockpit and started the engine. *Seawolf* burst into shuddering sound and advanced, roaring, in top gear into the anchorage.

There was an echoing roar as every yacht in the bay started up its anchor winch and its engine at one and the same time. There was a brisk movement, as of fry in a jam jar, and then one by one all the engines cut out again.

On *Seawolf* the roar of the throttle had weakened; the pulse slowed and a tinny rattling came clear over the water, together with some thin shouting traceable to Victoria. The trailing end of her dinghy rope had caught in the screw.

In the water, a long way behind, a dimpling pool located the swimming figure of Ogden. *Seawolf*'s engine cut and she slid forward dreamily, headed towards the sandbanks on the other side, Victoria steering. As we watched, the yacht lost way and began to slip sideways, impelled by the tide. Victoria, a silhouette against the saloon skylight, was seen to leave the cockpit and, running forward, to pick up the anchor and heave it successfully over the side. There was a distant ticking as the anchor chain followed, a splash as the anchor hit water and sank, and then silence.

'*The anchor chain!*' said Lenny. The ticking had stopped.

'The anchor chain?' said Rupert, but louder.

'It's got stuck in the hawse-pipe,' reported Johnson amiably. 'And there's poor Victoria drifting out again on the tide with a short-chain anchor punching holes in the yacht like a pickled ticket-collector. I think we should help her.'

Almost before he had finished talking, *Dolly*'s dinghy was in the water, with me in it. I was not being left aboard *Dolly* for anything, even though copper boots and kangaroo skin are not the best thing for nautical ballet. Then Johnson was talking to a slick white launch from *Evergreen* which had appeared with a uniformed helmsman, also rescuebent; and in a moment Johnson, Rupert and I had transferred to the launch and were tearing over the dark water to *Seawolf*, while Lenny started up the outboard and snarled off in *Dolly*'s dinghy to the lugubrious spot in the sea which was Cecil Ogden.

While *Evergreen*'s paid hand lashed motorboat to yacht and prepared to lead *Seawolf* gently back to civilization and safety, the rest of us boarded Ogden's boat.

Nearly helpless with giggles and madly pleased with herself and with us, Victoria helped us aboard.

Johnson disappeared below to the chain locker. Rupert started to throw off his clothes.

He wore a string vest. I wished very much I had stayed safe on *Dolly*. When he took off the string vest and started on his trousers, I marched below, leaving Victoria. I am broad-minded, naturally, but not in public. Then my attention was arrested by other things altogether.

Seawolf was not, I declare, an irredeemable misnomer. If a Wolf Cub tried to train for all his badges at once in an area roughly the size, shape and smell of a large dental cavity, the result would be the inside of *Seawolf*. She was floored and halflined. Above waist level were merely the ribs of the boat, with a shelf tacked on to the wood here and there. Hinged to the mast was a let-down table of rough-cut mahogany, with a brass plate on its underside: … *In token of esteem and affection for his thirty years' service to the Presbytery,* I read.

There were evidences, too, of the esteem and affection of the Navy, in the form of a standard pair of naval binoculars, a naval issue raincoat (American) and, on the benches, a pair of rubber-stamped charts. The Air Force had contributed a couple of fire extinguishers, British Railways a towel, and the Northern Lighthouse Commission a miscellany of objects, including three Brasso tins and a clock.

The light, of a theatrical isolation, came from an engineer's inspection lamp slung on a festoon of flex. The bedding, which lay rolled up under one of the benches, was as supplied by HM Prisons. Beside it, under this and the second bench opposite, was Ogden's working equipment: old chocolate boxes filled with rusty screwdrivers, mouldering insulating tape, wire clippers and nails, tacks, hooks, hammers, odd bits of chalk and a spirit level, inscribed clearly WIMPEY. There were some engineers' waste, and a number of old, dirty flags strung together, with some anonymous cans reeking of spirit and oil, which clinked together as *Seawolf* began to sail up to her tow.

49

There was another clinking too, which I was investigating in the fo'c'sle, a kind of after-care unit for nail-sickness, when a whoop from Victoria in the bows told of success with the chain: a moment later and from above there came the squeak of a hand-operated winch and rhythmic crash from the chain locker as the anchor was brought up from the sea to the bows. Soon after that, *Seawolf*'s gentle sauntering stopped; Johnson spoke, and there was a splash and a racing rattle as the anchor was thrown in again and the chain ran out, properly this time, to reach the sea bed. Casting a last, fascinated glance at my immediate scenery, I prepared to return to the saloon.

On the inside of the cockpit door was a painted legend, insufficiently sandpapered off, reading LADIES. I was studying it, entertained, when it flew open and the owner vaulted down the stairs.

I was not tempted to laugh now: indeed I was not. Cecil Ogden was wet, cold, tired and in a towering temper. 'Who the hell gave you leave to break in and meddle down here? You've squawked before all the zombies in Europe, and that makes you the bloody Queen of the May?' His eyeballs were bloodshot, but his ducking had practically sobered him.

Before I could answer, Johnson spoke matter-of-factly behind me, 'It's nothing to be ashamed of, the building of a boat with your own hands, Ogden. Madame Rossi is a friend and a guest of mine, not a Hennessy, you know.'

Then Ogden's long, high-boned cheeks flamed under the streaming tails of his hair; and he muttered, directing it somewhere between us, 'It's the end of the season, that's all. After a hard season's wear, you can't expect the same service from the best engine there is.'

He was almost sober, as I have said; but the whole boat still reeked of spirits. Of course he didn't want strangers exploring his fo'c'sle unaccompanied. But it wasn't the boat he was ashamed of.

But now Victoria emerged from the chain locker, talking excitedly; the man from *Evergreen* in immaculate uniform appeared in the cockpit and began testing the engine; Lenny, rather wet, vaulted into the cabin and announced *Seawolf*'s pram in good order and tied to its parent again; and last of all Rupert, a godly figure quite nude but for a pair of bathing trunks, appeared glistening negligently on the stairs and announced calmly that the rope was freed from the screw. As he said so, under the surgical fingertips of *Evergreen*'s skipper the engine stirred, chattered and then boomed into life.

There was a deafening cheer. The paid hand from *Evergreen*, his face severe, slowly entered the crowded saloon and confronted Cecil Ogden. 'I think that'll be all right now, sir, although your clutch, if you'll pardon my saying so, is in a verra poor kind of condition. Would there be somewhere I could wash my hands, sir?'

Pressing back, we gave him passage through to the galley. There was no tap. He put an oily, efficient thumb over the open vent of the old trawler pump, and after a moment the water gushed into the sink, which he hadn't yet plugged.

Alas, he had not yet noticed – why should he? – that the sink and the waste pipe were not united. Water, falling straight through the hole, filled his immaculate shoes.

There was a sorrowful silence. Then Johnson, his voice beautifully modulated, recalled that we were on our way to a cocktail party, and led the way out.

6

On *Evergreen,* the first person I saw was my manager, Michael Twiss. There he stood among the flood-lit geraniums with his blow-waved hair, doeskin jacket and Italian belt with the silver and ceramic clasp, looking blanched about his small, well-shaped mouth, which was smiling politely. He had been encountered ashore at the Lochgair Hotel by our host and hostess, May and Billy Bird, who had invited him aboard while he waited to join *Dolly.* Damn, damn, and a triple-force damn.

Why? Why join *Dolly* now, at the start of her voyage, instead of at the end, at Tobermory? To Johnson, who welcomed his change of plan, Michael said merely that he had decided to take up the original invitation. To me, as he uttered smiling politeness, his eyes were eloquent with *tepidita.* For the second time tonight, someone was in a passion of rage with me, poor Tina Rossi. And this time, again, I knew very well why.

But of course Michael was at his most charming. Beside him, in any case, in open-necked shirts and clean trousers, were the Buchanans of *Binkie.* I was still wondering what they had managed to talk about when I found myself among the scatter cushions in the deck saloon, my feet in the bulwark-to-bulwark carpeting and my wrist bones creaking under a tumbler six inches thick, full of single malt Talisker.

'Eee, lass,' May Bird, dispensing drinks from a commode like a Hammond organ, was screaming to me. 'You're a right dishy girl for a singer. And don't tell me it don't always 'elp. My 'Arold now 'ad a nice little tenor, but never the looks for it; and 'is Dad and me, we kept 'im off the stage. I won't say the Navy pays well; but it's safer.'

She dimpled, like a very old window-pane. 'Takes after me. The only way I could ever make the Winter Garden Torquay, legitimate, was to marry old Billy-boy here.'

May Bird was small and fat, with bouffant hair, very yellow, and a short sleeveless dress in pink cloqué. The diamonds in her ears were real. Billy Bird, her husband, showed his age more: pink and round and white-haired, with stagey lines all around the mouth. They owned, Nancy whispered, a large public house and dance hall in Liverpool.

I did not care, just at that moment, what they owned, apart from a radio telephone Johnson could use before I was pounced on by Michael. I sat drinking and smiling until I saw Johnson and Billy Bird get up together and disappear into the passage which led to the wheelhouse: a faint crackling ensued, and was cut off as a door shut.

After an interval it opened again: there was more crackling, a faint burst of uproarious laughter, an unidentifiable booming, and then the voice of our host, embarking on something I could swear was a limerick. Johnson came back. 'Mrs Billy, you've been letting him get into bad company. That's a new one since last year.'

Pouring vodka as from a hot water bottle, Mrs Billy laughed like a crow and said, without lowering her voice, 'An' what the 'eck was Cecil Ogden doing this night? And a good drop in 'im, an' all.'

She didn't wait for an answer. 'That Victoria wants her head seen to.'

Victoria, in vivid discussion with Rupert over The Lovin' Spoonful, which is an American disc group, put out her tongue and returned to her giggle. 'All the dead-beats, that's what she picks up. All the washed-up old trash. I tell 'er. They don't appreciate it; and she'll get a pay-off she doesn't expect, one of these days.'

'Where *is* Ogden?' asked Bob Buchanan. Without their woolly hats, he and his wife looked like brown pickled otters. They chose to drink gin.

'Sulking,' said Lenny under his breath. He was right, too. With Victoria beguiled from his side, Ogden had shown no inclination to board Johnson's liner friend *Evergreen*; and had stayed on his own yacht to towel and change. Later, he was supposed to motor *Dolly*'s dinghy over to *Dolly*, trailing his own recovered small boat; and I wouldn't trust him to do even that, but that he wanted to collect a pair of substitute oars Johnson had offered him. Like Lenny, I found riling the permissive atmosphere concerning Ogden. As for Victoria, she would learn too late that in this world one must look out for oneself.

Johnson sat down beside me.

'Well?' I said. There are some things which are beneath me, and I do not mind delegating those. I disliked having had to abandon this particular inquiry to Johnson, but it was necessary. Perhaps Johnson was as well known as I was. But he had an excuse through his burglar for making it, and I had no excuse at all.

So I said, 'Well?' in a tone no doubt less than patient; and Johnson stared down thoughtfully at the pitcher of Scotch in his hands, glass to glass, and said, 'Would you like to know why Michael Twiss is actually here?'

There was a short silence, broken by a distant rendering of 'Any Old Iron'.

'I can guess,' I said gloomily.

'Quite. Why didn't you tell me,' said Johnson pleasantly, through both parts of the bifocals at once, 'that Dr Kenneth Holmes was on Rum?'

Damn. 'Because I wanted to find out for myself first what really happened in Rose Street,' I said sulkily. 'How did you hear about Kenneth?'

The owl-like glasses inclined. 'If Kenneth Holmes really killed Chigwell, what on earth do you imagine you could do anyway? Although I must admit he's still in the running. The police have found no trace of my burglar or your small, warty friend. Nor, I deduce, have they yet found the late Mr Chigwell, with coat hanger or without. Lastly, if you wish to know, I learned of Dr Holmes's whereabouts in the same way that Michael Twiss did: from the radio news.'

'He's dead,' I said blankly.

'He's not dead. He's the Ministry's chief explosives engineer, now doing prototype instrument work for the Nature Conservancy on Rum, and he has been called in to advise after the bomb outrage on the submarine *Lysander*.'

'The nuclear submarine? The one undergoing trials somewhere up here?'

'Correct. She was returning to her base in South Rona and had passed outside Raasay when the explosion occurred. It could have sunk her, and the damage to instrumentation was considerable, I quote, but she was able to return under her own power. A navigating officer, a naval scientist and a leading mechanic in the affected compartment lost their lives. You are not alone in suffering tribulations at sea.'

He was pipped. 'You're angry because I came with you under false pretences,' I said gently. 'I'm sorry.'

'Goodness me. Dear girl,' said Johnson, and rapped his pipe smartly on a big onyx dish with a chromium model of *Evergreen* stuck on its rim, 'I want your face, that's all. I don't want your confidences.'

He was a cool customer. Perhaps he and I had more in common than I thought. A man who knows his own mind, under some circumstances, can make a very good ally.

The idea sustained me, or nearly, through an evening of nerve-wracking ennui. We were shown over the boat, not missing a deep freeze or a centrifugal windscreen wiper, by May Bird, who then put on a frilly apron over the pink cloqué and served a large, expensive meal which she had cooked herself, no doubt by radar. After this, having sung comic songs to each other without cease over the radio telephone, the neighbours arrived from the floating trattorias all around, each boatload slightly plastered but prepared to sink its trayful of vodka and remain to join in the good, clean, innocent fun. A little complex of cigars and emba minks settled down to high-stake poker in one corner, but I did not join them. I never gamble.

Halfway through all this, Michael caught me. By that time it had occurred to me that if we were going to have a row, we might as well have it masked by the bedlam on *Evergreen* rather than amid the gentlemanly hush of *Dolly*. I allowed Michael Twiss therefore to whisk me into an empty, heavily upholstered cabin where, leaning arms folded against a bleached walnut wardrobe, he fixed me with his why-the-hell-all-the-*portamento* basilisk stare.

'Right,' he said. 'Now we know why you were so bloody anxious to get a date fixed at Edinburgh. Your gorgeous big chemist is working up north.'

My Mr Twiss was a sharp little man: sharp of feature, sharp of voice and filed to a positive barb where his ten per cent was concerned. After Johnson, I was getting more than fed-up with the carping, but it was no good getting riled. I said, 'You have a coarse little mind, Michael. Calm down. You needn't call in the Salvation Army just yet.'

'I told you to drop Holmes,' said Michael. Having to keep his voice low was a little handicapping his style. 'It's bad for you, and bad for your career. And if it's all so damned innocent, why hide the fact that he's not in London but Rum?'

'Because he asked me to,' I said nastily. 'He's important. He's a scientist, remember? Anyway, how did you find out?'

Same story. He had heard a news broadcast about the explosion on the submarine *Lysander*. Why the hell they had chosen this moment to broadcast Kenneth's name I should like to have known. Filling my lungs, I settled down on the mock ponyskin bedspread, and proceeded to handle my manager.

It wasn't a jolly encounter, but I did it, eventually. After all, if I'd been itching to fling my cap over the opera house and live the life of Riley with Kenneth, I should have done it long since. I reiterated, wearily, that nothing mattered to me, either, but my career, and I was not likely to jeopardize it. That my painting by Johnson was not something to abandon lightly, nor was my promising new friendship with Hennessy. That provided Michael also came aboard *Dolly*, what the hell could I do that would shake his shirtmaker's confidence?

He was not easy to placate, but he granted me so much, angrily, on my final, clinching argument that I had no other dates anyway. I was not walking out of the big slot in the Württembergische Staatstheater Ballet in order to snuggle with Kenneth. I was on holiday; and that was bloody well that.

Then May Bird's voice hunting us began to ring through the passages, and we had to abandon hostilities and return to the gig.

I wasn't sorry. I had begun to feel that there were either too many or far too few people around. I wanted people I knew on either side of me, and a good solid wall at my back.

Johnson said as much, too, later on, when the saloon had been cleared for the Birds' double act and we sat on the carpet behind a row of motor cruisers in beaded dresses, falling about laughing. The jokes were all about the Prime Minister, lodgers and Sheffield Wednesday, but they still fell about laughing, and May Bird, pleased as hell, gave them an encore, tripping back on her fat little feet in their ghastly pink satin shoes. Johnson murmured, 'Stick it. It won't last for ever. And you're safest in crowds. You couldn't slip a stranger in here. They know each other too well.'

'It isn't worrying me,' I said.

The bifocals inspected me: I could feel them. 'Isn't it? You're not only mixed up with a vanishing boyfriend and a murder, you know. You're in the middle of some damned big cock-up to do with nuclear submarines. Or hadn't it struck you?'

'It's struck me all right,' I said gloomily. This was what was known as a dilemma. I wanted protection, all right. But I didn't want Johnson Johnson supervising any meeting with Kenneth. The situation with Kenneth was delicate enough as it was.

'D'you really want to go on?' said Johnson. 'The canal should be safe enough, but we'll have to spend the night in Crinan basin tomorrow.'

Billy Bird, in a straw boater, had joined his wife, and someone was working a record-player. It burst into sound. Billy tipped his hat over one eye and picked up a cane. May sidled behind him, kneecaps crossed; plump hand arched on his shoulder, and they both plunged into song.

'She's… ma… lady love; she is ma
    dove… ma… baby-love.
She's… no gal… for sittin' down to
    dream…'

57

It was all there: the cocked eyebrow, the nimble reverse, the one-step, the little unified skip. The audience stamped with delight. 'I want to go on,' I said, and smiled. I could see my wrapped-around hair shining in his glasses, and my citrine topazes. 'If I may.'

'It's your risk,' said Johnson. 'We'll be with you all through the canal, and at night you can lock the cabin door and we'll tarpaulin the hatch. Although anyone who knows boats can usually tell the moment we're boarded. The rest of the time we'll pick you a bodyguard. If your manager doesn't object.'

'Object! He's the one I need guarding from,' I hissed under my breath. 'He doesn't like Kenneth. He'd stop me meeting him if he possibly could.'

'I see. Then in that case,' said Johnson, taking out his pipe, 'we'd better not chat in his hearing about your body in Rose Street. Or Kenneth's body, as it might prove to be.'

> 'She is de Lily… of Laguna…
> She is ma Lily… and ma Rose.'

And exit off, with Billy's straw hat held high over his ruffled white head, and May's diamond earrings swinging, one beat behind.

It seemed a long time before the party ended and I was finally back in bed on *Dolly*. The weather had changed. Coming out on deck we had found the water quite black, freckled with grey where the white caps were catching our light. The air moaned in, making the geraniums shake.

Now, half-asleep on *Dolly* between my monogrammed sheets I could hear the wind and waves still, and the creaking of wood; and buzzing among them, my own tangled thoughts. I wondered, now, whether I was right in pursuing Kenneth like this. Why not, indeed, forget the whole affair, leave the country, let fate and the police take their course? Johnson would help me. Hennessy, even.

I thought about it, and I might even have acted on it if Johnson and Michael hadn't both been so keen that I should. I am an obstinate woman, and I dislike being pushed. By anyone, anywhere.

Then I must have slept, for how long I don't know; for I was wakened by a sound I could swear was a human voice, calling my name. '*Valentina!*' it said. '*Valentina, my sweet!*'

I sat up, my heart giving huge, exhausted beats like a worn-out dynamo. I was dreaming. That was a name only one man, ever, had been permitted to use. I listened again.

The wind. The sound of a thin rope, whipping. The clink and gurgle of waves on the hull. The creak of decking over my head, and a muffled thud. Then again a voice, the same voice, the same guarded whisper, so careful not to waken the rest: '*Tina! Valentina, come quickly!*' It could only be Kenneth.

Then I swung my legs out of bed slowly, and took my dressing-gown slowly, and opened my door. Where would the others be? Johnson had stayed on board *Evergreen.* Lenny and Rupert were in the main saloon bunks, and Michael had the big stateroom forward, at the other end of the boat. Unless Lenny and Rupert heard and opened the door into the cockpit, I was safe. I stepped into the cockpit… There was no one.

No one on the deck to right or to left. It was very dark. The sea was black: the sky black and starless. No lights showed now on land, and none in the bay but for the tossing sparks of ships' anchor lights. Far across, in *Evergreen,* a single window was lit.

I looked in front. Among the tangle of dark shadows made by mast and rigging and coachhouse roof, I could make out nothing alien in the dark: no warm, waiting presence with muscular body and rough, uncared-for brown hair. The air round me was damp and sharp and I shivered, and shivered again as in the dark the queer whine in the rigging rose a tone and then another, and fell, whimpering like a child. Then from behind me came the whisper again. '*Valentina! Tina, my darling!*'

I turned; and there on the roof of my cabin was the kneeling shadow I looked for, black in the black night. The wind rose. I stretched out my hands. The orchestration high in the wire rigging was rising fast to a scream. The presence on the cabin roof, as if stirred by the wind rose up over me. *Die Fledermaus* – a man, a whirlwind, a muffled, cloaked bat.

It rose. It fell. I felt the warmth of its flesh. And then all the howling darkness about me was resolved in a single sharp blow over the shell of my skull that lifted me, hurled me, propelled me over the edge of the cockpit and into the sea.

'She's coming to. How do you feel?' It was Michael's voice, full of anxiety for his investments. I opened my eyes.

I was in bed in my cabin on *Dolly*, but the swaying motion had stopped. It was still night: the lights were on and someone had undressed me. The someone was bending over me now, on the other side from my manager – May Bird. I thought of the whisper, the howling in the rigging, the blow from which my head reeled and ached, and the sight of the black water rushing to meet me; and my eyes blackened and my heart thumped again. May Bird, her brightly painted face raddled and puffy said, 'Now you lie still, love. *Dolly*'s boom never killed anyone yet, but you had a right do all the same. Johnson's gone for a doctor.'

Michael looked sullen, and I knew what he was thinking. Bad publicity. A drunken party with some second-hand concert artistes in some dead-and-alive spot in Scotland, ending in a spectacular ducking. I said hoarsely, 'I don't want a doctor. I'm all right. What happened?'

I didn't want a fuss either. If Kenneth was there.

Soon everybody had explained what had happened. The wooden crutch for the boom had blown down in the wind, a lashing had given way, and a sudden gust of wind must have brought the heavy spar hard over just as I stepped up on deck. Luckily, to men used to the sea, the slightest change in a boat's motion means action. The bump, the lurch and the splash as I went over had both Lenny and Rupert awake instantly, and they fished me hastily out. No one mentioned seeing anyone else. Johnson had been summoned over the RT and had brought Mrs Bird: Michael had slept through the whole thing and had had to be wakened. We were now in the canal basin where we had motored.

If it was Kenneth who had called me, why did he go? Or was it Kenneth at all? Sitting up, feeling sick, I listened to Rupert and Lenny in furious argument about their bloody crutch. I didn't know whose fault it was and I didn't care, though Lenny was perhaps protesting the most. He swore he tested it when we all came back from *Evergreen*, and it was quite secure then. I was examined and pronounced lucky to have a hard head; Michael swore the doctor to secrecy; and finally I persuaded everyone to let me have my own way and proceed with the cruise as we had planned.

But I wondered. Oh, God, I wondered. If I was right.

7

On the following day, Wednesday, the sun shone and the day's slow motoring through the Crinan Canal provided all the convalescence I needed. While Rupert and Lenny leaped up and down cavernous walls, threw and received ropes, switched engines on and off, heaved open lock gates in the company of curious sunburnt men and their dogs, greeted oncoming boats and dispensed, for four solid hours, more invidious regional gossip than fifty women in fifty teashops could do in a lifetime, Johnson continued to paint me; and as he did so, I talked.

Afterwards, I wondered if it was the gin or merely the blow on the head which made me so loquacious. Or perhaps, when there is violence in the air, one has an instinct to make one's will to society: to be known and to be understood.

I am not ashamed of my past. On the contrary, I like to remember how I, from nothing and less than nothing, have become Tina Rossi, with ninety thousand pounds in the bank, and cinnamon diamonds.

Nor am I bitter. In the war my father's family in Poland were killed. I suffered nothing but to be born in Fife, Scotland, where my father flew with other exiled Polish airmen, met and married my mother, and then died in a crash. I never knew him – or my mother, who died when I was born.

I was in an institution of one sort or another until I was seven. Then I was at school, and finding out that children from a Home were regarded as different; and also finding out what 'bastard' implied. My father had married my mother, but the result was the same. He was a foreigner; she was a potato picker; they were both absent, and my mother's relatives were largely unemployed and unemployable. It didn't do to shout back or to fuss. I changed the subject, made a new game, admired a hairclasp. My teacher had by then discovered that I had a talent – a high, true voice – but it didn't do to make much of that either. I hated it when I was singled out to deliver a song. It destroyed in a minute all the laborious progress I had made.

Later, when I was passed from one foster home to another, it was different. A talent brought the household some credit. I sang in church choirs, and was spoken to by ministers' wives, but the attention I attracted was fleeting. In those days one moved without warning. I would hear a strange voice downstairs, and my foster mother of a year or less would shout to me to fold up my clothes. In half an hour I would be packed and walking downstairs, to the nameless persons waiting below.

Sitting in the train with a strange woman, in a shrunken coat with my battered bag on the rack, I never wondered where I was going. Places were all much the same. The woman might have two children of her own, or three, as well as several she was paid for; and human nature being what it is, the best of the clothes and the food went to her own. I learned to keep house in a dozen different ways in a dozen different sorts of places, from stone fisher cottages on the windy, raw east coast to a shepherd's timber house in the Borders. Every woman had her own way, and what I learned to do in one place I had to unlearn quickly at the next.

I moved on from one to the other without regret, and bent all my mind only to making myself acceptable and useful as quickly as possible. I worked hard, and I smiled all the time. And while I was smiling, I decided that one day I was going to be rich, and famous, and sought-after. I would imagine, while writing my weekly letters to all my foster mothers and to the lady superintendents of the homes, how I would gradually break the news. I was a constant letter-writer in those days.

Not all of this I told Johnson, but enough. He made few comments, but neither did he express surprise or pity, or even admiration. He was, after all, wealthy and spoiled. Perhaps because of this, I went on to tell him of the later years, when I was put out to service in my northern village; and when, taken into the shooting lodge that season, I met Chase Ruddyman and his friends, over from Hollywood. He was due to make a big film in London when the shooting was over; and he took me back with him, to help staff his leased house. I was a very hard and a good worker; and this was what I had worked for. Also, I sang as I worked.

The rest is very well known. I was cheerful, I was hard-working, I had no self-pity. I made Chase laugh with my mixture of shrewdness and naïveté, and in time he discovered my voice. Chase and I have never been lovers. I was too remote from his world for that; and besides his taste never ran to women – all the world knows that. All the world knows too of the household he kept; actors and adventurers and artists, all the café society of the inter-pretative arts. He was the first man I had ever known to be careless with his wealth. All he got, he spent – on luxury, on sensation. His presents were kingly; but next week, after playing all night at a gambling club, he might be a pauper, and his secretary would be on the phone to Madrid, feverishly fixing up a new contract, a new film. Or, unexpectedly, a new backer would be charmed into the circle, and his tailors and his wine merchant would breathe again.

It was he who sent me to the Vienna conservatoire for my initial studies; and then, when the money ran out, it was my teacher in Austria who passed me, on his own account, on to Vittioni in Milan. I repaid my debt in work – and sometimes by selling a sudden, fabulous present from Chase Ruddyman. I wrote all the time to Chase, and his secretary wrote back sometimes. He would have honoured his obligations to me, I know, if he had not been killed in that plane crash. Planes have been fateful for me. But in this world you can get anything you want, if you are ready to work for it. I have no time for the idle.

I was launched from Milan, through an introduction to Giulini by the Conte and Contessa, who paid for my last year of training. They are still my very good friends.

'The prettiest coloratura soprano in the world,' said Johnson, setting down his glass. It was hot. We were tied up beneath the willows in a stretch of water so quiet that one could hear the bees humming in the meadowsweet. The towpath was deserted, and beyond there were only the flat bogs and mosses of Dalriada, and the blue sky. Lenny was below, passing up fresh salmon sandwiches, while Rupert did something among the ropes for'ard. Soon, we should be at the end of the canal, and the next day we should race.

'And it was then that you met Michael Twiss,' added Johnson, tilting his hat over his bifocal glasses. The cockpit smelled of varnish and salmon and Chablis and turpentine and the oily reek of paints; and then there was a little lift of air in the heat, and it smelt of meadowsweet. I glanced forward, where Michael was lying, stripped to the waist, in Bermuda shorts of impeccable cut. I could see the top of his thick lacquered hair, and his rib-cage, and his feet. Michael never put on weight, whatever he ate.

Yes, it was then that Michael Twiss, ambitious and out of work, stranded by a cheap engineering company that went bankrupt behind his back, met the Conte and the Contessa, and smiled and worked hard for them too, and finally met me.

I wasn't interested. I have seen back in Scotland what happens when one meddles with men. Children happen, and a room and kitchen in Pollokshaws, and hard work where there is no point in smiling, for most people you meet are worse off than yourself.

Then I realized that Michael wasn't interested either. That I was not a girl, or a passing entertainment, but a paycheque in prospect for the intense Mr Twiss.

I had never known Michael's origins, and I had never asked. He had been in his time many things, and had had many trades, but always his work had ended in disaster not of his making. Unlike me, he was embittered. He blamed not his intelligence but his birth, his accent, his lack of schooling, his lack of friends. But in fact he possessed many virtues: a quick brain, an ability to copy and to learn, and a capacity for work like my own. By the time he joined Milanese society he could pass for a gentleman, and when he left it he *was* a gentleman, and dressed and spoke like one. For he had made himself indispensable to my sponsors, and was fast becoming indispensable to me, too.

For my début was a sudden, overwhelming success. I touched on it lightly with Johnson, but when I speak of it, to myself, my throat is choked with the thought. At last it came, what I had worked for; and because of Ruddyman's friends, and all the others I had met and cultivated since, other things came, far more quickly than I had a right to expect: recordings, concerts and, finally, films.

For all this I needed a manager. For my money I needed an advisor. For my new career, I needed grooming. For my voice, I needed a coach.

Michael became all these. It was Michael who, watching the Italian society we moved in, changed my hair to its present French roll; and then employed a hairdresser, whenever I appeared, to vary its style so that I photograph always differently. All my clothes were made finer: my shoes were made of thinner leather, my gloves were kid wisps; my underwear and dresses were of silk that made me more slender yet. And the pounds he forced me to lose!

I was given a style: the jewellery I must wear; the hats I must eschew. And then, he set to work on my voice.

He cannot have known that this talent lay within him, this understanding of music. He had always been fond of it, he said. He possessed, I know, at a time when he had few possessions, an ancient radiogram with bakelite records, which went everywhere with him then. To begin with, he heard me with Vittioni, listening to my faults being explained; and to Vittioni's interpretation of the arias. Then, when he found me practising, Michael would act as Vittioni, correcting, reminding, forcing me to work on and on, improving until I was reproducing exactly what the master had said. He grew to know my voice better than I did myself; and then, as it came to light, to have a feeling for the music as great as my master's. The day came when, having done all that could be done on my Mozart for the next study, Michael made me go on to tackle a recitative and aria I had never before sung. I learned afterwards that he had spent all the previous night poring over it in manuscript. In any case, the result was climacteric. Before Vittioni, next day, I sang Michael's interpretation of Donna Elvira; and the master, silent for a long moment, suddenly rose and kissed me on both cheeks. Michael had made of me not a pupil, but a singer.

He went everywhere with me after that. I paid his living expenses, and a tenth of what I earned he took, and probably much else of his own on private business besides. He was rich and wore only silk shirts, and referred to the owners of opera houses by their Christian names – but very occasionally he still dropped his aitches. He had women friends, I knew, but he was discreet about them. And nothing, ever, was allowed to come between him and his chosen vocation, which was Tina Rossi.

But I said nothing of this at all to the bifocal glasses reflecting the bright cushions of *Dolly*. I merely said, 'Yes. I'm very lucky to have Michael: he's a genius for management. And he makes me work far too hard. But for Michael I should spend all my life lying on beautiful boats such as yours, being painted. Michael! Do you hear! You are a slave-driver.'

'Do I look like a slave-driver?' said Michael lazily. But I knew that this evening at Crinan there would be a handful of telegrams waiting for him; and he would go ashore and make phone calls; and then out of that damned pigskin dispatch case would come the score of someone's interminable opera, which I should then have to learn. I found I was frowning, and smoothed out my face. It was silly to be angry with Michael. Without him I should still be striving to do all these things. Without me, he would be nothing.

Then, it seemed, almost at once, we were on the last sunny stretches, and the canal basin, where we were to spend the evening and night, lay there before us.

Folded in greenery, with the blue sea beyond the lock gates and the green coastal hills and isles in the distance, the last stretch of the canal and the basin at Crinan itself was packed with yachts as with groceries. And not only yachts. Motor launches, small puffers, wartime conversions of ungainly size and unforgettable shape crowded the water, where also I could see the stout dark red belly of the Buchanans' sloop *Binkie,* the shabby decking of Ogden's string-tethered *Seawolf,* and the shining twin masts of Hennessy's yawl, the suave *Symphonetta*.

'Well, there it is, Tina,' Johnson was saying. He stood, pipe in mouth, conning her in, and waving cursorily from time to time as he was hailed from either side. 'All the essence of a paranoic scout camp financed by a brewery. Port, Rupert. We'll get in beside *Cara Mia*.'

'My God, is she there?' said Rupert, craning to see over the coachroof as he eased the tiller. 'Jane! Cindy!'

Two reclining figures, one in a man's shirt and the other in an arrangement of string fulfilling the minimum requirements of decency, rolled over on the decks of a big motor cruiser as we slid past, and waved. Victoria was there too, in her patched trousers and bare feet, with a screwdriver, half sunk, in her hand. 'And my God, Ogden will dig that,' said Rupert as he reversed and cut.

'He doesn't like the *Cara Mia*?' It was not hard to see why. Compared with this, Cecil Ogden's *Seawolf* was a cereal packet, with a hole in the bottom instead of a gift.

'Dotty sub-debs aren't much in Cecil's line,' said Rupert. 'The boat belongs to Moody the financier – that's Tim Moody over there.'

True enough, a young man came into view in very small boxer shorts and a peaked cap from the Aquatic Sports Club, Barbados. Two other boys and a large girl in a catsuit made their appearance, and there was a general clinking and pouring. Daddy, clearly, was absent at work in the City. Music, of a sort, shuddered out from the decks.

'Huddy Leadbetter's new single,' said Rupert thoughtfully, effecting a final clove hitch. He avoided looking at Johnson.

'Goodbye,' said Johnson lazily. 'Give them my love, and don't smoke anything I wouldn't smoke.'

In five minutes, Rupert had gone.

In five more minutes Michael too had gone, hellbent for the hotel and the telephone, leaving a fallout of Trumper's Eucris behind him. A succession of working parties began to move round from boat to boat, like bees preparing to swarm. The clinking of glasses, competing strains of tape, radio and record-player, and loud bellows of laughter, live performance, were heard all over the basin. Some of the parties came aboard *Dolly*, and Lenny served drinks.

Their jokes were all very long, and some of them were in dialect. They seemed to have had a very dangerous summer. Eventually,

Johnson said something about fixing dinner at the hotel and clambered ashore, leaving me to change in my locked cabin, with Lenny as watchdog. Trouble seemed unlikely. But then, trouble always seems unlikely.

I dressed in white cotton matelassé and uncut turquoises. I was very brown, from the South America tour, and my hair had bleached itself almost silver. After a little thought I let it down smoothly over my shoulders and brushed it with Givenchy's Le Dé. I had just finished this when a voice said, '*Hey, Missus!*'

I was no one's *Hey missus* now. I slipped on little kid slippers by Jourdain, and fastened my watch, that Byng gave me, in three colours of gold; by which time I had had three *Hey Missuses* more. Then heavy feet sounded on the deck over my cabin, there was a thud as somone jumped into the cockpit, and the same rough voice, 'Are ye there, Mistress Rossi? I've word from Dr Kenneth at Rum!'

And at the same moment Lenny's voice, damn him, said near at hand, 'Now wait a bit. Let's hear who you might be first... oh, it's you, Tom.'

And the first voice, softening, said, 'Aye, man. Tom McIver. I've a wee note for the lady. She'll be in?'

I ran to open the door.

He was from the puffer. He had a Breton beret and a three-day beard, and he stank of kippers and coal dust. But he had a message from Kenneth. I looked Lenny straight in the eye, and Lenny grinned and said, 'Tom McIver's all right, ma'am. You'll excuse me. I'm cleaning the cooker.' And he disappeared, tactfully, across the saloon and into the galley.

I asked McIver in, and said, 'He's here? Dr Holmes is in Crinan?'

Mercury cleared his throat. Under the bristle his big face was scarlet. 'Na, na. He's no on Rum either. You've maybe no heard of the *Lysander*'s accident?'

'Of course I've heard.' If I was short, it was because I was cold with alarm. If he wasn't on Rum, where the hell had he gone? Or did the idiot mean he was dead?

'Aye. Well.' The stupid man shifted from one great foot to the other. 'He's been moved from Rum to South Rona, Dr Kenneth, while they look into that business. The submarine was on trial off South Rona, ye'll ken.'

Where the hell was South Rona? My face must have betrayed my exasperation and dismay, for the man added quickly, 'It's not far away: it's a wee island next to Raasay, ye ken.' And as my face remained blank, 'Just over from Portree, Skye. There's nothing on it but a few wee huts where the sub. crew and the scientists stay. Well, he's there now; and he canna get to Rum, and I was to seek you out, mistress, and gie ye this.'

I snatched it. It was an old OHMS envelope, sealed over with sticky tape, with a scrap of paper inside. On that were a few words only in Kenneth's big, personal writing. *Don't come now. Don't come ever – it isn't safe. Goodbye. I love you.* There was no signature and no need of one. It was Kenneth, I knew.

I looked at it for a long time, and I smiled as I looked. Oh, he was still afraid for me, still protecting me. He was giving me the chance to retreat. But he must know perfectly well that he had also now given me an address where I could reach him in privacy far more easily than before. For South Rona was only a short sail from Portree. And in three days' time, I should be in Portree on the *Dolly*, on the race's last call before Rum.

I touched my friend's kippery arm and said, 'Thank you for bringing this. I know you won't speak of it to anyone else... Did you see Dr Kenneth when he gave you this? Is he well?'

My friend had removed his beret, at last. He cleared his throat. 'Oh, well enough. Aye. They're all a bit pressed, ye ken, since the accident.' He paused, and then said, 'Would there be a reply?'

I hadn't dreamed a reply would be possible. Now I realized that this puffer was probably taking regular supplies to South Rona for both lighthouse and base. With the mellow evening sunlight all about me, and the convivial sounds from the concourse, the lap of water and the distant Niagara of the locks, the cry of gulls and the sundown song of the land birds, with all the saltwater togetherness going on all around me, I thought of a dead man swinging slowly in a cupboard in Rose Street and said, 'Yes, there's a reply. Tell Dr Kenneth... tell him that there has been a death in the family, and might be another. Tell him... particularly to take care of himself.'

Say it exactly like that. And tell him that on Saturday I am coming to Portree on *Dolly*, and that he must not fail to meet me privately there.'

There was a pause. I could not tell whether Mercury was shocked or approving, or whether he had even absorbed what I had told him. I dared not put it in writing. The high-coloured, unshaven face showed no reaction. After a moment though, McIver said, 'He mightna manage to cross. There's a fair stramash on the now, with the submarine boys, ye understand.'

'Then I'll come to South Rona,' I said.

There was another pause. 'Ah,' he said. 'But the boat you're on isna going to South Rona, though. The race only calls at Portree.'

'I know. But other boats must make the crossing sometimes from Portree to his island; your own, say?'

It was a risk. I wanted no publicity. Tina Rossi in this land of porridge and peasants being smuggled from one place to the next in a puffer – that would be a manquet for *Oggi*. Already, as I waited for the slow-witted creature to answer, approaching footsteps resounded on the quayside.

I drummed my fingers. Rupert or Lenny I did not mind. But I had no desire to be found by Michael in conference with this man.

It was too late. The seaman had actually drawn breath to answer when the footsteps halted on the quay above *Dolly* and a loud, commanding, and familiar voice demanded, 'And who the hell may you be, bothering Madame Rossi? Get off this boat before I get the owner to put you in charge!'

I smiled. 'Mr Hennessy, can't I have an admirer in the shipping lanes? This gentleman simply wanted to shake my hand because he has all my records. Don't be angry with him, or you'll leave me with no public to sing to!'

My friend from the puffer, who probably could not tell the difference between Beatrice di Tenda and the Fairy Queen from *Iolanthe,* looked surprised, but said nothing except, 'Well, I'll have to be getting back.'

'I beg your pardon,' began Stanley Hennessy, a little less heated, but I was already suggesting kindly to the pufferman that he should call for a beer when Johnson returned. Anything, anything to hear more about Kenneth.

'I'm sorry.' The fellow stared stolidly back. 'I'll have to go, mistress. We're due out on this tide: we're in the sea lock as it is, and the boys are waiting.' He must, God save us, be the skipper. Hennessy looked as if he were bolted to the deck: clearly he would not leave while McIver was there. It was hopeless.

'Well, goodbye, Mr…'

'Tom McIver. Just call me Tom.'

'Goodbye, Tom. And thank you. I hope we'll come across one another again.'

'Oh, aye. Ye don't have to look far for the *Willa Mavis*… We'll be at Portree on Saturday,' he said. And, unsmiling, he put on his beret and left.

It was a pleasure, after Tom McIver had gone, to greet Stanley Hennessy and to give him, out of Lenny's hearing, a sketch of life on the *Dolly*.

He wanted me to dine with him that night but I had, regrettably, a prior engagement with Johnson and Rupert at the hotel. I agreed, instead, to post-dinner liqueurs, if my hosts would permit, on *Symphonetta* alone. He wanted advice on the hanging of my Rhu menu portrait.

To be frank, I had forgotten about that picture of Johnson's. There was a better one half finished on board. But I agreed. I do not antagonize people like Stanley Hennessy. But I make them pay highly for what they buy.

Dinner was pleasant in the hotel overlooking the islands, with the moon risen, a round pallid primrose over its field of satin and hessian on the dark sea. Within, it was warm and smoky and comfortable, with talk and laughter filling the room. Rupert had not come back and Lenny was busy elsewhere so I dined with Johnson, at a table which was soon pushed against three others to allow the quips to be heard, and explained to me. Crackling with animation, Johnson behaved like a cobalt bomb, and towards the end did a small charactersketch of Thalberg which had me in tears. Then Michael Twiss joined us.

I knew by his face at once what had happened. There was one thing and one thing only that rejuvenated Michael, despite his copy of *Be Young with Yoga*, and that was money. The particular sleekness this time, the little, crisp gestures as he joined us were due, I was sure, to the fact that he thought he had separated Kenneth and me.

And so it turned out. A contract – a big contract, the largest even I had ever been offered – to sing *La Gioconda* on Friday at the Colón. Which meant, of course, flying tomorrow from Abbotsinch to London, and to Buenos Aires on Thursday.

'No,' I said. And I thought, it was a strange thing that never, even in my recent career, had I had so many lucrative offers from abroad as I had had now, just before and just after singing in Edinburgh.

Michael smiled and said, 'Tina, my dear,' as if reproving a child, 'we'll discuss it later. It will be a beastly wrench for us both, I know, to give up this marvellous voyage, but Mr Johnson will have to forgive you. A great singer belongs to the world.

'Is this chair taken? Do you know, I'm quite hungry?' Bloody Michael. Bloody-minded Mr Manager Twiss.

Being Michael, of course, he would not risk an explosion in public; and neither would I. But once the tables around us had cleared, and we had nothing to do, Johnson and I, but watch Michael finish his disgusting pudding, I opened my attack. I was not accepting any engagement in Buenos Aires. Or, it appeared, in Mexico City the following week. I had announced that I was taking a rest, and that was what I was proposing to do.

'Tina, we can't bore Mr Johnson with all this.' Michael was furious at having to discuss it here and now. 'You know how concerned I've been about this whole trip. The continual draughts are bad for your voice. You can't practise; you haven't done a single half-hour of exercises since Saturday. Now you are throwing aside a contract which may never be renewed. You know how touchy these people are. Once it gets about that you are snubbing them, other people will hold off.'

'Let them,' said I. 'Do you really think I'll starve?'

Michael was really *aufgeregt*: his face had gone quite pale under his suntan, with red spots on the cheeks. He said, 'It's easy to say so; but you don't have to smoothe down these bastards and fight through new bookings. It isn't good enough, Tina. You promised to give all this up if an offer arrived. You can't expect me to manage you unless I can depend on some simple co-operation.'

He had finished, and we were standing up, while Johnson was paying the bill. I had just enough sense left to keep my voice down. 'Then don't,' I said coldly. 'If ten days' holiday are going to ruin my voice and all my future engagements, then it's exceedingly sad. For ten days' holiday is what I am going to have.'

Johnson was occupied still with the waiter. 'All right. Take them, ducky,' said my manager. 'And then try singing without me. You'll be having a damn sight more than ten days' holiday, my sweet. You'll be lucky if you sing in anything better than "Radio Scrapbook 1903" for the rest of your life. *What can you do without me?*'

'Save money,' I said.

'Hullo! Has Mr Twiss gone?' inquired Johnson, turning towards us just then.

'He had to rush out,' I said. I was more shaken than I tried to show. In some ways Michael was my genius: it was true. But there were other things besides singing. And for the first time... for the very first time in my life, I was becoming a little weary of work. So, when Johnson said with sympathy, 'He was a bit upset, I'm afraid, about your new contract. I feel guilty because, of course, I very much want you to stay,' I replied at once, 'I mean to. Michael is a little neurotic. He'll recover... And now in any case I must leave you – I hope you forgive me – to meet Mr Hennessy on *Symphonetta*.'

In the warm, dark air of the terrace, Johnson's bifocals shone like old bottles. 'Of course. Of course,' he said. 'I'd forgotten. The wolf of Crinan. You'll enjoy seeing over his boat, but don't let him bore you. I'll send Rupert over if you like in about an hour to fetch you both over. Or is that presumptuous?'

'No, Johnson,' I said suddenly, 'you are a man, I find, of considerable experience.'

'In some things.' He took out his pipe, and the harbour lights flashed on his glasses. 'I have only one rule. I never offer advice.'

To hell with Johnson, as well.

*

74

Stanley Hennessy's yacht was magnificent and so, I must say, was he. Large and charming, he waited by the companionway, and below my feet sank into bearskin while one of the three silent helpers, in white jacket, served coffee and salignac. Later, brandy in hand, I was taken on tour.

I had never seen so much electrical equipment. *Symphonetta*'s engine room was like a small bakery plant, so hygienic and sparkling. Her electronic gear was the equal nearly of *Evergreen*'s, and she had a wardrobe of sail that would outfit the America's Cup.

Nor did Mr Hennessy swear, as do the Buchanans, by the maps and tips of the Good Book alone. On the chartroom shelves were over seventy Admiralty sheets, all of the Scottish west coast.

When I mentioned *Evergreen* back in the saloon, Hennessy was amused. 'My God, the pride of the Fol de Rols! Don't say you had to spend an evening in the only floating Wimpy Bar with its own cabaret. I should think those two poor old things are certifiable by now.'

He got up, after knocking the third brandy back. 'Madame Rossi, I'm a lonely man, and you're good for me. Come. I've boasted about my boat long enough. Come and show me where this lovely drawing should hang.'

Guess where. I let him take me as far as the master stateroom, because when he got there, he slid open a baize-lined drawer in a dressing-table and produced, not the drawing, but a small leather case containing a marquise and baguette diamond bracelet worth maybe four thousand pounds. The case said Wartski, and it looked new. He must have followed my thought, for he said thickly, 'It wasn't my wife's. It's for you, Tina. For you.'

It was a gamble he took. It is a gamble they all take. I have a name, a standing; I cannot be forced. If I choose to sleep with them, they have been lucky, this throw. If I do not, and nine times out of ten, ninety-nine out of a hundred I do not, then they must act the good loser, and hope for my interest next time. For the jewels I keep, always.

Anyway, that night I had enough on my mind without Stanley Hennessy. I smiled; I heard my voice automatically saying the right, the routine things; and I brought him back to the saloon because he had drunk a good deal. With the bracelet clasped on my wrist, I allowed him to kiss my hand, and then my arm. Then I retired for a cooling period to a room with a lock; and when I returned we talked about his sugar and cotton estates, and his family shipping line to Latin America, and his other interests abroad. He was like all tycoons, utterly hypnotized by himself. I did not mind. These days, if I subjected myself to boredom, I first made sure of my fee.

All the same, I was glad when Rupert's hail came from the quayside. It was amusing to see Hennessy's temper flare: he had spent an hour creating for me an image, and here was Rupert, all careless young gentry, to spoil it. 'I really doubt,' I heard Stanley saying on deck, 'if the lady is interested in beer-parlour juvenilia.'

Rupert's voice, still mild, said, 'It's not quite as ripe as that, sir, although I won't claim that everyone is stone cold sober like yourself. We thought she'd like to hear some mouth music and a bit of piping, maybe. Won't you come yourself, sir?'

'Where? To *Blue Kitten*?' *Blue Kitten*, I recalled, had the pipes.

'No – we're all on *Cara Mia*, Tom Moody's boat. Madame Rossi?'

I was up on deck, in the lamplit darkness, by the time he called me, but Stanley Hennessy, his back to me, did not give way. Instead he said drily, 'I imagine your young beat friends would interest her even less. Mouth music! More likely readings of Genet and reefers.'

Rupert was angry too. 'No doubt. Do come, sir,' he said, 'then if anyone falls in the oggin, you'll know what to do.'

For a big man, Stanley Hennessy was very light on his feet. One brandy less, and he would have lifted Rupert clean over the side. As it was, he caught him a glancing blow on the jaw which Rupert, swaying, almost entirely deflected. For a moment, he looked like replying; then turning quickly, he stepped down to the quay, breathing hard. He had seen me.

'I'm sorry, Madame Rossi,' said Rupert. 'Mr Hennessy, I apologize. But you'll admit you're pretty damned ready to run down me and my friends. You can't expect everyone to lie down and take it. Will you ask Madame Rossi if she wants to come?'

'Stanley.' I put my hand, with the diamond bracelet on it, on Hennessy's arm. 'We're all tired, but I mustn't offend Johnson: he *is* my host. Forgive the boy. To be young is to be silly, we know.'

'The boy can go to hell,' said Hennessy forcibly. '*After* I've seen the colour of his five thousand pounds.' And, white with temper, he led me on to the quay, whence, in silence, Rupert and I walked to Moody's big motor yacht.

Really, men are impossible.

On *Cara Mia*, which was an expensive mess, there was everybody, except perhaps Cecil Ogden. The dotty sub-debs had become, if possible, a little more undressed, and the resident males had become a little tight. But Johnson was there, his feet up, and there also were the QC from *Blue Kitten* and *Mina's* professor with guitar, and a CA's family, and the two Buchanans from *Binkie*, in clean shirts, exchanging blood-curdling reminiscences of something named, impossibly, the Cooing Sound. I recalled one of Johnson's remarks during dinner. 'You haven't lived,' he had said, 'until you've had a ten-tonner read you his log book.'

The tape had changed to what Rupert, jeering, referred to as quiet, showbiz pop. And indeed, it was not overloud, except when the pipes and the guitar were playing together.

That was the party I sang at. I remember in the middle saying impatiently to Johnson, 'Shall I sing?'

He didn't even lift his damned glasses from the duet of 'Westering Home', but merely remarked, 'Depends what you charge.'

So, of course, I sang. There is a rather good ballad, which takes a lot of experience and breath control, but has an impact quite its own, particularly at drunken parties. I launched into it in the first perceptible pause in the riot, and you could have heard a mouse sneeze by the second bar.

Whatever Michael may say, absolute rest does my voice nothing but good. It came, high and pure and child-like, and I can tell you, sustained head notes are hell. Victoria was crying.

'Perhaps the moon is shining for you in the far country...
But the skies there are not island skies...
Do... you not remember the salt smell of the sea?
And the little rain?'

I gripped the last note in my diaphragm like a nut in a nutcracker and diminished it, and it was magnificent. I can usually tell to a second how long a silence will hold before the applause breaks out, but that was a record. Then I sang the Waltz Song from *Romeo and Juliet*. It couldn't miss. And it didn't. Who needs Michael Twiss?

When we finally went home to *Dolly* the sky was pale in the east and Rupert's arms were tightening round the matelassé as he lifted me on board in a way that made Johnson's bifocals twinkle like butter dishes. I said, 'What a silly encounter that was, Rupert, between you and Hennessy. What on earth did it mean?'

Rupert put me down in the cockpit. Johnson, following, said with interest, 'Yes. Tell her. Me too, Rupert. What did it mean?'

In the flood of light from my cabin, Rupert visibly blushed. 'It was my fault. I took a swipe at him. But he has bloody bad manners at the best of times. And to imply that everyone under twenty is a layabout or a junkie or a ponce just because his Frederick got hooked on amphetamine and jumped into the sea is a bit this side of too much.'

'His son?'

Johnson had switched on the saloon lights, and forward I saw Lenny busy with cocoa in big jugs. 'Yes. His wife died of cancer some years ago, while Hennessy was playing about with some starlet. Then the son drowned himself off *Symphonetta*, and Hennessy wasn't a good enough seaman to save him. Hence the killing drive for perfection ever since. He'll blame anyone except the boy. Rupert went to school with him, you see. Hennessy can never forgive him for knowing the story.'

I took my cocoa from Lenny. It was steaming hot. And in my bed, I knew, would be an electric blanket, with my nightdress on it, folded and warm. Already, the dawn air was stirring my hair.

On my arm, Hennessy's diamonds sparkled and danced. I said, 'All the same, Rupert, it was unfair, surely, to throw the thing in his teeth.'

'All right, I apologized,' said Rupert, eyeing Johnson as if he and not I had made the remark. 'But don't run away with the idea that Mr Stanley Hennessy is a figure of tragedy. It's a safe bet that a few hundred daddies lose their Fredericks for every cargo the Latin Shipping Line carries.'

There was a little silence. Then, 'That's only a rather uninformed guess, Rupert,' said Johnson gently. 'Let Tina make up her own mind.'

I said nothing, but I was not very surprised. I had heard of gun-running, of course. And at least some of Mr Stanley Hennessy's superb equipment for *Symphonetta,* I had already noticed, was made in regions of Europe and Asia where British yacht owners rarely drop in.

I thanked Johnson, then, for this pleasant evening, and I closed the door of my cabin, warned of our early start tomorrow, when of course the race proper would begin. As I brushed my hair, relaxed in my lovely swansdown, I saw the pale sea in the distance rising from the night's gloom, stained opal and pink in the dawning. It was beautiful.

It was coming to me that it was not impossible to survive without Michael. Now he had moulded me, the mould could not be broken. I knew I could not sing, without him, the great roles which would keep me among the first names of music. I have the voice and the application, but not the instinct or the heart. With a great many aunts, it is safest not to develop a heart.

But I could enjoy, as I had done tonight, the applause of the herd. It would give me my living, and all I wanted in moral support. My film work would go on. And I need not, at last, work so endlessly hard.

Michael did not mean, I knew, what he said about leaving me. He would be on board still tomorrow. He had made a fortune out of me, after all. But I – I owed nothing to Michael. Not now.

I went to sleep thinking, Thursday morning. In three days I should be in Portree, and the *Willa Mavis* would give me news of

Kenneth. Would he come? Would he come as I asked, to Portree? And if he were struck, if he couldn't freely sail from South Rona, who then whispered to me in Lochgair, the night I was struck by the boom? Or did I imagine it all?

I fell asleep, and dreamed all night of Wagner.

8

It was a short night. At six, a cock crew, it seemed under my elbow, and I heard beyond my door and the cockpit the saloon door slide open as both Johnson and Rupert emerged to pad about on the deck. A smell of coffee seeped through, indistinctly, from the galley. From the fo'c'sle, there was no sound. Michael, I took it, was sulking. Who cared?

By six-thirty we were in the sea lock with *Binkie*, and Rupert was rolling about on deck roaring with laughter to such an extent that I dressed and emerged. I wore ski trousers, a man's printed lawn shirt and suede boots. Everyone else wore large dirty woollens with yellow oilskins. Bob and Nancy Buchanan wore their small woollen caps and sat on *Binkie*'s coachroof, subsiding with *Dolly* in unison as the lock water ebbed, and relating, it seemed, the stop-press or aftermath of the Club's night out at Crinan. There was no sign of life on *Cara Mia*, but the basin was full of exhaust fumes, as the competitors moved about, ready to emerge.

The puffer *Willia Mavis* had gone out long ago, on the same course as our own, bound for the south end of Mull, but not before losing a coil of old rope and a loo lid to Ogden. Victoria, with the seat round her neck, strolled along the lock gate high above us just before we sailed through, and confirmed this, grinning. Her feet were still bare, and she looked as if she could do with a long sleep and a bath.

'Cecil Ogden should be in a bat-house,' said Rupert irritably after she had gone; but Johnson, perched up at the tiller with his bifocals repeating the first sun said, 'For God's sake don't go all Bunny Mother now over Victoria. She collects bums. If you want her, you'll have to go round the twist first.'

We were jilling about in a brisk wind, manoeuvring for the starting line, and Lenny, Johnson and Rupert appeared and disappeared among ropes and sails and tackle while they talked. 'She'll get no thanks for it,' I said. I know the Victorias. It begins with their ponies, at seven years old; and then they look for a man pony, because a grown-up man they could not manage or match.

The sail to Iona at least was fast: this much nearer to Kenneth, although Johnson and Lenny and Rupert were too occupied to be entertaining, and Michael was sulking still, with occasional bursts of chat directed at Johnson, usually about some tired, old soprano he once knew in Florence who ended up doing budgie-seed jingles. No one could be more childish than Michael when he didn't get his own way. I hoped he was going to be sick.

On either side, the sunlit islands slipped past, wooded, pink with heather or rusty with bracken; some with small white houses, some with sheep. Soon we turned our backs on the mainland on our right and flew west, our main and mizzen sail full, for the south end of the island of Mull. Somewhere ahead of us, over the blue glittering water, was Hennessy's *Symphonetta* who must not be allowed, Lenny said, to obtain too much of a lead in case the weather changed and we had a bad beat to Barra. Rupert said nothing.

Around us were the other boats of our class – sixteen now, Lenny said. Two had dropped out at Ardrishaig and two more at Crinan, due to affairs of business, family, and poor winter upkeep. Now we were widely separated.

'Funny thing,' said Lenny to nobody in particular as we went spinning past *Binkie,* 'their Sniffa went off at Crinan, and they slammed the saloon door in me face.'

'Who did? Bob and Nancy Buchanan?' said Rupert. 'You were sloshed, Lenny. They entertain every layabout that has been in port.'

'Not this time,' said Johnson amiably. 'They had the cabin door locked all through the canal. Was it a gas leak?'

'Naw,' said Lenny. 'Drip from the waterpump into the engine compartment. Fancy that, now. Getting nearly as particular as *Seawolf,* aren't they, as to their company?'

Why waste time talking about workmen? Johnson's hand over mine adjusted the tiller, while I saw Lenny below spilling cream and whisky into the coffee. The sky was a pale, shining blue, laddered with shimmering floss where the high cloud was streamed by the wind. On the horizon, as we opened the Sound of Iona, the mid-blue of the sea met the sky in a filming of mist. If only the damned tub were a helicopter.

At teatime, we anchored off Iona island itself, with its cathedral, foursquare as a fishing boat, perched above a thumbnail of sacred white sand in a blue and purple and emerald sea. Rupert fled ashore to check in, and even Michael strolled on deck to study the form. Hennessy and his *Symphonetta* lay there already. But our other rivals were behind us, with one rare exception. Ogden's *Seawolf,* sailed, Johnson said, like a one-legged tricycle, had somehow got into the anchorage first.

Victoria herself, whom Rupert brought back from the checkpoint to celebrate, was filled alternately with jubilation and with gloom. By flogging both themselves and *Seawolf* to death, Cecil had got to Iona in excellent time but a state of disrepair so extreme that their departure this side of Christmas seemed (said Victoria) highly unlikely. Even now Cecil was on board *Seawolf* (said Rupert) mending the rudder with string. And since *Seawolf* was temporarily out of commission, Ogden had sent Victoria (said Rupert) to go to Staffa in *Dolly* for her share of the champers. *Seawolf,* when mended, would follow. It looked to me, just then, as if Victoria had had just about all she could take of *Seawolf* and Ogden.

I had heard – who hadn't? – about Duke Buzzy's champers. The Duke, who sailed Buckingham Palace with stabilizers, was in the habit of awarding an annual prize to any Club yachts venturing to make the extra short passage to Staffa. The prize took the forms of two crates of champagne left, as a rule, in the recesses of Staffa's large cave.

Two years out of three, had said Rupert, nobody got the champagne, either because Duke Buzzy wasn't sailing that way that year; or he was sailing but couldn't put a launch in to deposit it; or because the Duke got the champagne in, but none of the Club yachts managed to get it out. Outside the island of Staffa, said Rupert, there was virtually no anchorage. If you were agile and lucky, you could drop a hook there for a short time in calm weather. If not, not. And absolutely bloody not.

Today was calm. And Duke Buzzy's *Vallida*, said the checkpoint, had not only sent the crates into the cave, but Hennessy had already been there for his pick. The remainder, Johnson with *Dolly* was now going to lift. 'What about the race?' I demanded of Rupert.

He looked surprised. 'This isn't part of the race. We've checked in,' he said.

I said, with what patience I could manage, 'I know. But shouldn't we give the champagne a miss, and take advantage of the whole thing to check out? We'd have a head start over everyone but Hennessy, and we'd soon catch him up.'

'It isn't done,' said Rupert. And added, 'Don't you want to see Fingal's cave?'

O heresy! The quick answer was no. I stood as we chugged over to Staffa, and Johnson pointed out the low green hills of Mull on our right, and the long mouse-like ridge of Coll to our left. Ahead, dimly indigo on a mist-bed, floated still others: a flat cockscomb of rock called, it could not be, Eigg; a stub to the left of it named, they said, Muck; and beyond, a toothy fragment of the Red Cuillins of Skye.

To the left of these, wild and high and quite prodigally hilly, like a sketch by a child, was the island of Rum where Kenneth's laboratory was, and where Kenneth himself ought to be. I stood staring by the bare pole of the mainmast while Johnson dropped anchor beside a whorl of stacked peats made of pumice-stone, and I plodded down the companionway as soon as the dinghy was lowered. I wasn't going to be left alone on board *Dolly* with Michael.

Then I saw Michael was in the dinghy already. Pride would not allow me to return. I got in, Lenny started the outboard, and we went snarling off.

I recalled that Michael had already played the Mendelssohn overture five times on Johnson's tape since we came alongside Mull. I was going to Staffa because I couldn't avoid it. Michael was going to see if Felix had flunked on his homework.

Also we were both going because we noticed suddenly that we had an audience after all. The steamer *King George V* with, Rupert said, six hundred concert-going tourists had heaved into sight and dropped anchor, prior to disgorging all six hundred into Fingal's cave. We should, said Rupert, manage to reach the cave and come back before the first boats arrived. The path used by the tourists, he also kindly made plain, ceased before penetrating the inmost bay of the cave. They wouldn't even see Duke Buzzy's champers.

We landed, and Johnson, declaiming ('…The pillared vestibule, Expanding yet precise, the roof embowed…'), helped ashore first me, then the barefoot Victoria. Lenny, prompted by Johnson, got back into the dinghy and departed to lend first aid to the unfortunate Cecil, drifting behind us on *Seawolf*. The rest of us set off, all five, along the volcanic footpath which leads from the minuscule harbour, past the PRIVATE PROPERTY notice, and into the mouth of the phenomenon known as Fingal's cave.

I forgot, as fast as I heard it, all that Johnson then told us of Staffa. What is columnar basalt? I didn't know, nor did Michael. I knew that the cliff surrounding the jetty was made of thick charcoal columns, some half fallen, some upright, some faggoted sideways to show their neatly packed ends, like a stack of shorn logs. Bleached to honey, they sank below the green water, and from the boat I had seen them continue, a cropped host of columns below the green sea; a razed forest, a broken city of temples, the upraised sliced face of each stalk glimmering jade and veridian and turquoise like a handful of coins.

Here, our path was a honeycomb of truncated columns, sealed together here and there, by courtesy of Messrs MacBrayne. Above to our right the dark ribbing towered, creased as elephant hide, up to stony tissues and the green sward on the top; while the sea swirled and lapped below on our left, and ran in and out of the petrified stack behind which *Dolly* lay.

Behind me, Michael walked carefully with Rupert, saying nothing. Ahead, Johnson was talking gently to Victoria about Cecil Ogden. It was possible, I supposed, that Victoria was sustaining her friend in his weaknesses purely for his own good and not her own. Possible, but extraordinary. What good would Cecil Ogden ever do anyone, after all?

The causeway ran like a ledge round the south-east cliff face of Staffa, and then turned sharp right. I cannoned into Johnson, who caught me, black eyebrows lifted. I turned, and there was the cavern.

If anyone cares, Fingal, I am told, is a mythical Celtic giant. His cave is nearly seventy feet high and forty feet wide at the entrance, with the sea running inland to its full length of over two hundred feet. If anyone cares.

To me, it was a black booming vault lined with columns, grey, rose, lilac and charcoal, of natural basalt. Uneven, crowded columns hung from the roof and stuck up through the opaque peacock water, thinning here to bright green, which lay surging and lapping below us, darkening as it moved away from the sunlight and into the depths of the cave.

On our right, the causeway we were following turned along the right wall of the cave and continued, guarded from the water by iron stanchions and wire roping, almost to the far end, where a barrier had been erected. Johnson leading, we started along it.

It was dark. We walked on the honeycomb, which fell away on our left, stalk upon broken stalk, into the deep sea-floor of the cave. To my hand, on the right, were the massive ribs of the fall, its surface pitted with loving inscriptions. Behind us, in the bright blue day at the cave mouth, the next wave had entered – a swell that darkened the vent and ran, silent and spume-spotted, into the unquiet sea of the cave, easing like oil over the drying stalks of its margin.

It rolled below us, thick, thundery green, and on to where the cave narrowed and ended. There was a growling, rising fast to a roar. A storm of glimmering foam flashed at the cave end, rearing high in the blackness, then retreated. And as it declined the cave gave forth a new sound: a great, tinny clatter of laughter, a pouring of primeval scorn, a vast, roaring, continuing rattle of inhuman amusement.

My skin rose in goose pimples and Johnson turned back, still talking about Ogden, and stood with me at the wire fence which guarded the drop. 'Queer, isn't it,' he added. 'It's the stone beach at the end, getting sucked back by the tide. What d'you think, Mr Twiss? Too many minims?'

Michael's face was silkily white. Some things frightened Michael very easily. But I knew he would not give in. He was hypnotized by the sound.

Johnson glanced at him, and at Victoria, and at Rupert who, having gone ahead to the end of the path, had vaulted the barrier and was hunting, whistling, for the champagne. Johnson said, 'I have had an idea. Ringside seats, with refreshments, before the masses arrive. No, not the champagne. Duck under there and sit down, and we'll see what *Dolly* can do.'

What *Dolly* could do was to produce five polythene sachets from Johnson's hip pocket, with a dry Martini with olive in each. Trying to drink a dry Martini from the snipped end of a sachet is a task calculated to preserve anyone from mysterious terrors. There was a good deal of giggling, and Victoria dropped her olive. Michael jumped down after it.

It was to annoy me, no doubt, but it was a sad mistake, for athletic Michael was not. There was a clatter, a cry, and as Johnson vaulted down after him, Michael disappeared into the water.

Only for a moment. The swell lifted him again as Johnson's arm reached him, and single-handed Johnson slid him on to the rocks, where he lay, cocked at various levels, seawater running out of his mouth. Johnson gave him a few experimental pressdowns, evacuated the rest of the water, and turning Michael over said briskly, 'It'll sell for tinning. Has he fainted, do you think?'

We were all standing above him by then, cautiously, with our Martinis fizzing inside us. I said, 'He always faints. Should we leave him, perhaps, for *King George V* to retrieve?' I was in no mood for meeting six hundred people in this bloody cave. Waving from yacht or dinghy, yes. Within touching distance, emphatically no.

No one answered me. Victoria, kneeling, was taking dear Michael's pulse. Rupert, sitting, was stacking champagne in a haversack. Johnson, the only one standing, said, 'Rupert!'

He was looking down into the water. Rupert joined him.

What was it? Michael's wrist-watch? Another Martini? The olive? A twittering noise outside caught my ears and I said, 'Listen.

People outside on the causeway. The *King George* must have landed its boats.' No doubt I sounded annoyed. There was slime on my printed lawn sleeve, and I had no wish to sign autograph books.

Rupert said simply, 'Christ!' I walked forward to see what they were staring at.

It was a mine. A new mine. A live mine, rather fetchingly patterned, bumping to and fro here in the cave.

I had not come so far, I had not achieved ninety thousand pounds and all those small safe vaults of diamonds to die under ground with a shipload of trippers. I turned to scramble back up the path just as Johnson's hand took a grip of my arm.

'No! You would only attract them here quicker. Victoria, get out fast. Warn the *King George* people off. This is a small one as mines go, but it could bring the roof down and pretty well swamp the causeway and boats... Tina! Give her a chance to make herself heard, and then follow the crowd to the boats. If they see you first, they won't listen – they'll mob you. Rupert and I will stay here and do what we can.'

He was a fool. Before he finished speaking a monstrous wave had begun its slow roll from the mouth of the cave and glided past us, towards the black, lazy orb at our feet. The mine lifted, glinting on the massive green back, and subsided, swaying, as the comber passed on and with a roar, a crash and that appalling death rattle of stone, hit the end of the cave.

Soon, with the next wave or the next, the mine would glance sideways against the tiered wall of the cave. Or in the end, with all the press of water behind it, it would be hurled by that roaring fury against the beach of smooth, chuckling black stones, and buried here, in this ridiculous hole, I should die.

'What about him?' said Rupert. I had forgotten Michael existed.

Shoeless, stripped to the waist, Johnson was already half into the water. It was twenty-five feet deep. What did he think he could do? But he turned and said formally, in my direction, 'That is up to Madame Rossi entirely.'

Hell... oh, hell! Who cared about Michael? But how would it look, afterwards, if I abandoned him now? If there was an afterwards.

I knelt, and grasping Michael by his Turnbull & Asser silk shirt, I began to shake him like a half-eaten mouse. At the same time I addressed Johnson with clarity. 'Why don't we get out? You could carry him. What can you do here?'

'You'd be surprised,' said Johnson. That was all.

What Rupert and he did, in the end, was to enter the water, one on each side of the inlet, and attempt to trap the mine as it rolled in towards the end of the cave in the folds of Rupert's oiled nylon anorak.

It was a crazy scheme. In the first place Johnson, treading water on the far side of the inlet, had no foothold or handhold at all, except his left-handed grasp of the anorak. And Rupert, in the water below me, standing on some submerged counter with sea up to his waist, and a right-handed grip on the anorak, and in his left hand an improvised rope made of torn shirting and scarves, which stretched up over the stone walks at the water's edge, to the iron stanchions by the path, where it was lashed. As Rupert gripped his end of the wretched rope and took up his stance, a wave began its slow lift inwards towards them – and on the back of the wave, came the mine.

It took its time, this moving green plateau of water, which washed Michael's arm at my side and slid neck-high to Rupert where he waited in the water. With one hand, Rupert held fast to his improvised rope, and between his body and Johnson's, brilliant green in the water, stretched the thin German stuff of the anorak. The mine swam slowly, steadily towards them.

The wave engulfed Rupert. I saw him take a deep breath, his hand whitening on the rope just before the swell arrived, lipping his chin, mouth and nose. Then it passed him, dragging him backwards, and, passing silently with it, the mine nosed its way into the fabric between the two men.

For a moment, it breasted the wave and might have brimmed over the anorak had not Johnson moved inwards, stretching it high. It bobbed, rolling, dragged by the current round Rupert's body. He moved too, gently, to hold it fast in the trap. Then, with a roar, the wave broke without harm on the black beach behind, while there, between Johnson and Rupert, the mine remained in the water, caught fast in its shawl. This time, we were safe.

They had hoped, I suppose, to lift the mine in its anorak out of the water and lay it somewhere on the basalt, where at least it wouldn't be buffeted. In that they were unlucky. When, between that wave and the next, moving with infinite care, they enveloped the mine and tried gently to raise it, the nylon began to tear and give way. They had reckoned without the mine's sheer, unhandy weight; and the push of the water, and the lack of any adequate handhold or leverage. Before they were prepared for it, the next wave was upon them, and the next. I could see Rupert, the anchor man, muscles rigid, easing back with the roll of the mine. And Johnson, unanchored save by the anorak sleeve, was resisting each wave to avoid falling back on its surf, unshelling the mine like a pea from its pod to rush on to the beach and explode.

Three waves went by. I don't know what made me look at the rope, Rupert's lifeline tied above me to the fence by the path. But as I glanced at it, under my eyes the improvised thing started to vibrate. It stretched, elongating suddenly like wool, and one by one, under my eyes, the knots began to dissolve.

There is an instinct of the scullery, of the domestic crises of innumerable aunties over the years, that can serve me crudely yet. As the free end flew past me, I caught it, and hung on.

I hung on, sideways, my fingers scraping a handhold among the stony pillars and discs, and held Rupert half-drowned on his perch until with a shattering roar the wave broke at the cave-end, and the jeering chatter, louder, louder and louder, described its dying withdrawal.

Then I looked. Rupert, glistening, saluted me with a wave of the rope-end. Johnson was treading water again in much the same place, spouting sea water like a small table fountain, but safe. And between them in its yellow calyx the mine rocked, also unharmed and secure.

Beside me on the rocks, Michael Twiss snorted suddenly and groaned. I gave him a smack on the face, and then, as he sat queasily up, I dispatched him up the rocks to hang on to the rail. Now, if I held his hand and Rupert held mine, we could make a chain long enough to let Johnson in turn touch the opposite wall of the cave.

He would not have much of a grip, but enough perhaps to save us all until help came.

The next wave arrived, and it worked. It was an interesting achievement and I had forgotten all about my diamonds, perhaps because Michael was so frightened. With a score or an agent he was a man of acid and iron, but physically, I knew so well, he acted as do the underfed and unloved in the back streets where he was born.

After that, each wave was a fresh calculation: how big this time, how far the mine would travel, how much play to allow it. Deluged every few moments anew, clinging to slippery handhold or water-soaked rocks, the men in the water couldn't hold on for ever. I remembered as they probably did, that Lenny was not at the jetty but holding Cecil Ogden's hand in his impossible boat. The steamer passengers by now would be safely embarked, other yachtsmen warned off. Who was going to risk returning for us?

'I am betting my bottom dollar,' said Rupert at this moment, emerging, rather green in the face, from the last hideous comber, 'on Victoria.' He paused. 'All my other dollars, I need hardly say, Madame Rossi, are on you.'

He was a likeable boy. No one could leave him to drown.

He was right, too. Behind the rolling emerald of the next wave I could see a swaying of something at the cave mouth. There was a shrill hail, and a shout, and there was Victoria in a boat of magnificent scarlet, together with half the crew of the *King George V,* hell-bent for death, glory and danger beside her.

They rode up the long waterway towards us like the Valkyrie, laden with canvas and netting; and working in teams of two or three at a time, trapped and cushioned the mine where it floated.

I watched them, with Victoria, from the cave entrance where Johnson had sent us. Michael had already disappeared, walking quickly. I saw Johnson finally haul himself out of the water and begin, dripping, to hunt for his jacket, which lay on the causeway beside me. On the premise that if he was bothering about jackets, the mine must be safe, I climbed down and took it to him. I also took to him the revolver which had fallen out of its pocket.

He thanked me profusely. 'Used to lose rubbers out of my schoolbag as well.'

'Do you usually carry a gun?' I inquired.

'Every portrait painter should have one. But it's my clasp-knife I'm after. In this pocket. Here we are.' He bent over the mine, did something, and straightened.

'Yes. Well, if all the good helpers and those who have provided the tea and buns will kindly get the hell out of it, I think I can remove the sting from this gentleman.'

'That's a job for experts,' I said. 'Don't be an ass. Now it's lashed, it can't joggle.'

'Doesn't matter if it joggles or not,' said Johnson. 'And if I hadn't been having an osmosis like a bloody buttercup every two minutes I'd have spotted it earlier. It isn't a trembler mechanism at all: it's the kind you set off by radio signals. So unless you know anyone with a transmitter and evil intentions, we are all perfectly safe.'

Which in its way was the insufferable, ultimate irony of Fingal's horrible cave.

Rupert, I remember, talked all the way back to the jetty and was annoyed when I didn't reply. I was busy, thinking. About, for example, Johnson's revolver.

We set off much later from Iona, under sail. I remember, through a haze of champagne, discussing the whole business with Johnson.

He was pleased with himself; no doubt because he had employed the old Navy touch without blowing his head off. I found there were advantages, as well, in being a popular heroine. Today, the six hundred passengers of the *King George V.* Tomorrow the world. There was, I remembered, an airstrip on Barra. Reporters could come by the planeload. Or a television team, at the least. I should give my first interviews there.

Without Michael. Of that I was sure. He had said nothing more about Kenneth or the cancelled South American tour, and Michael didn't as a rule lie down to defeat. But if he was still on board, it was for a reason. And it wasn't to bolster my ego with journalists, I was sure.

But instead, I had a new standing with others. Victoria had kissed and apologized: 'We did think, all of us, that you weren't mad about poor Johnson and us and our junketings… But you were super. I'll never speak to anyone again who says you weren't *super*. And the drip-dry non-seat chic bit just wasn't Madame Rossi at all.'

I related then, I remember, an abbreviated version of my childhood, with grateful results, and was sorry when she returned to Ogden and *Seawolf,* which awaited off Staffa, duly mended by Lenny. The race forced itself unfortunately on the attention every time one looked at Rupert, who wore the expression of a man now worrying about five thousand pounds. On sailing time, only Hennessy and *Seawolf* had beaten us. On handicapped time, our likeliest rivals were Hennessy still, *Seawolf* from her recent fast reach, and the Buchanans on *Binkie.*

With the surface of my mind, through a meal of Chinese water chestnuts and snow peas, I made all the appropriate noises. But I was both glad and relieved when at midnight, Johnson leaned below from the cockpit and asked if I should like to come and see Ardnamurchan light from the deck. With my little gold alpaca coat pulled round my shoulders, I followed him up and kneeling, looked out to sea.

In the summer night, the Inner Hebrides lay all about us, black on the indigo sea. Above us, the uninterrupted sky stretched, a light, dense ultramarine, its ghostly clouds and small, sharp white stars suspended over the bright winking lights, near and far, of a constellation of lighthouses, and the grey, dimly voyaging waves here below. To our right, a dark mass and the fitful beam of a lighthouse announced the furthest west land mass of Britain. Ahead, and much nearer now, were the islands – Muck, Eigg, Rum, Canna, already seen from off Mull.

Behind and around us on the pleasant seas and warm breeze were the dim sails of the cruising yachts, wake and canvas gilded, like ours, by the faint radiance of escaped cabin light. I drew the saloon door shut behind me, not to dazzle Johnson's eyes, and went to lean where he was resting, his pipe between his teeth, his arm on the tiller, his bifocal lenses trained on the waves, the sails, the burgee, the other boats, but never on me. He said, 'There's Rum. If

Rupert could be trusted not to have kittens, we could call on your friend there tomorrow.'

I forgot about the gun. Idiot that I was, I thought only that here was a man self-sufficient as I was myself, who had shown no scruples about walking out on a corpse, and no sentiment afterwards. Since Crinan, my mind had been changed for me, radically. I said, 'Dr Holmes isn't there. They've moved him to South Rona. I'm to meet him on Saturday in Portree.'

'How do you know? Oh, Tom McIver,' Johnson answered himself, centring me briefly in the short-focus lenses. 'Lenny mentioned he came round at Crinan. Was the message from Holmes?'

I told him. 'So Kenneth Holmes warned you off, and you replied that you weren't having any, and made a new assignation,' said Johnson. 'The bulldog breed. And now the mine. They *are* keen to keep you apart, aren't they?'

'Then the mine wasn't a coincidence?' I said.

The bifocals tipped upwards. 'Coincidence, hell! That mine was so new it was a wonder anyone recognized it as such. I did, because it's a hobby with me.'

'So did I.' There seemed no point now in failing to mention it. 'Because I saw it last night. On an identification chart in Hennessy's wheelhouse.'

There was a long silence. Then, 'Did you, indeed?' said Johnson thoughtfully.

I knew what he was thinking. With the tide as it was, that mine was planted – if it had been planted – no more than a short time before *Dolly*'s party arrived. And Hennessy had been at the cave just before us. I said it aloud.

'Yes. Hennessy could have carried it,' said Johnson. 'It wasn't big. A small packing case or a reinforced kitbag would hold it. Also, from what you say, he had the radio equipment to trigger it off.'

I sat down and hugged myself in my alpaca coat, and the silver of my Mexican earrings pattered cold on my cheek. I said, 'But it needn't be Hennessy. There must have been other boats, too.'

'Not so many. I checked with MacBrayne and Iona,' said Johnson. 'The puffer *Willa Mavis,* of course, but she had passed hours before we arrived on the scene. Duke Buzzy's *Vallida* had long since gone, too, after chucking in the champagne. Lenny and Ogden brought *Seawolf* over, but that was after we were all in the cave, and if Ogden's got a children's telephone set, never mind a shortwave radio, I'm Alexander Graham Bell. The *King George* arrived afterwards, too. So did *Binkie*, while we were all in the cave, but the Buchanans didn't go ashore, and I don't suppose they've got an RT. Apart from one or two fishing boats who passed through earlier and were miles away while we were there in the cave, that's the whole list of suspects.' He glanced up at me.

'You realize that someone has been carrying that mine, from Crinan or Rhu, with just this sort of purpose in mind? Stick it near a boat and trigger it off, and there's nothing to show afterwards why any yacht got blown out of the water.'

I don't get excited either. Not easily. 'Why didn't this one get triggered off, then?' I asked. 'And anyway, how could they be sure of doing it at the right time?'

'Binoculars,' said Johnson. 'That's why it had to be someone who was within reasonable range while we were inside the cave. And frankly, I don't know why they didn't explode it. The boat with the shortwave radio maybe couldn't get within binocular range at the time. There may have been someone with us they wanted to spare. They may have meant simply to give us a fright.'

'What do you mean,' I said. '*Someone they wanted to spare?*'

'Well,' said Johnson, his gaze fixed on the streaming burgee. 'Someone might have an accomplice. Are you sure now, for example, that your Lochgair ducking was nothing but an accident?'

I stared at him, but there was nothing to be seen of his face but the glittering glass. Lochgair, where the unhitched boom had knocked me into the sea. They had all sworn it was the wind in the crutch. Lenny had declared it was in perfect order when he went to bed, and he and Rupert were both sure that no one could have boarded *Dolly* that night unheard...

And yet – I was thinking – and yet, I heard a whisper that night using the words Kenneth uses. Who else would have known them?

Who else? What about Michael Twiss?

But I was his golden disc-making goose. Why should he try to kill me?

Now, of course, we had quarrelled. But we had patched it up then. Unless, I thought slowly, he planned to quarrel and did not intend patching it up? For Michael, and no one but Michael, knew in which banks, all over Europe, I kept my money under all my various names, and where my jewels were. If I were to die…

I had not considered this before. But if I were to die, Michael Twiss would be rich. Except that Michael, too, was there in the cave.

Except… No. Put it another way, said my brain. Except that Michael, too, was there in the cave far longer than he had intended. Unconscious, after his fall.

I could face, until I had thought all that through, neither the upper nor the lower reaches of the bifocals. I made an excuse, abruptly, to Johnson, and locked myself into my room.

9

That night, I had to use sleeping pills and Michael knew it: I saw it in his sharp, cologne-imbued face the next morning. I behaved as usual, to Michael, to Rupert, to everyone. Johnson would, I believed, give me protection. The rest was my own affair, after all.

On deck there was nothing but sunshine and sea, although Rupert's silent anxiety dimmed his exuberance. The night's progress had been abysmal, the winds freakish and contrary, dropping now to something near calm. We were nowhere near the island of Barra, our next port of call. But the twelve yachts still left in the race were doing no better than we.

Only Johnson showed no signs of impatience. He had, I saw, clipped his easel into place behind the cockpit, and when we all adjourned there with our coffee, with Lenny at helm, I sank into my allotted place, back to the saloon. I wanted the portrait finished.

For the moment, smoking, Johnson painted in silence, timing his strokes with the roll of the boat; and it came to me that he also knew that time was running out. The techniques, too, had altered. Now, the glistening coils of colour on his palette were swept off in hodfuls, and laid on the canvas like satiny twill. The reek of linseed oil came in snatches, allowed by the wind. Rupert hovered with turpentine on a rag, vociferating as he lifted from paint and varnishwork the flying flecks from Johnson's sables and hogs.

After a bit, it got easier and Johnson said, unexpectedly, 'No advertising could do justice to the planes between your cheekbone and jaw. Hence your voice timbre, I suppose.'

This was true, of course. I have widely spaced cheekbones, with big and resonant hollows within them. Inside, my palate too is arched very high, which gives me my head tones, along with the spaces inside the head, I explained. With age, my range would probably drop, but provided I kept in good health and maintained my technique and breath control, I could sing lyric and even dramatic roles for thirty years yet.

'Will you?' said Johnson conversationally. 'Without Michael Twiss?'

I am Tina Rossi, *cara diva* to Visconti, Serafin, Karajan, Bernstein; *Madame* to the world. I did not need Michael Twiss to tell me how to move, to speak, to dress any longer. Michael Twiss's interpretation of Marguerite, Titania, Tosca, Norma, Lucia, Nedda, Rosina, Ameria and Imogene were all on record, in my voice: I had only to replay them to study them. While Colbert La Berge could earn me five thousand dollars for one *Quando rapita in estasi*, I should not starve. I had spent all night thinking that out.

So: 'Galli-Curci managed without Michael Twiss,' I said now mildly to Johnson's inquiry. 'And Adelina Patti. And Jenny Lind and Luisa Tetrazzini. One can always find managers.'

'But you mean to go on with it?' he asked, all his attention on the planes of my face. 'Don't you get tired of living out of suitcases, of planning every day of your life three or four years ahead?'

'Why?' I said. 'Do you think it is better to be of the moneyed idle: to sail, to fish, to form little parties for Bermuda and Ascot, to sleep a little with whoever appeals, to ski, to gamble, to attend charity balls and weddings and hunt balls and first nights and public luncheons and private supper parties until one dies in one's corseting?'

'Isn't that why you learned to sing in the first place?'

In my mind only, I answered. Not quite, it isn't. I learned to sing for fame, as well as for fortune: for that moment when the thunder of the orchestra is suspended, the choirs stop, and my voice is revealed, single, pure and celestial, embarked on a passage of tender *bel canto*. I do not want to lose that elation, that power, that applause. And how can I start leading a life of style, leisure and luxury when I have no friends?

Then Johnson said placidly, answering himself, 'No. I'm sure you have a true vocation. But there is a halfway house, you know, with time for new friends, new relationships. Lots of people work like hell just because they are lonely.'

Almost… almost I was tempted. But not quite. I am not Cecil Ogden with my Victoria.

'They are lucky,' I said. 'To have solitude, freedom from one's poor lame dogs and one's admirers and overpowering friends… What bliss! To stay on Barra, for instance.' I gazed where Rupert had pointed out to me the hilly ridge of the Outer Isles, where Castlebay, Barra, was to be our landfall today. 'To retire to Barra. To go native on an unknown island where no one has heard of me… There *is* an airport?' I said.

There was an airfield, of sorts. And save for Sundays, the Glasgow plane arrived there each day.

The wind freshened after that, and soon after lunch, I looked through the starboard porthole to see a low whaleback of sunlit moorlands on the right, beyond a black perch. By the time I was on deck, we were passing the creamy crescent of Vatersay's beach, and low hills ahead of us were sliding slowly towards our port flank as the harbour of Castlebay, Barra, opened out on our right.

It was a wide bay, limpid blue, with white and grey houses scattered around it and climbing the base of a tall, rounded hill, below which lay the jetty, half masked by a big MacBrayne's cargo boat, with a trawler tied up at the side.

Between ourselves and the jetty was a rock rising clear out of the sea, with the square walls of a castle on it. From its roofwalk, a strange flag was flying. I stared.

'On the starboard bow,' said Rupert helpfully, 'the Red Hand of the Macneils, denoting that the chief of the clan is in residence at Kishmul's castle… there's *Symphonetta*, damn her.'

There indeed was *Symphonetta*, her poles bare, and, looking through the glasses, one could see *Symphonetta*'s power boat tied up by the trawler, with someone in glistening white oilskins therein. Stanley Hennessy had lost no time in checking in. His mouth shut, Rupert scanned the rest of the bay.

Four others, including the Buchanans of *Binkie* were in, or sailing in just behind us. Ogden's *Seawolf* was not yet in sight, though there were one or two strange boats also anchored, including a steam yacht just taking position with a good deal of fussing, having been thrown out from the quay by the steamer. It was a pretty sight: the water reflections like blown silvery dandelion clocks running over hull, flank and sail of the moving boats, while the long, dark wake of the steam yacht slid sideways in bars underneath them, making the smaller yachts tilt, their reflected sails twisted like corkscrews.

'*Vallida*,' said Rupert with unwonted clarity, indicating the steam yacht. 'The tourist element. Or Duke Buzzy's annual *weekend relaxe* or *semaine tonique* with friends.'

'Why not?' said Johnson. 'The chap owns half the shooting and fishing rights north of the Highland line, not to mention several distilleries. You enjoyed his champagne.'

'Tourist element,' repeated Rupert firmly. 'That oceanic bingo-box there will be shoulder to shoulder with Middle European industrial creeps getting a little free fishing and losing their gold bridgework at blackjack. Look at them.'

I took his binoculars. 'I'm looking,' I said. A vast power boat laden with bald heads and shooting-lodge men's wear had put off from *Vallida* and was whipping off on a line for the jetty. Stanley Hennessy, I noticed, was on the steps of the jetty, awaiting them. Naturally. It came to me, suddenly, that I should like to visit Duke Buzzy, too.

As it happened, I had plenty of time. For the first time in recorded memory (said Rupert) the Royal Highland Cruising Club had let down its members. The checkpoint officials who should have been there, prepared on the pier, had been detained at Glasgow airport, Abbotsinch, by the fog. There were no reporters there, either.

As the bay filled up with furious yachtsmen, a hasty checkpoint, set up by Hennessy, took unofficial note of their times. A little later a small enclave of senior yachtsmen, again led by Hennessy, declared that no one shoud set off for Rodel until the Club officials had ruled on procedure.

That meant until an Olympian decision was arrived at in Glasgow. There was a lot of argument, which we watched from the gate of the pier and I wondered, looking at Hennessy, why he was so anxious to enforce a pause here at Barra. Everyone, of course, could do with a rest: we had been at sea, after all, since the previous evening. And since only sailing times counted, the running order of the race would be unaffected. But it disturbed me and Johnson, perhaps seeing my face, came over and said, 'We'll be later in Portree than we thought. You did warn your friend, you said, didn't you?'

I knew what he was thinking, for I was thinking it too. If anyone wanted to get rid of Kenneth, he was safer on South Rona than anywhere else. That base would be guarded. But if, on the other hand, he were hanging about in Portree, he was badly exposed to attack.

I had begun to have other misgivings. The press, for example might be in force there, hoping for news leaks about the *Lysander* disaster. The Portree hotel, into which I had booked by wire from Crinan, might be full of high-ranking officials brought to Skye by the same thing. For a while, I could avoid recognition, with a headscarf and dark glasses, if they thought I was on *Dolly* still with Johnson. If I could persuade Kenneth, we could leave for the mainland almost immediately, by hiring a car.

Now, I was going to be late. More, I didn't like being stuck here with all these yachtsmen. With all these yachtsmen and Michael. And the steamer had gone.

'Come on,' said Johnson. 'Let's hire a car, and show you around.'
He did.

Barra is a delightful part of the Western Hebrides. In spring, the primroses cover the machair in acres. In summer, the surf rolls in along miles of unoccupied silvery beaches, with untouched sand fine as milled silk running out under the blue and green water, without pebble or rock. The children are charming, the people gentle-spoken and courteous. After two hours, I could have seen Barra in hell.

Back at the pier, the Caribbean tan and glistening waves of Stanley Hennessy waited. He was just back from *Vallida*, with an invitation from Duke Buzzy for me.

Just for me.

I saw Johnson open his mouth to make my excuses. I thought of that mine, and the diagram in Hennessy's wheelhouse. I also thought of the diamonds and all those middle-European gentlemen in tweeds. I wished now I had asked Johnson to lend his revolver but I hoped he would understand there was safety in numbers. For I wanted to go on board the *Vallida* very much indeed. 'I should be delighted,' I said. I saw Johnson's bifocals still gazing after me with melancholy as *Vallida*'s power boat set off over the bay, carrying Stanley Hennessy and myself to His Grace's *weekend relaxe*.

I had wondered, when dressing that morning in my black quilted silk trouser suit, with the white frogging and detachable ermine-trimmed hood, if I hadn't over-egged the pudding a trifle. In the event, I was glad I had put on my black opal earrings as well. It was that kind of a call.

The *Vallida* of course was a steam yacht, built in Edward VII's day, all mahogany and close carpeting and brasswork polished like twenty-four carat gold, with some gold polished like twenty-four carat gold as well. Plodding over the Axminsters to arrive at a stateroom, I was conscious of the Greuze over the wrought-iron radiator and a fighting-force of after-shave lotions, divergent in all except cost.

In my room was a marble washbasin, a bidet, a Degas and six gold-encased lipsticks with the Duke's proper initial. The top drawer was full of unused feminine clothes in cellophane packs. I didn't look at the others. I returned, slowly, to the steward awaiting me, and he showed me into the saloon.

That was like Brighton Pavilion, and would have boasted a baby grand piano, save that on *Vallida* no one boasted. One practised the art of the self-evident, drawn to a point. Then the Duke, tall, pink and hairless with a bright, pearly smile, came forward to greet me, and, with a large neat whisky in hand, I was taken on tour.

I do not remember now all their names, but they were all bald, German, and thoroughly weekend relaxed. Hennessy, at ease among them, patted my arm as I passed. The last guest in the last Louis Quinze armchair was Michael Twiss. 'Hello,' he said. 'My dear. His Grace thought you'd be busy. But I knew you'd be delighted to come.'

The bastard. I sat down, smiling, beside Duke Buzzy. How had Michael got himself asked to *Vallida*? He had gone off, of course, in Cecil Ogden's old wooden pram. Was Ogden on calling terms with the Duke? I looked at Michael again in his pale sharkskin suit. I knew that self-satisfied glitter. New contacts. New fields opening up. Michael couldn't shoot, or hunt, or run a distillery. But then, a dozen years before, Michael knew nothing of music.

I refused, automatically, the Duke's invitation to go to bed with him straight away; and he rose, smiling without impatience, to make way for two heavily built middle-aged men who sat on either side of me on the Duke's Chinese brocade, with no packing space to speak of. My drink was renewed. So was theirs. We exchanged badinage, of a sort.

I have seldom spent a more uncomfortable hour. Relays of whisky appeared, but no food. Hennessy watched me ceaselessly as the Duke's guests, in rotation, took their turn on my sofa. He watched me, but talked of electric switchgear, and the programming of steel supplies, and the trend on the Stock Exchange. They all did. I was the light relief. I began to wonder how to get myself out.

In a moment, the problem was solved for me. The steward tripped. And I received four Scotch on the rocks straight down the white frogging and the black quilted trouser suit.

Amid the sibilant, middle-European hissing of sympathy, the Duke whipped out some monograms and dabbed at me uselessly, then commanded the steward, with satisfying acerbity, to lead me out and find me something to wear. There was a practised air about the whole scene which I found even touching. This sort of thing I can handle.

So I came to exchange the saloon for my stateroom where, the steward said as he left me, I should find a selection of clothes.

I knew that. I have met Duke Buzzies before. I shut the stateroom door firmly behind me, and looked for a key.

Naturally, there was none. And the furniture, of course, was bolted to the floor. Ah, well. Peeling off my soaked quilted jacket, I crossed to the long wardrobe lockers and opened the door. It was full of expensive dresses on hangers. And among the hangers, dropping outwards towards me, was a man.

I cannot deny that, for perhaps a second, I was not fully conscious of my surroundings. One's nerves are not sixteen-core hawsers. I choked as he hit me, and could not see properly, while the pressure of blood drummed in my ears. These things are bad for a singer. Then he had his hand over my mouth and I realised that this was not the large, dead, cold-eyed Mr Chigwell but someone small, and spare and agile, with large powerful hands and a gold tooth that gleamed as he smiled.

He smiled now. 'Go and sit down,' said the man whom I had last seen leaping from another wardrobe in that awful Edinburgh flat. 'And if you scream I'll wring your beautiful neck.'

I sat down. 'They'll miss me.'

'Not for a while.' He was wearing a chief steward's uniform. He locked the door with a key taken out of his pocket, and flung me a dress from the locker. 'But you had better put one of these on just in case.'

It was not the one I should have chosen, but that was not the moment to think of it. I said, undressing shakily, 'I haven't told anyone. I promise I haven't.'

He sat down and crossed his legs, damn him, like a man at a strip-club. 'Not even Johnson?' he said.

It was a choice of evils. I don't gamble with money. But in life, I take risks. If I have to. 'Oh, I told Johnson,' I said. I picked up the dress. It wasn't bad. 'I had to, goodness. He was there in the flat. But he agreed to do nothing about it for my sake, because of the scandal.' I paused. The thing was hell to put on: all hooks and eyes and wiring and cutaways. I got it half on, and then took the rest of my clothes off underneath it. It was that kind of dress. 'If anything happened to me, of course, he'd do something at once. Or if anything happened to Kenneth Holmes.'

Show over. Mr Gold-tooth uncrossed his legs. 'Nothing will happen to Kenneth Holmes,' he said. 'Unless the police discover he murdered the landlord.'

I didn't believe it. I said, 'You can't get away with that. Putting the blame on him for the murder. Why should he kill Chigwell, anyway?'

Gold-tooth grinned. 'Because Chigwell was a Government agent,' he said, agreeably. 'And Kenneth Holmes – didn't you know? – blew up the *Lysander*.'

There was a blank pause. I dropped my hands from the last hook and stared at him. 'You can't—'

'I can.' Someone tried the door and then knocked on it. He paid no attention, and neither did I. I said, 'I'll damned well tell…'

'Will you?' He was still smiling. Outside the door, someone was calling my name.

'Will Tina Rossi really tell her private life to the world? And if you do, will it save Dr Holmes?'

'What else can I do that will save Dr Holmes?' I said. And sang out 'Wait a moment!' to whoever was banging outside.

Gold-tooth cracked his enormous, powerful fingers. 'I could always try to replace him by someone expendable,' he said. 'If I were properly paid.'

In my black, sling crocodile bag – how did he know? Maybe he didn't – was Hennessy's Wartski bracelet. You don't leave anything uninsured like that aboard an untended boat. Grimly, I hauled the bag open.

I'd been afraid of this. But it was the only way, I supposed, to save both Kenneth and my reputation. I could, I hoped, one day replace it. And if Hennessy were the man behind Gold-tooth, I hoped he'd understand, when and if he found out.

I tossed the bracelet to Gold-tooth and he caught it, just as the door opened under a master-key and Duke Buzzy walked in. Mercifully, before he was properly over the threshold, Gold-tooth had vanished once more into the locker of dresses, and the door was fast shut.

It had a key-hole, I noticed much later, so Gold-tooth must have enjoyed what came next. Even I did, and I'd a lot on my mind.

If Hennessy was surprised, in due course, by my carefree return to the saloon, he showed little of it, although I did think his manner constrained during the Duke's rather forceful farewells. Then Hennessy and I got into *Vallida*'s power boat, waved to the row of middle-European gentlemen, and tore off into the sunset. Michael Twiss, I learned, had already gone off home to *Dolly*.

I didn't want to go off to *Dolly:* not to a tête-à-tête with Michael Twiss with that queer look in his eye. I wasn't very happy about

Hennessy either. I'd bribed Gold-tooth all right. But I hadn't bribed whoever employed him. I said a cheerful goodnight to Stanley Hennessy and dropped him on *Symphonetta*. He hadn't said a word beyond admiring my dress and Duke Buzzy's horizontally stranded red fox fur coat. My trouser suit, after all, had been ruined.

Vallida's helmsman was accommodating. I chugged about, looking for company. In the end, it was a light on *Seawolf* that attracted me. Victoria. Or even Cecil Ogden would do. *Vallida*'s powerful boat stopped; I shouted, and on deck stepped not Victoria or Ogden but Lenny Milligan. I said, 'Where's Victoria?'

Neither the furs nor the cutaway dress disturbed Lenny a whit.

'On shore. I'm getting her guitar for her. Ogden's on shore too, elsewhere, trying to produce instant friendship with *Vallida*'s chippy and plumber. Care to join Victoria's party? We're all at the croft over there.'

He nodded towards the other side of the bay, and I saw some dim, stone-built cottages, thatched and splayed at the corners. 'If you want to hear the real Gaelic bit, that's the place. "Kishmul's Galley", sung right on the Metro-Goldwyn-Meyer set. I bet,' said Lenny with cheerful malice, 'you ain't heard "Kishmul's Galley" yet, or some of the other warbles they've got. The flamenco of the north. Proper groovy, it is. They've even got a bunch of Macneils staying there, hung up waiting for the Chief, and all set to twang the old 'arpstrings in the great 'All. No kidding,' said Lenny, helping me into *Dolly*'s dinghy and making nautical conversation with the *Vallida*'s boat crew at the same time. 'This you must see.'

Revolting, of course. But *Dolly* was the alternative. So I thanked the Duke's retainers, and I tipped them, and I allowed Lenny Milligan to motor me yet again over the bay, while I considered what on earth to tell Johnson. I even toyed with a fancy to tell him the truth.

It was the kind of occasion that sticks in one's mind. You bent low, entering the house of Duncan's Peggy; and the windows were small as Johnson's bifocals, and sunk in the walls. The hens came in with you, and a few more dogs; and some of them stayed inside and some of them didn't. Duncan's Peggy herself came to the door at Lenny's shout, peering through the blue haze of peat and pipe and cigarette smoke, and said, 'My word, the bonny lass you have there, Lenny Milligan. Come away you in, and take off that coat: you'd think there was a furnace in it here, with all these big sweaty men. Have you supped?'

I stared at her queasily, and Lenny said, 'Don't show your ignorance now: she's off Buzzy's yacht. When did he start handing out free meals?'

'Don't answer that,' said Johnson's mild voice and, emerging in turn from the haze, he took my fur like an old mac and, pipe on my shoulders, steered me into the room.

'And relax. If you drink too much at Duncan's Peggy's, you get made an honorary member of the Clan Macneil.' And he sat me down and began introductions.

I had been grossly misled. The peat fire was not in the centre of the room, but in a tiled fireplace with a tall mantelpiece, whose ornaments served to prop up a variety of over-bright postcards and bundles of dog-eared envelopes, mostly with foreign stamps. A deep-sea household, then, with sons who had flunked out on the fishing and ventured into the big world. I could imagine the trash they sent back to her – the plushy carpets, the brassware, the Cape Verde tusks. Or did they send her money instead?

So far, apart from Lenny and Rupert and Johnson, all the men and women in the room had been Barra folk, of all shapes and sizes. No one mentioned the cutaway dress. Then Victoria came in and exclaimed, 'Madame Rossi! Duncan's Peggy, can she hear "Kishmul's Galley"? And the Macneils must sing again, would you? Madame Rossi must hear you!' and a group of three men, sitting politely on the horsehair chairs furthest from the fire got up and bowed and said, Yes, of course.

Their voices were a little different from the rest, and I tried to pin it down, while the preparations for the regional dirge were begun. Then I had it. They must be the exiled Macneils, come to pay their respects to their Chief. From Canada, perhaps.

Then the talk died down and a woman's voice, unaccompanied, sang 'Kishmul's Galley' through to the end.

It is set in Barra, of course. Sung, normally, by a strong untrained soprano with poor breath control and a bad piano accompaniment, it is something to make angels flinch. Angels, that night, would have broken out into a pistular rash.

As it came to an end, and the applause broke out, Duncan's Peggy said in my ear in a kindly, low voice, 'She is a woman of great age, that; and had it from another of the same, so the notes are likely authentic. The School of Scottish Studies have her, of course. But she would take it very kindly were you to mention that you might sing it yourself now, one day.'

So they knew I sang. I wondered what they would expect me to contribute. Vilja, of the *Merry Widow*, perhaps. Would they have heard of the *Merry Widow*? As I spoke to the woman who had sung, I thought, well, they appreciated that. But this is their culture. If I ask her for an encore, *she* may even sing Vilja from the *Merry Widow*, at that, and they will applaud even more. And out of the corner of my eye – oh, shades of Kenneth, and all my overbearing aunts, and all the frustration and boredom and unrewarded patience I have ever exerted – I saw the outline of a harp, waiting for the Celtic twilight to fall on it… and after that, I anticipated song after song from the exiled Macneils…

But suddenly, a pile of cucumber and cheese sandwiches had appeared mysteriously under my hand, and a cup of strong tea at my elbow, and a weatherbeaten man with a two-day beard and no collar on was observing, 'The School of Scottish Studies has this one too, Mistress Rossi, but I will English it for you as I go along, and you will maybe enjoy the one or two jokes in it…'

It wasn't a bad story, if you could make out the accent. At the end, when I clapped him with the rest, I noticed that the plate of sandwiches was quite empty and I had no recollection of eating one. 'They taped eight hundred of his,' said Johnson's succinct voice. 'Dates from the days of illiteracy, of course. Did Buzzy give you a bad time on *Vallida*? Hennessy shouldn't have taken you.'

'I can look after myself,' I said. They were wheeling forward the harp.

'So I see. We've had a message from Glasgow,' said Johnson. 'Permission to sail for Rodel, at last. What else of interest occurred on *Vallida*?'

They had taken the harp cover off, and someone was tuning the strings against a guitar. The pedals clattered and knocked. I wondered what his expression would be if I said, 'I've found Chigwell's murderer.' Mild congratulations, probably: no more. But I couldn't risk it. I had bought Kenneth's safety, I hoped. I wasn't going to put any strain on Johnson's problematical conscience, and have all that good work undone. For, apart from anything else, if Gold-tooth were picked up, another would just take his place. Another, or *the* other. It took two to operate that trick with the mine. It took two, come to think of it, to get me on Duke Buzzy's yacht. Then the harp tuning stopped, there was a clattering of chairs, and the Macneils settled down to perform. They turned out to be one of the coolest harp, guitar and tenor sax combos I had heard outside Harlem. 'Bald-headed Lena' belted out over Castlebay, Barra, and no one seemed surprised except me.

I knew the long-distance halves of the bifocals were watching. After an interval, when they had to break off to retune the harp, Johnson remarked, 'Don't underrate them. Duncan's Peggy has reared a surgeon, a police chief and a Minister of State besides Rupert. Education in the Highlands, you ought to know, is a sectarian rite.'

I shifted my chair back a little. 'What did you say?'

'I said Rupert's mother isn't the only one to be proud of her sons.'

'I can't hear you. I thought you called Duncan's Peggy Rupert's mother.'

'If I did,' he replied, 'Duncan's Peggy ought to have mentioned it. But she's annoyed with him for throwing over one of his girlfriends that she liked, and when he displeases her, she's apt to ignore him.'

'You mean,' I said, 'that *Rupert, Rupert Glasscock* was born and brought up on Barra? But how could he...? The public school, the commission – one doesn't pay for all that out of haddock.'

Johnson was informative, if indifferent. 'Scholarships,' he said. 'And brains, naturally. Rupert's father was lost at sea a good while ago, but he has plenty of aunts and uncles who chipped in. He comes back to get his earholes clipped for the good of his soul every half-year or so.'

'But don't they long to get away, too?' I asked. 'If they had brains, if they had scholarships, why in God's name didn't they get out of Barra?'

'To be a Buzzy?' said Johnson.

'Yes. Hush,' I said. 'The harp's starting again.'

People describe me as cold. I have my emotions, it is true, under control. I am not a John Gordon, but I have common sense. I am not, as a rule, nervous.

I was nervous then, setting sail from Barra on that next leg of the race, the last before my call at Portree.

I had reasonable cause. The glass was dropping. It was a tricky sail, Rupert said, because at low water the Rodel anchorage dried out to a quarter fathom at the edges. To get in, we had to time our arrival exactly. And with the strong seas that were promising that night, with a contrary wind, we had a long plod ahead of us.

I did not tell Johnson how hard I tried to get off that bloody island, by boat or by plane, that Thursday night. I didn't trust Gold-tooth. I wanted to get, fast, to Portree. And I didn't want to spend any time at all in the near company of Michael Twiss. Michael was hanging about to see if I really was going to meet Kenneth on Rum, and no doubt to forestall that meeting if possible.

When I couldn't get direct to Portree, either by boat or by plane, I took my own simple precautions. I listened all through supper to Michael engaging Johnson in light, sophisticated conversation about Cortina and Beirut. (I could tell Johnson a thing or two about Michael in Beirut.) And afterwards, when Johnson and Rupert had turned in, and Lenny was up at the helm, I mentioned to Michael over the Cointreau that I required him to place all my papers in order before leaving my employment, as from now. Any negotiations in progress I should wind up myself.

I also remarked that before leaving Barra, I had sent letters by plane to my lawyers, halting payment from all my accounts in the event of my unexplained death. Even the Swiss ones, as well.

Neat in his zip-up Swedish co-ordinates, Michael heard me, the long lashes fluttering on either side of that thin, high-bridged nose. His reply, I remember, was lightly obscene.

I did not wait for more, but, retiring, locked myself in my cabin, where the score of *Don Pasquale* lay already open to hand. At home I had my secretary, my accountant, my pianist, my housekeeper, my maid. I was in no hurry to find a new manager. I could manage, alone.

We entered the anchorage at Rodel, Harris, with a good steady wind, about mid-afternoon on Friday.

It was a good anchorage. There was a frigate lying already outside; and the basin, as we made ready to enter, was crowded with boats, though not with either *Seawolf* or *Symphonetta,* which must have picked their way through before high water, and gone.

Rupert stalked grimly on deck. Under the eyes of a Royal Naval boat crew, the staysail slammed down like smoke; the mainsail followed. With textbook precision, sheets flew, canvas collapsed; and seizing the anchor with passion, Rupert hurled it into the sea. Unattached, alas, to its chain.

10

After her departure from Rodel, an air of thoughtfulness descended on *Dolly*. It may have been the weather, which was certainly stinking. It was certainly due in part to the burden of financial anxiety which was visibly weighing on Rupert. It may even have emanated from Michael, who, aside from being sick all that evening, must have known that, assuming I were meeting Kenneth in Rum, he had only twenty-four hours at the most in which to prevent such a meeting. If that were his intention.

As for Johnson: he knew, as I did, that Kenneth was not at Rum, but might be waiting for me even now at our next call, Portree in the island of Skye.

It was none of his business. In order to keep my mouth shut, he had said, he had asked for my company and my portrait to paint. He had had my company, on which he had made few demands, and those all legitimate. He had painted my portrait, or most of it, and could finish it on dry land at any time he cared to arrange. The fact that this was somehow mixed up with the *Lysander* had not seemed to affect him: he had made no patriotic gestures and had displayed in the other kind, the ease of infinite practice.

Best of all, he had shown no lasting pique on being left out of my arrangements with Kenneth. I didn't want any intrusion on those. He had, presumably, come to terms with the fact that I proposed certainly to leave him at Skye.

I raised the subject, I remember, over supper, when Lenny had taken the wheel and Michael, I could be sure, had retired as far from the odour of food as the boat would allow. We were spanking along at about seven knots, Johnson said, although in what direction he was not fully certain. The indications were, however, that we should arrive at about 1 a.m. in Portree. Then, he added, filling his obnoxious pipe, if we were to catch the tide south, *Dolly* would have to leave an hour or two later, and certainly not after 4 a.m. The black eyebrows, I noticed, were raised impossibly high.

He might be taking it lightly, but I wasn't. If Kenneth wasn't waiting to meet me – and why should he be, in the small hours of the morning? – I should have to rouse the night porter at my hotel, since I couldn't linger till daylight on *Dolly*. I hardly realized until then how much I had depended on *Dolly*. But Johnson's tone had been final. Five thousand pounds was five thousand pounds, after all. And, what was more, when *Dolly* left Portree harbour, she would be taking Michael Twiss out of the way. On the other hand, if I had to cross to South Rona, it must be done, somehow, tonight. For after daylight tomorrow, no one would dare sail out of Skye, so they said. Tomorrow, I had remembered, was Sunday.

I said to Johnson, 'I shall be sorry to leave. But I must. Can I do it without Michael knowing?'

Johnson grinned. 'After the Sound of Raasay,' he said, 'I think you need have no fear of Michael Twiss being able to stop you.'

I remember that day I wore my ciré rainsuit lined with lynx fur, and ribbon tweed with Diorama for evening; and his bifocals were as excited as deadlights. But he was effective, I grant, to the end. Just before one in the morning I was discreetly roused from my bunk, and, taking only my pigskin case with my night gear and jewellery, I dressed and climbed for the last time on deck.

It was raining. We were in a wide, land-locked harbour with a long pier ranged on our left, ribbon-built on its more distant side with ships' chandlers, cafés and shops. From the pier, a road led dimly uphill towards a crowding of houses and shops set above and among trees, with, high on the left, the flat white face of a biggish hotel. That was where I had booked.

I thought of my flat in Grosvenor Square, and my deep bed with the peach linen sheets renewed daily, and my bathroom carpeted in Mongolian fur, with the handmade soaps and the flagons of essence, the invisible record-player, the thick warm bathsheets all waiting; and I sighed. When I had met Kenneth.

There were perhaps a dozen yachts in the basin, of which I recognized five as fellow-competitors. Only two of these mattered: Hennessy's *Symphonetta*, and *Seawolf*, with Ogden and Victoria. *Binkie*, our only other close contender according to Rupert, had entered the Sound on our tail. Most of the rest had dropped out.

It didn't matter to me any longer who won Hennessy's five thousand. Five thousand is nothing in my kind of gamble. I went, soundlessly, to descend into the dinghy with Rupert, who waited to row me on shore. On the companionway, Johnson held my hand lightly. 'Have you hated every second of it? Apart, I mean, from the Russian roulette?'

'I haven't hated it at all,' I replied. And this, surprisingly, was perfectly true. Without Kenneth on my mind I should have enjoyed exerting my power on them all. I recalled my recital at Crinan, and Johnson's silent respect as I told him my history; and the moment when I walked downstairs at Rhu. I hadn't hated it, really.

Johnson had taken such precautions as must have seemed reasonable: I was to have Rupert's escort until I found Kenneth or until I was safely in my hotel. He said, through the short and long focus at once, 'You're going to have all the fun. I do envy you that. Try and let me know, if you possibly can, who murdered Chigwell. A postcard would do.'

I liked Johnson. I kissed him, I remember, then. And I wasn't drunk that time: the reverse. Then I remembered that time meant money to Rupert, waiting to hurry ashore and check in. I got into the dinghy, and as Rupert lifted the oars and pulled out and away I saw the anchor light of a big boat, a puffer, hitherto masked by the rest. It was the *Willa Mavis*, thank God. Tom McIver had kept the promise he had made me at Crinan, and had brought her across.

The row to the quayside took time. The dark water was uneasy, even in this sheltered anchorage, stirred by the driving squall whipping the Sound of Raasay outside, and beaten by the increasing rain. I had left all my public appearance clothes on board. I was dressed in black rainproof trousers and boots, with a short, shining black mackintosh and black turban. By the time Rupert drew into the jetty, I was glad of them all.

Tied up at the seaweedy steps of the pier was a big old rowboat with *Willa Mavis* on its stern. It was empty.

In the whole of Portree only one window was lit – that of the big fish and chip shop on the pier, showing a couple of young men inside smoking, their feet up on tables. One of them was half-asleep, the other was reading a paperback. At our footsteps, the second put down his novel and peered out past the unlit neon sign in the window. The checkpoint, Rupert said.

He added, 'Come in a moment, will you Tina? Then I'll take you on up to the hotel.' And, swinging my suitcase, he went on to sign *Dolly* in while I lingered in the doorway. At the back of my mind, as I looked out into the quiet harbour, I heard him explaining my presence to the two checkpoint staff. He did not, discreetly, say who I was; and by now, of course, my dark glasses were on.

I slipped them down, momentarily, as I watched. Was that a dark figure, standing out from the line of retreating shop doors and windows, a bit further up? I stepped out, to show myself, and in the darkness a cigarette flared. It *was* someone, a man. Then Rupert joined me and, still swinging my suitcase, walked with me up the pier and towards the steps which climbed to the hotel. As we passed the place where I had noticed the smoker I glanced casually sideways, but there was nobody there.

Then, at the bottom of the steps Rupert said, 'Damn. Sorry,' and stopped. 'I was so bloody busy, hearing the latest yell about Ogden. I think I've put *Dolly*'s arrival in wrong.' Then he moved, saying again, 'Sorry, Tina. How loopy can you get? I'll take you up, and fix it when I get back.'

But he was obviously worried. I stood firm. 'Don't be silly, go back now. Take the case, if you like. I'll wait here for you, bang in the middle of the pier, and if you hear me scream, you're welcome to come running.' I smiled at him. 'Go on! Get it fixed. They may not believe you if you leave it.' Far off, I could see *Binkie*'s boat drawing in to the steps.

It was that, perhaps, which decided Rupert. He said worriedly, 'You'll stand right out in the road, now? And if anyone you don't know approaches, you'll shout?' He hardly waited for my nod before, my case jolting, he was gone, in the rain. Then I thrust my hands into my wet mackintosh pockets and waited, and the soft footsteps behind me got nearer and nearer. They stopped, and there was a touch on my arm.

I spun round.

It wasn't Kenneth. Hell! Hell! Hell! It wasn't Kenneth. It was that great lump of a fool Tom McIver. He said, 'Missus?' and in spite of all the precautions, you could hear him two blocks away. I found I was hissing. 'Where's Dr Holmes?'

The big head, its thick beret sodden, dimly shook in the dark. 'Canna get over. Like I told you. They're keeping him fast on South Rona till the submarine business is better cleared up. I was to look for you coming into the bay, and to tell you.'

I stared up at him. 'And I told you that I'd go to him if he couldn't come here.'

There was a long pause. Then McIver said, 'Aye. And Dr Holmes says if I canna stop ye, to go to Acarsaid Mor, and from there to the topmost house in the old village, and wait for him there. He'll see your boat coming, and join you.'

My heart had begun to beat again; deep, fleshy vibrations under my ribs.

In my pocket, for just this purpose, was a yellow roll of Scottish five pound notes. I felt for and put them into his hand, turning a little so that they caught a gleam of light from Rupert's lit fish and chip shop. 'Will you take me?'

There was a moment of silence. Far along the pier, two small figures emerged climbing from the pier steps and walked towards the fish shop without glancing my way: the Buchanans. The rain flashed about them, golden in the lamplight; then they disappeared inside and the sounds of voices, magnified by the quiet and the night, reached us thinly.

I inhaled deeply, smelling the stale seaweed from the rocks on my left, and petrol from some garage nearby, and tar and ropes and new wood and rusted metal and fish and all the scents connected with seagoing and ships. McIver opened his mouth to pronounce.

He never did speak. Something thrust on my shoulder. Light gleamed on flesh, on a tall body, on a fist travelling with fourteen good stones of force full behind it. There was a clicking thud, a

116

grunting explosion of breath, and McIver was falling, marvellously, inexplicably, like a kapok-filled corpse in a film, to lie prone on Portree pier.

'The devil! How much did he take from you? I'll have the police on to this! Are you hurt, me dear?' asked Stanley Hennessy, panting, with every indication of acute concern. And as I looked despairingly down, 'Don't you worry your head about him. He'll wake up in jail in the morning. He's thoroughly out.'

He was. The *Willa Mavis* wasn't taking me anywhere tonight. And tomorrow was Sunday.

There was only one thing for it. I stared at Stanley Hennessy, and my eyes filled with tears.

Half an hour later, I was on my way to South Rona on *Symphonetta*. First, I had to confess to Hennessy why Tom McIver had confronted me. I let it appear that in visiting my old engineer friend on South Rona, I was merely flouting authority, expressing my scorn of the security clamp-down which had interfered with our meeting.

It was a hard sell, but I did it. And in the end, as he began to dwell on the personal perquisites, Hennessy became quite amazingly keen. He had had three hours or so to spend in Portree before catching the tide south. He had had already, due to his early arrival, at least some hours' sleep. He was willing – in fact, he proposed it – to take me to South Rona, invite my friend on board for a chat and a drink, and bring me speedily back. That bit especially.

I did not mention, while expressing my thanks, that I had no intention of asking Kenneth on board, or that on the contrary this assignation would be strictly for two, and on shore. The way I expressed my thanks, he didn't notice the omission. Then Rupert joined us, with the Buchanans and the two young men from the checkpoint, who were persuaded to allow Tom McIver to repose in the chip shop until he came to. We said he was drunk. The rolls of notes I left in his pocket.

There were, unfortunately, two built-in snags in this happy arrangement. One I was prepared to endure because of my late Wartski bracelet. The other was the fact that, for all I could prove, Hennessy might be the man who wished to have Kenneth murdered.

In which case it was small wonder he was being so co-operative. And how shirty he would be to discover I'd used that same Wartski bracelet to buy Gold-tooth off.

Once aboard Hennessy's *Symphonetta* and slipping gently out of Portree harbour, however, I found both problems solved themselves neatly at once. Innocent or guilty, Hennessy did not deviate from form. Outside on the heaving waters of Raasay Sound, while his three white oilskin-coated young men downed sail and put on the engine, Stanley pressed me together and led me masterfully below.

Back to square one. Old man Bizet and boozet again.

I was wrong. But it wasn't Hennessy's fault. He hadn't got the length of nibbling my ear when we were interrupted by someone reporting a chart missing; and five minutes after that a second fellow arrived to ask advice about a slightly choked feed pump.

He had the look of a boy who hadn't had a square meal for a week, and was out of cigarettes most likely as well. I smiled at him and, saying 'May I?' to Hennessy, offered him one of the silver cigarette boxes before he went. Aided by me, he took half a dozen. Mine I let go out in the ashtray at once. I don't, of course, smoke.

It wasn't coincidence. The next to tap on the door had an anxiety about the echo-sounder. As Hennessy, cursing, ran up the companion, the lad turned round to me, and I gave him a wink.

He disappeared, a shiny smile covering his dripping face from ear to sou'-westered ear. They were ready for mischief and mutiny – and good luck to them. *Symphonetta* had arrived first at Portree because Hennessy had driven his helpers like dogs.

It seemed a good idea to go up on deck too, before the ship fell nominally apart. I gathered my hair again under the black oiled silk turban, finished my drink, and, drawing my mackintosh close, clambered aloft.

In the cockpit, Hennessy was saying, 'You damned, feckless set of nincompoops – if I thought this was deliberate...'

'Where is South Rona, Stanley?' I said. 'Is that the chart? Do show me how you are sailing?'

The acolytes melted to their tasks, and Hennessy pored over the chart. I had a good look too, for very soon I was going to be alone on the land inside all those soundings, where Kenneth and I were to meet.

South Rona is a rocky slip of an island, less than five miles in length and not much more than a mile wide anywhere, with no inhabitants save the lighthouse keepers at the north end, and a small naval base not far from the lighthouse which is normally deserted, except when the *Lysander* or a sister submarine was on trial. The rest of the island is ridged with rocky spurs and steep valleys, with bog and lochans in most of them, and, to the south-west, a rock-ridden haven called Acarsaid Mor, which seems to mean, simply, Big Harbour.

Over the hill from Acarsaid Mor was another bay, long dried out, with above it the roofless ruins of the old village. So *Dolly*'s maps said, and all those of whom I had discreetly inquired. I was here now to prove how well I had studied my lesson.

Soon, through the murk and the rain, a blacker shape appeared on our right, and one of the boys slithered to the bows, while Hennessy cut our power down to a whisper. It was the entrance to the anchorage opening up to us, and the black shapes merging into the blue-black of the sky were the hills of South Rona. From one of these, or from the lighthouse itself, Kenneth would have seen *Dolly* pass after midnight, on her way south to Portree. I wondered if he had seen and recognized *Symphonetta*, and if Hennessy's presence alarmed him. I wondered if he had turned back, or had been stopped by the security guards.

We were a long way from the base and the lighthouse, where his sleeping quarters must be. The other anchorage, at the north end of the island, was for lighthouse and naval use only. The pier there was for taking on stores, and for the *Willa Mavis* when she brought stocks for the lighthouse. Somewhere there, they had what remained of the *Lysander*'s wrecked special equipment, and their scientists would be working on it. Kenneth would not want a rendezvous there.

While I considered, we had crept to the head of the inlet and the boys had dropped anchor. Nothing stirred on the dark shore. Hennessy, out of temper already, looked through his binoculars and was inclined to be tart.

I have no patience with that kind of thing. While the boat was being lowered in a hurry to take me ashore, I looked at the chart once again. A mile of rough walking, it looked; with perhaps a stiff climb in the middle, and then I should be in the village. And I should know very soon after that what happened that night in a warm flat in Rose Street, Edinburgh, where there was a dead man about whom there had been no publicity at all.

11

Hennessy didn't go ashore with me in that launch to meet Kenneth. It took me some time to argue him out of it, and all the time I was sure of only one thing. If he insisted on coming, then I should insist on all three of his young men coming with him. As it was, he gave in when he did because he thought I was bringing my friend back on board with me.

Life, however, does not always work out like that. Instead of Hennessy, two of his white-coated young men, Shaw and Roberts, were to take me ashore. By Hennessy's orders. During the journey I took the chance to explain my dilemma, and to receive from Mr Shaw and Mr Roberts their most fervent assurances of help. I told them I wanted to keep this appointment in privacy. I could count, they said, on doing just that.

We landed. Shaw, who was going to be a doctor, and Roberts, who dreamed during law classes of being a front-desk fiddle under von Karajan, helped me out of the boat and up the stony beach into the undergrowth, while I felt for my whistle, my torch and my compass. I waved them goodbye and watched them return to the launch.

They made no attempt to refloat it. They were going to sit there, oblivious to signals, and wait until I should come back. That left Stanley Hennessy marooned in the harbour on board *Symphonetta*, with a rowing boat his only means of conveyance. By the time he got that ashore, Kenneth and I should be quite hard to find. I waved my torch again and, turning, set off.

Once, in my years of sycophancy, I learned my way about the night sky. It is a useful trick, to steer by in the dark. That night, the stars were half masked by the heavy, rain-sodden clouds, but it did not greatly matter. My way, from the very slope of the rock, was quite clear. And the darkness was welcome.

I told myself that *Vallida,* with Duke Buzzy and Gold-tooth, was by now safely in Stornoway, where Gold-tooth could catch a plane south with my diamond bracelet. I told myself that every boat on these shores would be checked by the look-out, and that there would be a cordon of some kind, whether of alarms or of men, through which Kenneth must come. That would be near the base. You cannot guard country like this. There are too many hiding places.

I picked my way over that ridge of bony, uneven ground, covered with tough grass and heather, until I heard the sea louder again on my left, and the broken shell of a path made itself felt, underfoot, winding uphill away from the sea, to the brow of a hill on my right.

Then I began to pick out, on either side of the path, dim against the black hillside, blurred by mosses and obscured by low clumps of dark trees, the squat shapes of houses, set here and there on the slopes. There were no roofs on these houses, no reflection in the empty windows of the thistles and bracken that waved in the wind outside. There, dim at my feet, they had a garden of club grass and buttercups, and the closed pink ragged-robin, bent long-legged in the dark.

The village. I stood still and listened. The topmost house, Kenneth had said. The wind, rising to one of its gusts, suddenly spoke like an organ through the vents and crevices of each tumbling, derelict house; and the grass and leaves and bracken, bending about me, roared and fumed like a marshalling of ghost locomotives, hissing pressurized steam. A stone fell, sharply, and I drew breath, my right fist clenched hard in my pocket. There was a heavy movement, and then the vanishing, trotting bulk of a sheep.

From tree to tree and wall to wall, I made my way uphill. That would be the house, higher up than the rest, with its end oblique to the sea. Kenneth, are you watching me? Are you waiting at one of the empty windows, your breath coming as quickly as mine is, or are you resting inside, on some fallen block from the chimney, your shoulders against the green-padded wall, your thin American raincoat, that you bought in Nevada, slung about your shoulders over the stained sweater and the untidy slacks...?

There was a doorway. Even its lintel had gone. I paused, and then walked slowly through.

'Hello,' said Johnson.

Once, at a very intimate party, I found myself introduced to my dentist. This was worse. Like a clenched hand opening, my diaphragm let fall all its breath. Then I clicked on the torch in my hand. It illuminated a square of unkempt, silky undergrowth, seeded with stones, and on one of the stones, as I had pictured, was seated a man.

Except that the two dazzling orbs, cat-like, which watched me weren't Kenneth's: they were Johnson's twin-arched bifocals. Of Kenneth there was no sign at all.

'How did you get here?' I said. And as an afterthought, 'I hope you remembered your gun?'

In the light of my torch he looked unwontedly businesslike, in some sort of proofed jacket and trousers in a dark peaty brown, cut like a battledress. At his side lay a stick, and an ordinary haversack, dark with moisture. The rain, I realized, had for some time eased off. Always smiling, while I looked at him he unbuttoned one of the big battledress pockets.

The first thing he took out was his pipe, which he stuck in his mouth. The second was his gun. It lay there in his hand, the small nickel pistol I last saw on the rocks inside Staffa. 'I'm glad you noticed it,' said Johnson comfortably, turning it in his artist's pussyfoot hand, until he had it trained on my heart. 'It comes in handy sometimes.' And he pressed the trigger, quickly and hard.

For singing, one must be in training. As his finger tightened, I dropped – but not before I had flung my torch as hard as I could straight for his head. As the bruising stones and nettles received me, I saw him incline gently, to allow the beam to arch hissing past him, while in his hand the trigger clicked fully home.

There was no report. Nor was there a bullet. Instead, a little flame minced up from the top of the gun and tilting it, Johnson puffed at his pipe.

It took some time to light, during which my torch lay shining green in the long grass at his back, while the little flame pulsed on his big brow and his flat glasses and his wet black hair, and his grin. Then the lighter flicked out, and there was nothing but the dull glow of the ash.

'You want to be careful,' he said mildly. 'Full of nettles, just there. Actually, I thought I'd protect my investment. It's going to be a good picture of you, Tina, this one. On reflection, I didn't want you either drowned in one of South Rona's lochans or chased by the security guards. I sobered up Tom McIver and got him to tell me the rendevous.'

'Then where's Kenneth?' I said. I limped round him, got my torch and limped back. I didn't shout. My brain was too busy. I could feel him watching me, but he didn't move. Grey in the darkness, his pipe smoke streamed out sideways in the wind, even in here.

'He couldn't get here. He left a note. One of the lighthouse men must have brought it. The guards are all alerted at base, and he couldn't get across the island in time. There's a parked Land Rover below the lighthouse on the road. He says he'll wait until dawn inside that.' In the light of my torch, which I had trained on him again, Johnson held out a white slip of paper. I could see the *Valentina* in Kenneth's writing outside.

'I don't need to read it now, do I?' I said. Pointedly.

'Maybe you don't, but I'd still like to know if that's your gentleman friend's handwriting,' said Johnson. 'I'd feel a bit of a twit walking four miles cross country on a dirty, wet night to have my virtue threatened by three lighthouse men in a Land Rover.' And as I hesitated still, 'Come on. Be fair. If he had written you a resounding farewell, I should have gone straight back and finished my night's sleep all cosy on *Dolly*. I nearly did, anyway. Who likes walking?'

'Who asked you to walk?' I remarked.

'Who asked me to hide a corpse in a cupboard?' he shot back. 'I thought something like this might happen – and I know this island while you don't. I can take you to that Land Rover. I'm as curious about Chigwell as you are. And a good deal better at fighting off autograph hunters. Unless you think I want to kill Kenneth Holmes, too.'

I stared at those glistening circles. 'Perhaps,' I said. 'But then, why wait for me? And where are the others? And Michael?' Especially Michael.

Johnson looked grave. 'Michael? We put him ashore to spend a few hours on dry land. He didn't complain. There's quite a swell running, you know… What he thought when he saw *Dolly* sailing out later is something I'm glad I don't know… Rupert dropped me off here at the beach: he and Lenny will be at anchor in Acarsaid Mor beside *Symphonetta* by now… That, by the way, was my other reason for following you. It seemed a pity – it really seemed quite a pity to see you fall into the satin boudoir of Stanley. We had a vote on it, and Rupert agreed.'

'I'm sure he did, Johnson,' a voice said interferingly. A damned, fruity, short-tempered voice, aimed from outside one of the windows. 'But then, your young friend is expert at shouldering women like a meat market bummaree out of gentlemen's rooms.'

Stanley Hennessy. I had underrated his rowing.

He continued, swinging himself dimly into the ruin beside us, in his neat blue parka and trousers, with his white polo jersey impeccable underneath. He addressed Johnson. 'Not a fault of your own. I need no reassuring. If ever I saw a bloody pansy from the neck down and a Friendship Club ponce from the neck up, that's you. What do those big, handsome boys pay you in, Johnson, for the introductions?' He had a gun, too, in his hand. I felt like a hen stalked by two foxes.

'Lessons,' said Johnson. He didn't move much, but Stanley Hennessy suddenly slid very fast across my line of vision, from right to left, and sat down. So did Johnson, but more deliberately, with Hennessy's gun twirling over his fingers.

'…In wrestling, actually. Not that I'm in favour of force as an argument. You hit me, and I hit you; and where does that get us? Now, if you admitted you were worried about Madame Rossi, and were hoping to locate and then dismiss her engineer friend; and I replied that I had exactly the same idea and am prepared to co-operate fully and most altruistically to bring this about, would we not be behaving like adults? And if I said further that Dr Holmes has sent a message arranging to meet Madame Rossi on the lighthouse road in a Land Rover and that I am prepared to share with you the task of taking her safely there and bringing her back again, would you have any grounds for objection?'

'Yes, plenty,' said Hennessy. 'You're mad. This place is full of security people. If he can't meet her this end of the island, then let's give the whole idea up and get back. I want some sleep if you don't. I don't like you or your associates,' he added. He had got up, and of course was feeling very sore. Those nettles would drive anyone crazy. And he was thinking, of course, of all that Blue Grass and the diamonds.

'You don't have to,' said Johnson, getting up too. 'But I'm the guy with the map and the torch and the Batmobile car. Madame Rossi wishes to go – so she goes. If you want to play, you'll have to be nice.'

'He'll be nice,' I said, and linked my arm into Hennessy's elbow. For a moment he resisted, and then his hand closed on mine. I didn't want either Johnson or Hennessy with me. But I saw I should take far too long to find my way over this rotten island in the dark on my own. And if these two didn't stop fighting, I should never get there.

The next hour was something I shall never forget.

To begin with, the rain came on full pelt again. Through it, we scrambled out of the ruin and uphill among the fallen stones and the weeds and the clumps of low trees, until we had reached a soft, reedy meadow where the moss gave under my booted feet. Here there was a broken wall to be climbed, and then we were on a rough path, avenued on either side with thorn bushes and juniper: the old hill pass out of the village. We crossed it – and that was the beginning.

I never knew exactly what terrain we traversed that night, but it seemed to be a chain of small glens, each blocked by a low, uneven hill and filled with bog or water. The men walked mostly in silence. It was not surprising, since Hennessy had just accused Johnson of selling his clients to Rupert, and Johnson had just knocked Hennessy flat. Johnson, leading, took us straight to the west, where a sunken path under a bluff guided us past a sea of brilliant green iris sheaths, high as a man. That was the first glen.

By now, our eyes were used to the dark and Johnson used his torch very little; but with his free hand he kept a firm grasp, behind him, of mine. Behind me, Hennessy walked like a shadow, coming to heel if I stumbled, his grip on my arm. A hen between two foxes. And at the end... what?

The third glen had a little lake in it, choked with lilypads, and an eerie sighing like surf came through the rain from its grassing of reeds. Climbing the hill at its end, Johnson's torch threw back a flare of magenta. We were standing knee-deep in bell heather, with all those silly fat bells. It was a riot. Give me a tarmacadam road, any day. But preferably now.

Beyond the brow of the hill, black against the dark blue of the night sky, was a tumble of rocky hills. I distinguished them, straining; and then suddenly their outline was as brilliant as if some theatrical switchboard had made an appalling mistake. It lasted only a second; then all was pitch-black again. There was a pause, ten... twelve seconds? And then the night sky was pale-lit again. 'Johnson?'

In the dark, as he turned, I could almost see the bland flash of his glasses. 'The lighthouse. We haven't so far to go now. How are you doing?'

Hell, how was I doing? Walking between two guns at night on a wild Scottish island. 'All right,' I said.

I suppose the last bit was the worst. Here there were no tracks in the valleys, only rocky bluffs to be climbed, padded with heather; and when one came to an end of these, flat bogs sunk with fat, soggy cushions, lit by the torch into hummocks of coral and green, with black peat pools between them, encrusted with scum. We could not trust our feet in the wet dark to these.

Johnson's light flickered on, tracing our steps in the mosses, showing a foothold on the grey-white rocks, seamed and patched with pale butcher's pink. He cursed mildly, once; and I thought he had bumped or grazed something, until I realized that if we were near the lighthouse, we must be near the road, and also the base, and Johnson did not relish having to show so much light. It was worse too, now that the twelve-second flash of the lighthouse dazzled the sky. In the blackness that fell on our eyes afterwards, our feet were invisible, and so was the bog.

It was, in fact, during one of those spells of reflected white light that the burst of gunfire came out of the dark, and Stanley Hennessy screamed.

We were standing on rock. While the shots were still echoing, Johnson's hands thrust me down, lying flat on the hillside. 'Stay there!' and then I heard the pad of his rubber-soled shoes as he jumped from boulder to boulder, away from me, to be lost in the sound of the rain. I strained my eyes after him. I peered through the darkness behind, where Hennessy had shouted, and where there was now no sound at all, and then jerked my head back. Thin and muffled by rain, a voice in the distance said, 'Got you!' and somebody squealed.

A moment later, a man's voice shouted in anger; there was another volley of shots, running footsteps, and then someone in blundering haste came downhill out of the rain towards me, from the direction in which Johnson had vanished.

It was not Johnson. As I lay still, the rainwater streaming down my neck and my whole body shivering, a hurrying figure loomed out of the dark, grazed one wet canvas toe on my ribs, and fell helplessly over me.

The shape was small, round and compact. The voice, crying miserably and despairingly, 'Oh! My! My pinkie's staved!' was the voice of Nancy Buchanan. She had just time, rolling over, to add in tones of soprano surprise, 'It's somebody! It's you! What's wrong? Are you hurt, Madame Rossi?' when Johnson swooped out of the dark, picked her up like an old cigarette packet, pointed her north and, smacking her bottom, said, 'Run like hell.'

She did. Straining my ears, I heard the small sound of her feet disappear. The trampling and bustling of a moment before had stopped also, and there was no more firing. For a long moment we both listened, Johnson and I, but wind and rain were all we could hear. 'What was she doing? Who was firing? Where's Hennessy?' I said. The loudest noise on South Rona was my heart.

'The security guards were after her. God knows what she's doing, but she and Bob were coming straight over here, so I headed them off. It was a fairly near thing, because we were all in the line of

fire for a moment. In fact, I think Hennessy may have caught it…
Look. Are you all right?'

'Yes,' I said, although I had to exert my singing muscles to say it quite steadily.

Above me, Johnson's shadow paused, was illuminated by the lighthouse, and then was invisible again. 'You're a hell of a woman,' his voice said; and continued immediately. 'I'm going to find him. Stay here. If you need me, blow your whistle.'

'Right,' I said shortly, but I was pleased. There is no particular credit in being born with courage. But it does come in useful. I could hear the admiration, despite himself, in his voice.

He had barely gone when I also heard something else. A groan, coming from below me, out of the bog. Since the whistle was for emergency only, and groans might easily turn to inconvenient, delirious shouts I gritted my costly capped teeth, and slithered downhill towards it.

In the darkness, certainly, something was moving. A man, a big man in what looked like a parka – only there was no longer a white polo necked jersey underneath. It was black, and all the face and head and wetly waving fair hair above it was black, black and fresh, welling blood.

Very small, very short, I blew a toot on the whistle for Johnson. He was correct. Stanley Hennessy had been in the line of firing all right. The only question was, who had fired?

In the end, I held the torch while Johnson got a polythene bag full of bogwater and poured it over Hennessy's head. Features appeared. Brow, nose, cheeks were in order. His eyes, still closed, seemed to have suffered no harm. Chin and mouth were intact. Johnson got more water and ran it over the thick hair and neck, when all became plain. He had had one ear shot partly through. 'Eureka! Jenkins!' said Johnson; and Hennessy abruptly woke up.

No one could have called him a coward. He opened his mouth to yell, and closed it when Johnson reminded him where we all were, and why. He opened his mouth again to express his feelings as Johnson, talking, began to dress his ear from the inexhaustible haversack; and shut it again when he saw me. He produced a large, resigned grimace; and when Johnson helped him to his feet he was able, without too much trouble, to walk.

It was I who told him about the Buchanans, and then Hennessy really did swear, and without apology. 'That prune-faced little couple of mantelshelf ornaments, dipping their ensign like maniacs to the Meals on Wheels van in Kilcreggan. My God, no wonder they seemed too stupid to be true. It was a cover-up. A cover-up for spying... *And you let her go, Johnson, you fool!*'

And that was true, too. It was then that I began to feel rather cold.

It was Johnson, too, who persuaded Hennessy it would be unfair to me to cast ourselves yet on the mercy of the guards. It wasn't hard. Hennessy didn't relish, clearly, the explanations that would follow, even though he was unwilling (he said) for me to run any more risks. I replied that having come so far, I was damned well going to see Kenneth, and he could go home if he liked. Thanks to the Buchanans, we were probably through the defence cordon anyway, and if the Buchanans were going to blow up the whole of the island, then good luck to them, I said.

I was perhaps a little hard on a man who had come all this way for my protection, and had been shot for his pains. If, that is, he *had* come all this way for my protection.

We were still arguing when we got to the next rise and looked over. Then Johnson suddenly said, 'Down!' and, trained in an hour like privates in the Borneo jungle, we dropped.

Not a second too soon. At last, we were in the full reflected glare of the lighthouse. And as, lying flat in the heather, the whole world about us was lit, for a pale space, by its backwash, we saw where we had come. Ahead and to the right, the lighthouse stood on its hill. From there, the road unreeled to our left, running west and downhill towards the long pier and the little harbour where the *Willa Mavis* normally tied up, and where now a smallish yacht rode darkly at anchor.

All the way up from the jetty, a single-track road was lit by tall, concrete street lights, which bestowed pools of light on the crane and the hundreds of oil drums lying stacked at the top of the pier. Above it was a big aluminum hut with double-louvred doors which Johnson said housed the generator. From there, and the black water tank beside it, the path struck up the low hillside beyond to a cluster of huts: the base. We could see the grooved aluminium walls on their brick batter, the windows carefully shuttered, and the floodlights manning the roof.

There were the laboratories, the mess-room, the dormitories used by the scientists and the naval personnel testing the new equipment on *Lysander*. There Kenneth was living, while the investigation into the submarine explosion continued. And there, high up on the winding, rutted road to the lighthouse which was the only paved way on the island, was a solitary vehicle, standing lightless and dark, parked waiting, next to the moor.

The Land Rover. And Kenneth.

There was time to see as much before the lighthouse revolved, and we were plunged into darkness again, except for the little, lit city below.

Then, with a silence and suddenness quite terrible, every other light we could see went instantly out, and the darkness was utter.

In the sodden, alien wilderness, the shouts of alarm and inquiry reached us quite distinctly from below. We waited, breathing lightly, trying to smell from which side the danger might come. Then Johnson spoke abruptly into my ear.

'Wait ten minutes, as near as you can judge, and then set off for Kenneth. I don't think anyone is likely to be watching us, but Hennessy and I will go off now in the opposite direction, and that should draw them away... Have you the nerve to get to that Land Rover alone?'

I answered, trying to sound bravely uncertain. All I asked in the world was a chance to get to that Land Rover alone.

I felt Johnson rise; then Hennessy got to his feet with a grunt. He pulled his parka hood over his bandages, patted me briefly on one shoulder, and blended with Johnson into the dark.

It was hard to believe that, after all his arduous journey, both Johnson and Hennessy were content to forego a meeting with Kenneth. It struck me that one or the other was far less interested in Kenneth Holmes than in the tumult now going on at the base. And that, distrusting each other as they did, neither man would move without the other.

It suited me. Nothing could have suited me better. There was nothing now but this dark, rain-filled hillside between me and Kenneth. And this was what I had come a long, painful way to achieve.

12

The rain had stopped.

On the steep road where the Land Rover was parked, it was dark and quiet under the overhanging hill, which masked even the revolving blaze of the lighthouse. Below, where the road joined the other paths to the base and the pier it was dark, but by no means as quiet. Men's voices, shouting, came clearly up from the waterfront, and the flash of numerous torches, borne at a run. As I watched, the disturbance swung away from me, and uphill. Up at the base, a big battery lamp suddenly switched on, then another.

But I was no longer looking or listening, for I had reached the Land Rover's nose.

If anyone had seen me approach, there was no sign within. The windscreen stared back at me emptily, and when, stepping lightly, I moved round behind, there was no sound or movement from the dark interior which the half-unrolled canvas concealed.

There was no point in whispering names, or in thinking of personal safety now. I was committed. Placing my hands where, on shooting weekends, I had been taught, I pulled myself inside the hood and up to one of the two lining benches. I arrived there, and Kenneth's voice, low and hoarse and quite unmistakable, said 'Valentina?' And Kenneth's arms, like a bear's in some huge, unyielding topcoat, closed hard around me. And we kissed.

It was the same. I don't know why, but there has never been anyone like him. I said, when I could pull my mouth away, 'You made me come a long way to find you.'

His lips in my hair, he didn't want to speak. At length he said, in the same low voice, 'I'm sorry. You shouldn't have come.'

'You need someone,' I said. He was shivering. 'You forget, Kenneth. Almost nothing can hurt me. I'm armour plate all the way through. You shouldn't have left me, in Rose Street, that night...'

His breathing quickened. As I spoke his hands tightened and my own pulses were a good deal less than stagnant: the kiss went on and on. To break it would be agony, but it had to be done. Now, of all times, I had to be clear-sighted. So I raised my two hands and said, 'Kenneth!'

He did not obey me at once, and I said sharply, 'Not now! Not now. The whole camp is awake.'

He drew a long breath, in the dark. 'I know,' he said. 'They're probably looking for me. I'm under suspicion.'

It was no news. Why else was he stuck here? And Gold-tooth had been quite confident. Chigwell was a Government agent, he had said. And Dr Holmes had blown up the *Lysander*. Just like that.

I wasn't taking the easy way. I said quietly, 'Under suspicion of what? Causing the *Lysander* explosion?'

He was grateful, clearly, not to have to tell me himself. Even so, there was a pause before he said, 'Yes. And not without cause. I probably did.'

This time I sat back, and no doubt my voice was impatient. 'My dear Kenneth, you are neither an idiot nor a traitor. Also, you were in Rose Street, Edinburgh, so far as I know, when the damned boat set off on her trials. Do you want me to testify for you? I could swear to the messages you sent me. And other people apart from your friend Chigwell must have known you were there.'

'Of course they do.' Now *he* was impatient. 'But I couldn't jeopardize your good name like that. In any case, that wasn't the point. The way it was worked, I could have been in a Gemini rocket and still set the thing off.' He stopped and said, in an irritable double-take, 'Was that damned fool Chigwell still there when you came? I'm sorry, darling. He swore blind he'd pack and get out.'

I said nothing. I was swallowing down my relief. Kenneth hadn't killed Chigwell. I knew it now, for an absolute fact. I knew my Kenneth Holmes to the bone. He was the most transparently honest man I have ever encountered. He said now, spurred by my silence, 'Don't worry. Harry Chigwell won't talk. He's discretion itself.'

'He certainly is,' I said. 'He's dead.'

There was a silence. Then, 'Oh, my God,' said Kenneth. 'Tell me.' And I did. Or as much as I told Johnson, anyway. There was no word, for instance, of diamond bracelets buying off anyone. I had no desire to go into the matter of diamond bracelets, or indeed of Duke Buzzy. Instead I said, 'Who *was* Chigwell?'

He didn't even hear me at first: he was too shocked, and too busy exclaiming over my unorthodox behaviour with a corpse. Then it dawned on him that my conduct was not quite so irrational when one considered that he, Kenneth, was the number one suspect. 'I didn't kill him,' he said then, blankly. I tried again. 'Who *was* he, Kenneth?'

It didn't help. Chigwell had been nothing, it appeared, but an old school friend he had run into the previous year, who had offered the use of his flat should Kenneth ever require it. If Gold-tooth was right and Chigwell was a Government agent, then Kenneth clearly was ignorant of it. I said, 'And why then did you leave?'

He didn't want to answer that. After a moment he said, 'Because of you, Tina. There were microphones in the flat. I found one under the table, and broke it. Someone was watching us: would have followed us, too. They wanted to hear what we said when we met. I thought I'd deprive them of that pleasure.'

'That sounds grim,' I said. I could hear my heart thudding. 'But why, Kenneth? Blackmail? Or what? Why should anyone want to do that?'

'That,' said Kenneth heavily, 'brings me back to the *Lysander*. The bloody sub. Tina.'

'Well?' I said. Sometimes he was so slow, one wanted to scream. But you forget that, most times, when you were with him. The wind, revived, sighed round the struts of the van and the canvas creaked and vibrated. The voices of men shouting could still be heard now and then, but comfortably in the distance. There was an immense sense of isolation, of space. Almost I had become reconciled to the darkness, to not being able to see more than the broad planes of his face. Kenneth's hands over mine were warm and heavily jointed, an artisan's hands. The hands of a scientific engineer of superior calibre.

He said, 'I didn't want you to know this; but your name and mine are already linked over *Lysander*. The defence people are curious. And that's why I didn't want you to come.'

'You didn't want me to come, and yet you told me where to find you?' I said and he must have heard the smile in my voice. But I wouldn't let him kiss me again, not just then. 'Tell me,' I said in my turn.

And that was how I heard from Kenneth that he and I between us had caused the destruction and worse than destruction on board the submarine *Lysander*.

It was simple enough. It concerned a new form of explosive, allied to a small electronic device sensitive to control by single or multiple sounds. He had been tinkering with it in the States, when we had been so much together, and I had given him one of my albums of records – *Tina Rossi Sings,* it was called. Original stuff.

So, purely as an experiment and as an indication of his state at the time, Kenneth had keyed the bomb to a phrase sung by my voice.

It was an experiment he had never concluded; and since he left Nevada the prototype and its plans and formulae had been left in a safe vault, inviolate. He would not say to me then, even there on South Rona, what form the device took, or even describe its outward appearance. But the device which exploded the *Lysander* was an exact copy of that very prototype. By some freak, parts of the bomb casing had been found. It was tiny, said Kenneth. Small enough to plant in a pocket, but powerful enough to wreck the immediate area where it exploded; and maybe even to sink the sub, if it hit the right place. That was all. Except that the bomb that killed three men on the *Lysander* had been set in the same way as his – *for my voice.*

I said nothing. After a moment, Kenneth went on. 'It was pretty clever, you see. They had the same album of songs in the submarine mess… everyone has it, I suppose. When the sub was in harbour they all used the record-player in the shore mess. It was only when they were submerged, on long trials, that the one in the mess was turned on, and when it reached that one note in your voice, it triggered the bomb. You must admit,' he added with an effort at lightness, 'being a fan of Valentina Rossi's has its drawbacks.'

I wished he would keep to the point. I said, 'So you're under suspicion. Why? Do they think you copied the plans? Or showed them to someone in Nevada?'

'They've not so far been very explicit,' said Kenneth. 'But they're asking a lot of interesting questions. Such as who had access to the lab besides me.'

'I did,' I said. 'If you mean the lab in Nevada. And who else?'

'No one,' said Kenneth, quite baldly.

There was a long silence. Then I said, 'If you are accusing me of stealing and selling your secrets, I can only deny it. I have no defence and no proof. Except that I'm here.'

'I'm not accusing you, my darling,' said Kenneth. 'I'm not. I'm not.' His arms, flung round me, suddenly tightened. His cheek, pressed against mine, was suddenly damp. 'I haven't even told them you were there. How could I, and keep your good name? It's just that they may find out anyway, if they trace the letters…'

'What letters?' This was what he had been longing to tell me, while the bloody rule-book told him he shouldn't. 'And *of course* you should have told them I had a key to that laboratory. Do you think I'd let you take all the blame?' I stopped. 'No wonder your boys are bugging your dates. What letters? Let's have it all.'

That was simple, too. He was being blackmailed: had been ever since his return from Nevada. Over his meetings in Nevada with me.

I heard that one out in silence, and the two dried-up steaks and the bottle of champagne in that damnable flat seemed a brave thing, when you knew. Someone had been bleeding him dry; someone with microfilm evidence of letters and notes I had written him, and of his letters back.

And to obtain that microfilm evidence, the blackmailer must have had access to that laboratory. For that was where Kenneth kept my letters to him.

Kenneth had had no reason to think that anything else in his lab had been tampered with. His precious device hadn't vanished, and the plans were intact. If he had not had my reputation to protect he would have reported the illegal entry, and asked the police to trace the blackmailer for him. It was not until the discoveries on

Lysander that he realized that the blackmailer was probably also a spy. And then he had been torn two ways.

He could keep me away from it, so that I should never know I was involved. Or he could meet me somewhere, somehow, and ask me who else during that long, hot idyll in Nevada could have had the use of my key. For the lab he was lent in Nevada had a special lock. No one could have picked it. No one had forced their way in otherwise. And there were only two keys.

He was, I think, right to take the second course. However silent he kept, those blackmail letters would have brought me into the story eventually. I had come to him there on South Rona at some cost and I was glad... A man of Victorian principles. It was part of his fascination for me.

But there was no future for either of us unless I cut through this tangle. There were two keys to the laboratory where Kenneth's papers and his sonic device were in storage. Two keys, he had said. His... and mine.

And I knew who could have had mine.

The shouting had stopped. Outside the Land Rover the rain had begun again, drumming on the canvas roof and reflecting, in half-tones and tones of differing texture, its descent on road, on grass, rock and bog. Dimly, through the van's windows, the hills appeared, remained and disappeared to the turn of the lighthouse, like a badly wired shop sign, telling me nothing. I said, 'I know who could have taken my key – and who had access to my letter from you. I know who must have been blackmailing you. No wonder he didn't want me to meet you... It's Michael, of course. Michael Twiss.'

'I wondered,' was all Kenneth said. And then, in the same careful voice, 'But it doesn't help, does it? We can't have him talk. And it only fouls up your relationship with him. I know what he does for your work.'

'We've parted already,' I said. I felt suddenly vicious. 'Michael Twiss and I. Do you think I care? Or would you rather be shot as a spy than have it known that I was your mistress?'

'Yes,' he said with perfect simplicity. And I couldn't shake him from that. So at length I said the only possible thing. 'Then I'll tell the police about Michael myself.'

'You won't.' His hands on my shoulders pushed me hard back on my seat, and kept me there. 'Why do you think I've tried to keep away from you? Valentina – it hasn't been easy, God knows, this past week. You must promise not to throw it away. *Promise!* Now, before you leave. Swear you'll never throw away your reputation and your career for my sake. You've worked so hard… and you've far more to lose than I have.'

It was quixotic, and it was crazy. I was shivering, too. I said, slowly, 'I can stop Michael's blackmail – that, at least; if only by threatening to expose him for your sake. But no threat of mine would make him give himself up in your place over the bomb. Kenneth, what is the worst that can happen to you, if they pursue a charge? They have no real evidence against you, surely?'

'I don't know. I don't know what they'll do to me, Tina. But ultimately, it *was* my mistake that killed those three men. And if I must pay for it, then I will.'

I had nothing to say. Kenneth moved and, cupping my face in his hands, kissed me lightly on the mouth. 'Don't worry. You've done all and more that you can. They can hardly shoot me. I'll go abroad, eventually: there's always a country somewhere wanting a scientist. We'll meet again. I'm sorry it was such a depressing story you had to hear, in the end. But I have your promise, don't I? Valentina…'

'Yes. I promise,' I said. And at that moment the lights came on, by the pier, the road and the base camp; and the faint illumination, striking up from the road under the half-unrolled canvas, showed me for the first time Kenneth's face. I stared at him, my hood back, and my hair fallen loose about my shoulders and brow, and he made a sudden little sound, a sound I remembered from long ago; and pulled me to him, bruisingly hard.

The world exploded. There was a mind-deadening roar, a shuddering, and a jerk under our feet that sent me cannoning into his stomach. Then our Land Rover drove smartly off.

It had everything. The seaside postcard, the horse-laugh, the Mack Sennett comedy, the lovers, locked in a clinch on the removable rug.

I can tell you what it is like when it happens to you. It makes you feel sick. Sick with interrupted emotion and outrage and shock. Sick and shaken and ill.

Kenneth was the first to recover. While I was still on all fours, and the car was pursuing a racketing descent towards the crossroads and jetty, Kenneth had his fingers on the back of the driving seat, and then on the neck muscles of the man sitting there, his hands turning the wheel. The car swerved. I shrieked. 'Kenneth! Let him go! It's a friend!'

I had my doubts even as I spoke, but I didn't want to be a road accident victim on South Rona. Kenneth heard me. Slowly, he let his arm fall.

'That's better, Dr Holmes,' said Johnson gracefully. 'Thank you, Tina.' Braking, he brought the car to a halt at the head of the pier.

Kenneth said nothing. But his face in the harbour lights, switched across and across by the shadow of the Rover's windscreen wipers, was disturbingly grim. 'That,' I said to him with precision, 'is Johnson Johnson. The man who helped pack Mr Chigwell away. His sense of humour conceals a love of dumb animals and a passionate feeling for cribbage.' I turned to Johnson and snapped, 'Have you been in the car all this time?'

He had, of course. Prone, I suppose, on both seats in the dark.

'I fell asleep,' said Johnson agreeably. The twinkling glasses were not unamiable. But he was not looking at me. 'Isn't it rather lucky? For *I* have no inhibitions about informing against Michael Twiss.'

'You bloody little spy,' said Kenneth blankly. I wished he would either shut up or beat Johnson into a pulp. I didn't much care which. There were times when Kenneth's Victorian principles lost their charm. Now I said wearily, 'I know. He heard everything we said. But he already knows all about Chigwell, Kenneth, and he couldn't have handled it better. I'm sure he won't make mischief, not now.'

'You're sure he won't make mischief? A man who would dream of climbing into that car and snooping on you through the whole of our...'

Words failed him. Words hadn't failed me, but I didn't dare use them. No wonder Johnson had set off so cheerfully in the opposite direction. It was merely the preliminary to coming cheerfully back. The show with the biggest TAM rating in South Rona. If I thought of one or two things I was grateful for, it didn't affect my natural instinct to grind his face in the windscreen.

Kenneth, recovering his breath, said, 'If he heard all that, he knows exactly how we're placed. If you denounce Michael Twiss, Johnson, you expose Madame Rossi to all I've been trying to save her from… If you really have a kindness for Tina, then keep quiet and let us both go. God knows, that way I'll pay any debt I have owing in full. And at least she won't suffer.'

'No. But then,' said Johnson mildly, 'what of all the future victims of the ubiquitous Mr Twiss? Including Madame Rossi herself? Hennessy got in the way of that bullet, but it was probably intended for her. Or didn't you realize Michael is finding her an embarrassment?'

I said, 'Wait a minute. Who shot at Hennessy?'

'Someone with a revolver,' said Johnson brightly. 'And the guards all had rifles: remember?'

'But you said Michael had something to do with it. Michael didn't come to South Rona.'

'Oh, but he did,' Johnson said. 'It was Old Home Week on South Rona tonight. The bloody place was like *Charley's Aunt* done by the Flintstones.'

I still couldn't believe it. 'But you said you left Michael ashore at Portree.'

'I did. One can only conjecture,' said Johnson, 'but I suppose he learned somewhere on shore that, far from being tucked up sleeping on *Dolly*, you had sailed into the Kodachrome on Hennessy's *Symphonetta*. Then, when he most wanted to be on board, he'd find that *Dolly* had disappeared, too… I don't suppose he wanted to be parted finally from *Dolly*, whatever he said. Anyway, he cadged a ferry from Cecil Ogden's *Seawolf*. I don't know what he told Ogden, but Victoria was ashore, having a bath and a kip-down with friends; so Cecil was quite free.

'According to the naval chaps here, *Seawolf* came in and anchored some time after we landed at Acarsaid Mor, and two men went on up to the lighthouse. According to the men there, they were Ogden and Twiss. Twiss left after a bit – he said to try and find me – and Ogden followed him later. Then they both boarded *Seawolf* and made back for Portree.

'I shouldn't,' said Johnson blandly to Kenneth, 'be blind to the fact that while Michael Twiss is about, Tina is really highly unsafe. That's why I make you this unrivalled sporting offer. *Dolly*'s here. I wirelessed to Acarsaid Mor for her. Come aboard *Dolly* with Tina, and sail with us to Portree to pick up Michael on board again. Then we'll get at the truth... How about that?'

There was a short silence. Then Kenneth said bitterly, 'And how do you propose to persuade the Navy to allow me to leave?'

'I don't,' Johnson said calmly. 'The Navy need never find out that you've gone. They know me. They know Hennessy and I brought Madame Rossi on shore for a bet, and Hennessy got mildly hurt in a clash with the security guards, and I've come back to collect Madame Rossi. We spun them that tale in order to get Hennessy's ear attended to: they've sent him back to his own boat by naval launch, protesting like hell. I've had a ticking off for getting mixed up with security, and I've made my peace. So long as no one prowls about their precious buildings, they're not all that worried. They'll never notice an extra passenger crossing to *Dolly*... and the *Willa Mavis,* if need be, can carry you back. Come aboard *Dolly*,' said Johnson. 'And I'll help you shake the truth out of Twiss.'

Kenneth didn't take much more persuading. I could see him registering the points as Johnson made them. It was a chance. And Kenneth and I had no other, if Johnson chose to inform the base of what he had just overheard. Kenneth would have his career wrecked, if not worse, for handing out gratuitous keys, and would also probably be accused of his friend Chigwell's murder. And I should have to face all that he was trying to spare me. Kenneth made a last effort. 'But if I come... how will Michael Twiss's confession make any difference?'

'In several ways,' said Johnson, surprised. 'For instance, *we* could blackmail Michael Twiss.'

We had, as he said, no real alternative. We were at his mercy, whether we liked it or not. We did as he said.

Forgathered on *Dolly*, with the lights of the base high above us, and the lighthouse shuttering and unshuttering its monotonous warning, I took Kenneth's hand. At least he was with me, and if one could trust Johnson there was hope, of a kind. The only trouble was, I didn't trust Johnson.

I looked at him, as he stood, hand on wheel, watching Rupert cast off, and thought of something he had never explained. 'Nancy Buchanan,' I said. 'What was she doing tonight?'

'Ah, yes.' His hand moved, and responding to the thrust of the engine, *Dolly*'s bows moved slowly round and she began, gently, to nose her way out of the anchorage. No one stopped us. Lenny, crouched in the bows, waved as she took up her course. 'Ah, yes,' said Johnson, and lifted his eyes from the chart. 'Clear, Lenny… If you want filthy villainy, take the Buchanans. No wonder they wouldn't let anyone down in their cabin. Little, Holmes, did we know.'

I'd had enough. I snapped, 'What did they do?'

'They crawled,' said Johnson, easing the wheel, 'across the whole length of South Rona, in the dead of night in a rainstorm, tripping over alarm wires with the precision of clockwork, until Bob actually fell over one of the guards who were watching him and made such a noise the poor chap had to raise the alarm. That was when the shooting occurred. And why we had so far been so little troubled.

'Then, considerably accelerated by circumstances and the general bedlam now let loose around them, the Buchanans carried out their pre-arranged plan. Bob, who is as you know an engineer, got in among the power machinery and disconnected it, while Nancy plodded on and created a diversion to let Bob carry out the next part of the plan. It was perfectly fascinating, and I'm told the Navy sat at its windows in rows and watched it like home movies.'

'They didn't stop them?' I said. It sounded like the silliest thing yet.

'They didn't need to,' said Johnson. 'They'd had a tip-off about the Buchanans. They knew what they were going to do.'

'*What?*' I said.

'You can see. They haven't pulled it down yet. Probably want to take pictures of it tomorrow and frame them.' Johnson, looking over his shoulder, waved generally upwards and back. We all looked.

High above the neat roofs of the camp, where the radio transmitter bore its tall web, floated a large, home-made banner, fully twenty feet long, and illuminated by all the battery spotlights the base was able to muster, as well as the intermittent glare of the lighthouse.

It said, with old-fashioned point, and less than old-fashioned spelling, BAN THE BOMM.

13

I think we made that journey to Portree in absolute silence. We weren't very talkative, either, when we found no Michael Twiss waiting to walk into our arms on the pier. For whatever reason, he hadn't wanted to come back to *Dolly*. He had stayed on *Seawolf*, picked up Victoria, and was off on the next stretch of race in Cecil Ogden's string-netted chicken coop.

I wasn't surprised, when I thought about it. And the more I thought about it, the more it concerned me. If he hadn't abandoned the race altogether, it was because he still had hopes of showing a profit. And I didn't want the profit to be my sudden demise, or Kenneth's. For Kenneth's death, one couldn't deny, would be very convenient indeed. If an accident happened to Kenneth, the blame for *Lysander* would go to his grave.

In the early hours of Sunday morning, after a brief debate carried by Johnson, we put off the engine, raised sail, and followed *Seawolf* on the next stage of the race, to the island of Rum. This really was my last sail, though I didn't know it, on *Dolly*.

I was tired to the bone. And although my world might be turned upside down in the next twenty-four hours, I was past thinking about it. I slept, half-dressed where I lay on my bed, and didn't waken until well after breakfast time, when the crash of a jarring boom sounded overhead and there was a jolting lurch, first to one side and then to the other, while every block on *Dolly* clattered and banged. It was dark, and until I switched on the little light by my bed, I thought we were still in the night.

When I saw the time, I jumped to my porthole and looked. Outside was a world of grey smoke, eddying and swirling above greasy water flowing in coils and whorls, which appeared and disappeared like oil under the grey, lightless veil. We were in the tidal race at the narrows of Kylerhea, the narrow sea passage separating the mainland from the south coast of Skye; and at the wrong state of the tide.

There is some comfort in adequate clothing. I had white kneeboots with me, and a white quilted tabard that slips over a hooded ski-suit in wool. I dressed, thrown this way and that against the side of my bunk as I did it, and went out into the cockpit.

Johnson was at the helm: a bad sign even if you cared for Johnson, and since the previous night I had reservations. At that moment he had eyes for nothing but the swirl of the current just ahead; and as the sails shuddered above me, slackly banging, I realized that, to add to the discomfort, the wind had almost totally dropped. Then he noticed me and said, 'Did you sleep the sleep of the just? I'm sorry about this. We'll be through fairly soon, but it's going to be a wearing journey to Rum. There's fog pretty consistently forecast, and we've still got the swell from the storm. Lenny'll make breakfast, if you can stand it.'

He and Rupert and Lenny had had, I suppose, relatively little sleep between them since we left Barra. Rupert, I saw on entering the saloon, looked a bit hollow-eyed, but he had just come off duty, and disappeared very soon into the spare cabin forward, leaving Lenny and Johnson on deck.

I did not want breakfast. I sat down in the saloon opposite Kenneth, who was sitting slack-tied, his head tilted back against Johnson's rough-weave cushions, expelling cigarette smoke in cancerous clouds. Under the table at his feet was a mess of upset cigarette butts and ash, and a chart thrown down from its ledge. I saw all the fiddles were up, and a table cloth, folded neatly in its place in the galley, had been soaked before being used. I had slept through some unpleasant weather.

Kenneth, I could tell from his face, had not slept at all. As I sat, his head came down, and putting out his cigarette quickly, he reached for my hands. It was then that he asked me to marry him, and I refused.

No one spoke much, after that. Once past Kylerhea, the boat was thrown about less, but still she rolled and pitched over the swell. Lying, one felt the pressures, like a massaging hand, move from side to side under one's body, and up and down one's shoulder and spine. The sea smacked the boat with strange, washboard thuds, mixed with a dull twang, like the sound of a cello. It reminded me, that persistent, irritating sound, of some slow-motion hand laundry, surging, trickling and rinsing all round *Dolly*'s boards. The other boats, now well ahead of us, would be suffering. Including Michael. It was odd, I thought, that one life, or two, might depend on Michael Twiss's weak stomach.

Then the fog came down, and it was afternoon when we crept into the anchorage of Loch Scresort, in the island of Rum.

Rum is an island of the Inner Hebrides, now wholly owned by the Scottish Nature Conservancy, who conduct experiments there. It is a mountainous, pear-shaped island, about eight miles across, and the only buildings of interest, including wardens' houses, post office, farm, school and school-teacher's house, are placed at intervals round a wide bay, which is the only anchorage the island possesses.

Set in a park inland from the bay is Kinloch Castle, in which the Nature Conservancy and other scientists like Kenneth live and have their laboratories, some inside the house, and some in the grounds. Apart from the scientists' wing, the house remains fully furnished as it was when it was built as a shooting-lodge seventy years ago.

The Warden's house was the Cruising Club's checkpoint. A confrontation with Michael Twiss was our primary objective. And Kenneth Holmes, Johnson had decided, should be our decoy. Kenneth, whom Michael did not yet know to be here. As *Dolly* felt her way into the bay, I said again, to Johnson, 'But will he be safe? How can you protect him?'

And Johnson, staring into the thick white atmosphere, said, 'I shall be behind him, wherever he goes. Don't worry. We haven't rescued him from his old-fashioned chivalry, you and I, to throw him into the bun-mixing machinery now. There's *Symphonetta*.'

It was, too, with her black stern and tall spars like a phantom, far on our right. She had come in, I judged with my new expertise, in the last half-hour: her sails were neatly stowed, but two of the boys were still working on deck. I waved as we passed and someone – Shaw? Roberts? – waved back. Beyond that, there was a squat shape identifiable as *Binkie,* with no sign of the Buchanans on board; and then, what we all were straining to see – Ogden's *Seawolf,* with Michael Twiss, we assumed, still on board.

We slid up beside her and executed, without fuss, the complicated manoeuvre of anchoring. Kenneth stood without moving, binoculars to his eyes. He was just saying, 'No one there. They'll be on shore, too,' when a voice at sea-level remarked, 'Ahoy, *Dolly*! I've got a passenger of yours. Did you know?' And looking down, we saw *Seawolf*'s little pram, with Cecil Ogden in it, alone.

Beside us, Lenny materialized with the companionway, and Johnson's most unctuous voice said, 'Does that mean you're carrying our Mr Twiss? Oh, good show. We wondered rather where he could be... Do come aboard.'

But Ogden's head vibrated gently under its pixie cap. 'You'll want to get ashore to check in. The rest are all there. They're dead set on exploring the Castle, but the lights are off. I've just come back for my torch.'

It was a wonder, I thought, that he had one that worked. Then I saw a number of objects packed under the dinghy bench: an old Tilley lamp, a coil of wire, and a hand brush and dustpan among them, with more under the tarpaulin behind. He had also two big milk churns full of water, and a bloodstained parcel of venison. The Nature Conservancy, clearly, was sustaining *Seawolf* on the next leg of her journey.

I don't know whether Ogden noticed our amusement, or cared. He had had a good deal to drink but not quite as much, I thought, as usual. On his long, knuckle-bone face was an expression of irony, and his eyes were half closed against the smoke of his drooping filter-tip as he looked up. 'Twiss is on shore with Victoria, if you want him. I don't mind keeping him, if you don't. I gather there was a bit of a tizzy.'

'Not yet,' said Kenneth, his voice deep. 'But there's going to be.'

'Dr Holmes.' Johnson made the introduction and added, in face of the open curiosity on Ogden's face, 'It's a matter of dispute between Mr Twiss and Dr Holmes.'

I was grateful for that, but Ogden was hardly likely to believe it, having chased Stanley Hennessy and me, at Michael's urgent request, all the way to South Rona; and knowing that Michael and I had fallen out already over Kenneth. I wondered if Ogden suspected that Michael was responsible for shooting poor Hennessy's ear, and if that was why *Seawolf* had left so promptly, with Michael aboard.

But whatever Ogden thought about us, he showed no more interest, having remembered, clearly, his leaking parcel and other acquisitions to unload on board. He pushed off busily as Johnson stepped into *Dolly*'s dory, and with Rupert at the helm and Kenneth and myself sitting aft, we made for the shore. Then, with leisure to look about, I saw that the fog filling this big sea loch was lifting, and that for the first time I was looking at the low woodland, the piled, shingly beach and the grotesque mountains of Rum.

The bay was shallow. Under the school-teacher's window the red deer were grazing, their rumps seaweed-yellow and umber. They looked up as we slid to the slipway, and I could see their long, soft spread ears like a hare's, and the large eyes, under their light padded arcs. Then they sprang off, but gently, with a flash of pink and yellow and green from the tags in their ears. For this was an island which culled its deer and also preserved them; and where no grass was unstudied. 'Where,' said Johnson, who had been pursuing this train of thought mildly all the way over from *Dolly*, 'only man can be vile, verminous and unsound genetically, and still never be shot.'

The walk to the Warden's house lay along the southern arc of the shore. Rupert was ahead, hurrying to enter *Dolly*'s time of arrival. Kenneth, Johnson and I followed at leisure, and I thought I knew why. It was to allow Rupert to reach the rest of the party and to spread the news that Kenneth was with us. Rupert was baiting the trap. Kenneth here was walking doggedly into it.

In steamy fingers, the sea mist was lifting. Speaking personally, I could never have built a house on that island. It was volcanic, said

Kenneth, but the volcanoes were extinct, which merely meant a lot of peaks and depressing black rocks and heather. The shooting-lodge people in their day had planted shore woods of birch and sycamore and Scotch pine and larch, with half-naked foxgloves and wild blue delphiniums growing under; but I shouldn't have bothered. If you want sport, you can get sport in the sun.

Kenneth told us as well, as we walked, how a hundred and fifty years before all but one family had been cleared out to America, so that Rum could become a single sheep farm. Soon after that, it had been sold as the deer forest it had been until recently. I wondered what happened to the four hundred who went, and if their great-great-granddaughters had maybe heard me sing in Carnegie Hall and assumed that I had come the easy way, from a long line of gentry.

It was at the main jetty, a big curving pier lined with red oil drums of rubbish, that we discovered Victoria. Tied up at the jetty was the big Conservancy launch, the *Sioras,* and her dinghy in two neat shades of green, the tarpaulin turned back. Ogden had mentioned, back there, that the thrice-weekly ferry from the mainland was due in later that day. And beside the *Sioras, Seawolf*'s dinghy was moored, with Victoria just climbing into it.

Johnson hailed her, with less than his usual tact. 'Hallo! Your lord and master back on shore again?'

Her long, swinging hair hid her face as she prepared to cast off, but her exceptionally clear voice was angry. 'If you mean Cecil Ogden, he's gone up to Kinloch Castle with his torch.' And she sat down, slamming the rowlocks into their holes.

Johnson said, in that mild tone we had all learned to distrust, 'The Warden's a good chap, Victoria. I shouldn't worry. The odd handout is part of his job.'

Victoria had an oar in her grip. 'I wish they wouldn't. Once Cecil put it all to good use, but he's getting lazier and lazier. Soon he'll just be a scavenger.' The bitterness in her voice silenced him. She looked at us then, defiantly, and said, 'Where's Lenny?'

'On *Dolly.* Fishing off the stern with a murderer,' said Johnson. 'But at your service, as ever. Something wrong?'

'Battery,' said Victoria abruptly. Lenny was a genius with electricity, I had learned, and generous with his help. I did not understand Victoria's tone until Johnson said, 'My, my!' with irony. 'And I was about to congratulate you on having the brightest lights in Portree.' And as Victoria for some reason flushed an unbecoming beetroot, he added, 'Hence the walkout?'

Victoria was still scarlet. I could see Kenneth couldn't understand either. 'It isn't a walkout,' she muttered. 'Not yet. I'm just going back on board *Seawolf*.'

And taking the dinghy, of course. It might not be a walkout, but it was an effective declaration of independence. Except that, wrapped up in his eccentric preoccupations, Ogden would hardly notice the worm had revolved. And could always cadge a lift, I supposed, in *Symphonetta*'s dory, or *Binkie*'s, or ours. He would have to, for I saw, as the mist continued to lift, that in fact ours were the only four yachts, barring the *Sioras,* in the loch.

We left Victoria, and resumed the rough, stony path round the bay. We saw no one. The path passed an oil store, became a bridge over a rushing stream joining the sea on our right, and passed a lime kiln, as old as the Castle. A midge stung, a needle-prick, and another; and suddenly there were voices, and we all drew breath and relaxed, for there was only a small tented encampment on the shore, and a smudge fire, and two lads in hooded anoraks bent over it, preferring suffocation to midges. They had come perhaps with the last ferry, and were going back later that night, having tramped the two permitted nature trails and defeated the midges. On the sodden hills, half-invaded by mist, I had noticed one or two others, but these had rifles. It was, Johnson said, the season for culling the deer.

There was another house, and on the shore, more deer grazing on seaweed; and then on our left a pair of white gates, with a barking big boxer behind them. Johnson opened the gate – and I did not wish to go in at all.

Inside the Warden's house, we found Rupert, rocking relaxed by the fireside, having signed *Dolly* in. Also there, to my sorrow, was Hennessy. But there was no Michael Twiss, and no Buchanans: they had all gone, with Ogden, to visit the Castle.

For a moment, socially inescapable, there was general talk, and I asked about the tame deer by the shore, and why the shear-waters had given the name of Troll's Hill to one of the peaks. Kenneth, greeting his friends, fell quickly silent. He wanted to reach Michael, and fast.

So did I, but I could see from Hennessy's slightly glazed stare that we should be lucky to escape trouble first. I couldn't blame him. After all his efforts to help, he must think that Johnson and I had made a fool of him. He had been fired on, rebuked by the Navy and then bundled back to his boat, without even the consolation prize of my company. And now I turned up with my engineer firmly in tow. Hennessy said now, glaring at Johnson, 'I see Glasscock signed you in. By your orders, I suppose?'

Johnson's formidable black eyebrows topped the bifocals. 'It was a test of initiative, actually. He did it all by himself,' he said. 'Why?'

Hennessy's voice rose. 'You don't deny you were motoring?'

Johnson kept his voice reasonable. 'We used the engine, certain-ly, as you did, to South Rona and back. At Portree, we changed over to sail. Why, didn't you?'

Now, as Hennessy turned his head, I saw for the first time the great square of bandage taped over his ear. Instead of a well-built, good-looking man with crisp yellow hair and a tan, he looked like Bugs Bunny. He said, very distinctly, 'Who knows when you switched your bloody tin topsail off, or if you switched it off at all until you got to Loch Scresort? I know my three louts sail as if they were farmers, but I'm damned if anyone could have caught up as quickly as that. Unless—' His voice was scathing. 'Unless your new recruit is an America's Cup man on the side? Is that it, Mr Holmes? Were you showing the *Lysander* some of *Dolly's* sailing techniques when she exploded?'

Outside, distantly, one of the guns banged, and somewhere in the house, a baby started to yell. The men's voices were not loud, but the temper in them was plain. Kenneth said quickly, 'I don't think this is the place to argue. I'm going up to the Castle. Coming, Johnson?'

There was a movement to the door, but Hennessy, behind us, took his time. 'What about Madame Rossi?' he said railingly. 'Isn't she going with you? You didn't get shot up as I did escorting her to a heavy date with somebody else. How naïve can you get?' He had just enough self-conceit to keep his voice down. 'You watch it, boy. You get the old carcass damaged and bang, you can't see her for dust.'

He was drunk, of course. By now, thank heaven, we were all almost out of the door. 'And you know what you pay for the privilege?' Hell's bells, he was going on. I stopped, to let him catch up. 'You know what I paid this little singing bird for the privilege of having my ear half shot off?'

Jealousy is always difficult to handle. Sober, he would realize he was killing any chance of kindness from me in the future. Drunk, he was going to make me look venal instead of practical, in Kenneth Holmes's eyes.

Which is why, at that moment, I tripped Hennessy up just a little, so that he banged his ear against the Chief Warden's doorpost. Then, as he stopped with a squeal, I said very quietly, 'When I have an understanding, I do not go back on it.'

After a moment's hesitation, Kenneth and Johnson, I saw, were now walking on. Rupert was indoors, talking still. Hand to ear, Hennessy said, his eyes watering, 'And what about the great Dr Holmes?'

'He doesn't need me any more.' I was not forlorn: I said it as a matter of fact. I think perhaps up to then all Stanley Hennessy's women had been of the weeping variety. He hesitated, and then, turning, lifted my manicured hand to his lips and kissed it. 'Do we start then afresh, Tina?'

He talked sometimes like a poor television serial. Outside his business he had trouble, I guessed, in aligning his ego and id. It does not greatly matter, when you have baguette diamonds to give.

I slipped my hand inside his and drew him along the rhododendron path to the Big House. 'We start afresh.'

But it was still the same damned old problem: how to get rid of Hennessy and Kenneth and Johnson, and find Michael Twiss. For, thinking over all I knew of Michael, if he really wanted to harm Kenneth or me, it would take a great deal to stop him. And of all of us, I thought I was best fitted to try.

The broad avenue striking inland through the trees from the Warden's house to the parkland surrounding Kinloch Castle does not take long to walk. There is a bridge to cross, over the river which generates the Castle's own private electricity; and then, across billiard-green lawns, one sees the red sandstone arcades and the castellated tower of the Big House itself, equipped, furnished and wholly deserted: frozen at the height of its effectiveness, when a man desiring to relax, and his wife and friends with him, bought an empty island and stocked it with beasts and built on it a modest palace like Blenheim, in which to live for a month yearly, killing trout and red deer.

The scientists' wing, formerly occupied by Kenneth, had been empty since his departure, and the caretaker was on holiday. Within, statuesque in the growing darkness, was the intact sepulchre of an Edwardian dream. And in that dream, somewhere, along with the others – the respectful, pattering footsteps of Bob and Nancy Buchanan; the derisive, ill-kept sneakers of Ogden – was a figure that did not walk at all, but stood silently waiting. Michael was there. Michael was there, and had chosen his place.

The caretaker's entrance was on the north side. Opening it with the Warden's key, Johnson stood aside while Kenneth, Hennessy and I filed in. Rupert had not yet appeared. As I entered, Hennessy's grasp on my arm, I saw the small, puzzled glance Kenneth gave me, and passing, without looking, I brushed Kenneth's hand. His fingers moved in recognition, then dropped as we walked on inside.

After the misty brightness outside, we were now lost in shadows. Footsteps echoing, we walked in silence through servants' quarters, along high-ceilinged corridors, their walls lined by bells rung long ago, when service was what it should be. There were signs of occasional life; a big kitchen stacked with chairs had been made into a cinema; there were ashes in the grate of a small sitting-room, tidily furnished, and a few toys.

Doors opened and shut. Johnson spoke very little, and the rest of us not at all. In a sudden warren of small rooms opening off to one side there was a glimpse of impressive period earthenware in a blue and white pattern: what would *Seawolf* choose for tribute from here? Then the public apartments appeared.

Walking through in the half-dark, linked to Hennessy, I was listening in the quiet above the thud of my heart. My nerves taut, I was listening for the first sign: the stir of a curtain, the creak of a floorboard below the thick carpet, a shot, even, which would finish this cold, nasty silence.

Somewhere in the house Ogden was wandering, and the Buchanans, talking naturally, flashing their torches on some particular treasure. The lighting fuseboard had failed us, said Johnson, but the power was intact. Here, with the tall windows giving on to the misty twilight outside, there was light enough still to see the mighty shapes of the dining room, the massive fireplace, the alcove cupboards for glasses and napery. Round the shining table, the chairs were almost too heavy to move. They came, Kenneth said, from the owner's steam yacht, the *Rhouma,* which had brought back most of the V&A standard bric-à-brac lying around us. Then we walked through an imposing arched doorway and into the main hall, which was two storeys high.

This, too, seemed empty. Saffron-coloured light fell, on our left, from a double row of Gothic oriel windows filling one entire wall, their glass stained with acorns and flowers. This wall gave on to the central lawns at the front, and contained the front door.

Glancing up, I saw, too, that a gallery ran, high above us, round the other three sides of the room; but I could see no one there. Kenneth, stepping carefully among the little mother-of-pearl tables, bent to straighten a leopardskin, laid on the parquet. There was a fine lionskin rug before the big, empty fireplace and the half-panelled walls were lined above with ruby velvet brocade. Gazing at the twin porcelain vases, each nine feet high, which the *Rhouma* had brought back from the Orient, at the heavy silk brocade curtains and the cut-velvet sofas with their trellised fringes and bobbles, I thought of the deer grazing outside, and the volcanic black peaks, and the row of red oil drums, filled with used tins of lager and baby custard and floor wax and dog food: all the bright-coloured symbols of modern family living, down on the bleak pier.

For eleven months of the year the Castle had been accustomed to solitude. Did it appreciate, I wondered, Kenneth's abstracted footsteps, running up and down to his lab, as he worried about Peter's blackmailing letters? The *Rhouma,* sailing stiffly on her corrugated blue seas, would have felt such sordid matters beneath her.

Kenneth moved through the hall and into the dark corridor beyond. I turned to follow him. On my right, someone screamed.

I saw Kenneth and Johnson both jump round; but Hennessy was quicker. Hennessy had vanished already into the black archway on our right, where the scream had modulated into a whisper and then into another, recognisable sound which was half a bright, social cough.

Nancy Buchanan's voice, pitched a full tone higher than usual, said, 'Mr Hennessy! Wasn't it silly of me! It's such an eerie place, don't you think? Have you been here before? I thought I was being hugged by a bear!'

'You were,' said Hennessy's voice shortly. He had nothing in common with *Binkie,* and held both the Buchanans jointly responsible, I had no doubt, for the accident to his ear. His immediate reaction on South Rona, Rupert had told me, had been to require the Navy to jail both Buchanans at once.

Now, I saw as I flew round the corner, he had dropped Nancy like a sticky sweet-paper and struck a match to reveal, looming over some cabinets, the life-sized stuffed figure of a brown bear, with Nancy's round, knitted cap depending from one set of claws. 'Free gift week,' said Johnson. 'Are you all right, Mrs Buchanan?'

'Yes! Yes. Oh, is that you, Madame Rossi? What a queer place, isn't it? There's a ballroom. Isn't the parquet lovely? Fancy bringing all these things here! Bob's upstairs looking at the hummingbirds: there's cases of them. Bob had an uncle that went to Jamaica. Wasn't that silly of me!' Hennessy, seeing Nancy beside me, had walked on, after Kenneth and Johnson. I followed, with Nancy between, still chattering with her small cough intermittent.

She was embarrassed, of course, over South Rona. I listened, thinking, waiting for her to make up her mind. Hennessy wouldn't bother me now she was here. But how did I now get away from Nancy? For upstairs, surely upstairs, Michael was waiting.

In the ballroom, she began. 'All yellow brocade, walls matching the curtains; think of the price! I wonder what he made his money on. I wonder if his wife chose it, or if they called in a decorator. Minstrels' gallery, see? And a wee hidden hatch in the panelling for serving their drinks...' She opened the hatch, proprietorially, and flinched as the cold eyes of Hennessy looked back at her from the other side. 'Oh... Hallo. That's the pantry. Going to serve us a glass of champagne, Mr Hennessy?' As he stared at her without replying, she gave her small, nervous laugh and led the way to the Napoleon room.

It was empty. A bust of the great man stared down on us as Nancy flopped into a seat below the hero of Kinloch Castle and burst into tears.

The aunties did that, sometimes, if they had ordered too much from the catalogue, and were afraid of telling their man. I put my arm round her shoulders. It was, of course, lack of sleep and reaction. She had wanted to have a wee rest before coming on shore, but Bob had said that the weather might change, and if she wanted to see Kinloch Castle, she had better come now. She had come, in the same way that she went to South Rona. Bob was hot for CND – it was only logical, when you thought of it, and she wouldn't let Bob down. He was a wee bit too inclined as it was to underrate the opposite sex. Nothing personal, I should understand, or ill-natured: just the way he was brought up. His mother did everything for his father, from the day they were wed. But last night! It was far worse than she had expected. Running through the night like a criminal; and the beastly banner so heavy. And spelled wrong, into the bargain. When they'd unfolded it, Bob'd just about died.

The guards had nearly caught them beforehand, but of course Johnson had helped. 'He's a lovely man,' said Nancy with feeling, and sent a sidelong glance over to me. I winced, but she didn't notice, absorbed in telling her tale.

So the Buchanans ran, and hid, and carried out their laborious plan, and nobody stopped them. And then, when they slipped away from the mast, the statement of belief, the act of defiance completed, a young captain had come forward deferentially to where they lay camouflaged in the heather, and had asked if they'd care for some cocoa.

That was all. They'd been treated like kids – and it hurt. That they had acted like kids didn't occur to them.

In this case I needed to do very little, beyond lending Nancy a handkerchief, as hers was all over paraffin. She wanted to feel understood, and I understood her. I told her she did what she set out to do, and it was over; and she must concentrate now on supporting Bob, who was probably feeling the same. She had not thought of that. She was as feudal in her way as her mother-in-law. She said doubtfully, 'D'ye think so? He hasn't said. But mind you, I hung up a cup the other way in the row, and he came out with a right nasty remark. It'll be working in him. You're right.'

She got up, her leathery face shining with recent tears and present admiration, in the light reflected from Napoleon's tall brow. 'It's being cosmopolitan that gives you the insight. We were going to Jersey ourselves for our holidays, a couple of years back, and then the Baby Blake seeped in its sea valve during the Tobermory races, and it all came to nothing again. Thanks.' She bent, and amazingly planted a prune-like kiss on my cheek. 'You're a good friend,' she said. Then she'd gone.

I rose, too, from the chair arm where I was perched, below the row of prints depicting the Emperor at Austerlitz, Jena, Friedland and Wagram. What about Falkirk was so non-cosmopolitan, when Barra could produce a Rupert Glasscock to order? Duncan's Peggy, who had never left Castlebay, lacked neither polish nor insight. How was that? By the same token, it did not suit Rupert to be applauded in Falkirk. He went for admiration to Duncan's Peggy, who mostly withheld it. It occurred to me that I was beginning to understand Johnson, too.

I was alone. I went out, and quickly and quietly continued through the rooms in that wing, looking for Michael.

It was not a house for the weak-nerved. In the drawing-room, all was glazed chintz and tapestry and slim, painted French furniture, but outside in the hall something glimmered in the half-dark: the carcass of a white rabbit, stuffed at the feet of a golden eagle, claws spread, yellow eyes staring at me in the gloom. There, beyond other glass cases, an armed Siamese suddenly faced me: he guarded a doorway, with his carved wooden twin opposite. I opened the door, and it swung shut behind me.

Books, from floor to ceiling: the library. A desk, furnished with leather books and bridge boxes, all stamped with the name of the house. A framed photograph of the steam yacht, the *Rhouma,* which I lifted to look at. Cold in my hands, the glass lit suddenly, scarlet as coal. As I dropped it, I heard the thing smash. And behind me, a voice said chidingly, '*Be careful!*'

I spun around.

Outside Kinloch Castle, the trees were quite black. They filled with darkness the tall study windows, and the windowed roundel of the small alcove-turret behind me. It was from the alcove that the voice spoke. And as it spoke, the alcove filled with red light, that light I had just seen, reflected, in the glass of the *Rhouma*'s dark picture. The glare came sliding over the room, from a pair of eyes set between a vast spread of bronze wings. Eight feet high, alone in the alcove, a bronze eagle reared over me, snarling; and by his great claws apes twisted and writhed.

'Be careful,' the voice hissed again; and out of the turret stepped the small, woolly figure of Bob Buchanan, swinging the red bulb of a torch. 'Oh, it's you; what a shame – I'll have given you a right fright. I was after your young friend, Rupert. My goodness, those were the days! Fancy scaring their after-dinner guests with yon thing!' He laughed, switching his torch from the red bulb to white, showing the determined grin and the bony ridge round his eyes: Bob Buchanan hadn't slept much either. 'It works from a wee red bulb in the ceiling, but you can get just the same effect with a torch... Have you seen Nancy?'

'She's looking for you. She thought you were upstairs with the hummingbirds.'

'I'd better go, then. I was, but I thought I'd come down. D'you know what they've got up there? A—'

He never did tell me. Before he could speak, the hideous rumbling began.

I know the sound of disaster. I have heard a building about to fall. I know the ringing, clamouring thump a steam cylinder makes when it is about to explode. When a roar like that begins inside a house one should run, and run fast.

I threw myself at the door, flung it open and flew out into the lightless hall.

There the clamour was frightening. Men's voices, shouting, weaved through and above it, echoing among the panelled grotesqueries. The house vibrated with thunder. I saw, huddled under the staircase before me, four silent figures: Hennessy, Ogden, Johnson, and Nancy Buchanan, their faces glowing with inexplicable light. My ears roared with groaning air under pressure. The eruption heaved up noise from its guts like a geyser, drumming tinnily between gasps. I fell on my knees beside Johnson.

The shuddering combers of sound rose, coalesced, fell into vast and shivering order and became, inflated beyond all human tolerance, the *intermezzo* from *Cavalleria Rusticana*, played on the organ. Played on an Imhof & Mukle electrical organ, from a roll of unwiding red paper, fitted under the stairs. Dumbly, with the others, I gazed.

Behind glass doors, the organ pipes glistened. And above, throbbing with passion, a triangle, two drums and a cymbal sat emoting for ever. The orchestration belted breathily into some climax; the triangle moved; and at the height of its palsied *fortissimo,* invisibly directed as Punch slamming a policeman, the row of truncated drumsticks jerked forward to pummel the drumskin, while, unasked, the cymbals quivered and clashed. Deafened we watched it flog itself hysterically through such a crisis. Trumpets blared; invisible hands pounded invisible keyboards; the drumsticks vibrated, halted, vibrated like flyweights boxing a punchball. Jangling, roaring, shuddering, the whole Teutonic nightmare landed with a thud back on to its tonic, and Johnson turned, his bifocals steamy with tears, and said, 'We were trying to turn on the lights.'

It was then, as the machine uncoiled an oily *legato,* and Nancy giggled, and Bob exclaimed and Hennessy craned purposefully into the mechanism, that we heard Kenneth's voice far above, shouting.

I was first on the stairs, with the other four pounding after me. Johnson was nearly level. I hissed as we ran, 'I thought you were to stay with him?' He did not answer. There were eight people in that house – nine, if Rupert was there. Could no one guard Kenneth? I could have cried with sheer rage, as we ran.

At the top, we hesitated; until another cry guided us. 'The lab wing,' said Johnson shortly, and led across the width of the house to where Kenneth's room was. We turned the corner, and stepped into a searing dazzle of light. In this wing, every lamp was lit, every door was open, and at the far end of the passage Kenneth stood, unhurt, his hand on the doorpost, and silently showed us, as we reached him, the chaos inside.

His locked laboratory had been opened and ruined. The original object, perhaps, was to search. If so, what happened next was the result of disappointment and temper. I knew from Kenneth that nothing of importance had been left locked here when he was taken to Rona. But whatever the reason, the vandalism was something that shocked. There was no fitting, no pane of glass, no piece of equipment left undestroyed. Papers littered benches and floor, some burnt, some destroyed with acid and ink. Every drawer and cupboard was open, everything of Kenneth's own, even his spare clothes, his blankets and sheets, had been ripped and scattered about. It was the work of an obsessive, a feminine, vindictive and familiar mind. I, of all people there, knew at once that it was the work of Michael: my Michael Twiss. I left them there, while they turned over debris and exclaimed at it; and I ran back through the house to find Michael this time, alone.

I did not turn switches, although the lighting, I realized, must now be on. I ran along the high gallery ringing the hall, where the saffron windows barely lit the dark ruby walls, and beside me, half-seen *bizarreries* alternated with the big secretive cabinets, heavy with doors. Glass glinted – the hummingbirds. I was on the first storey now, heading for the bedrooms, dressing rooms, bathrooms in the dark, silent wing where no one was sight-seeing, exclaiming over the period niceties; where Michael, surely, was waiting. Did he guess that Kenneth meant to unmask him? Did he know, I wondered, that soon the *Sioras* would be leaving the jetty to make rendezvous in mid-loch with the ferry from Mallaig – to receive post and to place on the ferry any mail, any parcels, any visitors wishing to return quickly from Rum to the mainland?

It was very quiet. I followed the corridor round, and round again. On my right, faintly, metal glimmered high on the wall and drew my eye to a display of weapons – swords, daggers, boomerangs, inlaid *samurai*. I turned my back on it and called, hardly stirring the air. 'Michael! Come out!'

Silence. Below someone had found the switch for *Cavalleria Rusticana* and turned the automaton off. Distantly, from Kenneth's room, I could hear voices arguing. An owl called thinly outside, and the trees sounded through the glass like a soft breaking sea. I said again, 'Michael?'

Opposite me was the dark mouth of a room. I had no wish to draw the others. On the other hand, it was only with an effort of logic that I found I could make myself walk through that door. In my hand was the little torch I had brought all the way from *Dolly*, switched to a thin, pencil light. It shone on a death's-head.

It was only a painting, a macabre motif. After a moment, I moved the beam, and it showed me a Jacobean four-poster, dark and carved, with the painted symbol of death at its head and foot, under the crown and dark drapes. The curtains hid nobody. The room, as I lit it inch by inch with my torch, was sparsely furnished and empty. I went out, and into the next.

I don't know how many I searched before I came to the bamboo-furnished bedroom. There, for the first time, when I called I sensed some kind of presence. I called again, and waited. When no one replied, I went right inside.

It was a big bedroom this time, with vast cupboards lining each wall. A bamboo lattice-work decorated the neat bed and its suite. But the sound I had heard came not from here, but from the bathroom beyond. It smelled damp. I paused there, controlling my breath, and then I said for the last time, 'Michael! I know you are here. Michael, come out and talk.' And when he did not reply, I switched on my torch.

Curtains. Ceiling-high cupboards. A wash-basin with wrought-iron legs. A bath, hooded man-high in mahogany, and tiered with knobs like an organ for every hydraulic device known to Edwardian man. I had got so far when the white light above me burst into unexpected, brilliant life. I gazed, dazzled at this wonderland bath;

and gradually I realized why, tonight, Michael Twiss did not come when I called. For Michael was here, in the bath; and his Trumper haircut was all ruffled and soaked, and his Lobb footwear fatally stained.

He was dead.

14

The torch in my hand was still on. I put it off, staring at the occupied bath. It did not occur to me to see who had switched the bedroom and bathroom lights on. I was gazing at Michael.

He had been shot. The light, dove-grey quilted coat which he bought with such pride for a long weekend with a marquess, was all spoiled and charred, and a spreading stain had soaked irregularly, like a bad dye, into the fabric. The untidy hair was unlike him, but there was no great change in the smooth face, which I supposed most people would call handsome; which in five years or less would have begun to show, under the skin, the traces of gross self-indulgence which had not yet marred his trimness. He had seated himself, one would guess, gun in hand, on the edge of the massive bath, under the knobs labelled WAVE and DOUCHE, and holding the gun to his heart, had fired and fallen tidily backwards, organized in death as in life.

So one would guess, except for two things, Michael was a man – had been a man – of no great courage and of immense spite. He was also a man of vainglorious ambition, who above all things loved life. If you knew Michael Twiss, you would know that of all men he was the least likely to kill himself.

You would also know that he did not smoke. And you would wonder why, therefore, the closed air of this bathroom held, as well as the faint unpleasant odours of cordite, of mustiness, of sweat, and of freshly shed blood, a tinge, already vanishing as I traced it, of recent smoke. I thought this; and a sharp voice at my shoulder said, '*What have you done?*' and I turned to face Hennessy, just as I thought: Kenneth smokes.

Then Hennessy said, 'What have you done?' again, and, stepping forward, shook me alive. I suppose my face was quite blank. There was suddenly so much to consider, so quickly. When did it happen? Not while I had been searching: I should have heard the sound of the shot. A little before, then. Of course... while the organ was playing. A machine-gun could have fired then and none of us would have heard it. And Kenneth was then upstairs. I realized that Hennessy was staring at me, his two hands still on my shoulders, my loose hair tumbled over them from the shaking. A little blood had come through the white bandage over his ear, and he was pale. It was not a nice sight, Michael folded into the bath. 'Tina!'

My eyes focussed on him, I felt his grip and I stirred. 'I haven't done anything – I've just come. Stanley, it's his own gun. He's killed himself.'

His eyes still stared into mine – cold eyes, of a chilly grey-blue, now the charm was turned off. 'Why?'

I said quietly, 'I told him not to come near me. I didn't want him as my manager any more... It was Michael who shot at you on South Rona, Stanley. He was jealous – of Kenneth, of you. That's why he followed me. And when he found it wasn't any good...' I bit my lip.

'Don't cry, sweetheart. It isn't your fault.' His tone had quite changed.

It was not hard to let my voice shake. I said, and it was true, 'I don't feel sorry. I ought to feel sorry for him, and I don't feel anything. I worked with him for years... He made me everything I am, *and I didn't like him and I'm not sorry he's dead!*'

I burst into tears, and Hennessy held me; and then Johnson's voice, cool in the background, said, 'Can three play? Who's dead? Oh, I see. The late Mr Twiss.' His bifocals, gleaming in the bright doorway, were bent on the bath and then, grieving, on me. 'Madame Rossi. You've been a bad girl, haven't you? Well, let's telephone the police.'

Hennessy snapped at him. 'She didn't do it. It's suicide.'

'Is it?' The black eyebrows shot up. 'There's blood in the bed-room. Suicides don't usually shoot themselves in one room, and

165

then run quickly backwards and jump into the bath. It was meant to look like suicide, let us say. By someone with a rather poor torch.'

I couldn't see his eyes, but his voice was colder than Hennessy's. Behind him in the bedroom Rupert had suddenly appeared. Beside me, I felt Hennessy fractionally recoil. He said harshly, 'Is that true?' And then, 'The gun's there, in the bath. Fingerprints would show… Tina said it was the gun that shot me.'

'Very likely. She would know,' said Johnson softly. 'After all, he was her manager and intimate friend, was he not? Who was just about to give to the world, wasn't he, Tina, all the sordid and unprestigious details of your warm friendship with Kenneth Holmes? Was that kind, Tina? You may have saved your own reputation, but where has poor Kenneth's hope of exculpation now gone?'

It was then, for the first time that I could remember, that I began to feel a true, chilling fear. 'Where's Kenneth?' I said sharply.

'Here. They're all here,' said Johnson agreeably, and I saw that they were, huddled behind in the bedroom: Nancy, Bob, Ogden and Kenneth. Only Kenneth moved quickly forward, pushing past Johnson and Rupert and Hennessy to my side, where no one wished to be, and said hurriedly, 'Valentina! You didn't do it, of course? You couldn't have!'

It sounded like a cry from the heart, and my mind boggled and the blood ran from my heart. For if Kenneth himself had abandoned me, my only bulwark had gone.

Except myself. I was alone when I was born, and I am no worse off now. Use your common sense, Tina. I said, 'If he was shot in the bedroom he must have been carried here. I couldn't do that.'

'He's a small, lightly built man.' Johnson's tone was one of gentle conjecture. 'And as a singer, you are an agile, muscular woman. He was not afraid to stand close, either, to the person who shot him.'

'Do you think, after all that has happened, that Michael would want to stand close to me? In the dark, anyone might have crept up to him without his knowing.'

'Exactly,' said Johnson, and I felt my colour rising along with my fear of him. I said quickly, 'Another thing. I was with someone else all the time until just before the organ was stopped. I heard it stop while I was standing beside those wall weapons. I hadn't time to shoot him.'

'You had, provided you went straight to this room.'

Damn him to hell. 'But I didn't. And I can prove it,' I said. 'Mr Hennessy came in here behind me. He can swear that I had just arrived when he switched on the light.'

There was a short silence, and I felt the cold closing in on me again. Surely, surely Hennessy saw me? If I was at the far end of the corridor when the organ stopped I couldn't have been here, killing Michael. On the other hand, he might have run along the long gallery in the dark, as I did, and unlike me, have simply turned in to the first room he saw, seeing nothing of me or Michael until he switched on the light. I looked at him: his well-brushed waving fair hair, his smooth skin rosily tanned from Caribbean beach and Riviera golf course, his sailing, his shooting; his whisky. The charm was utterly absent, and I knew, suddenly and absolutely, that my last guess was right – and that he had no alibi for me.

Then he said, laying his hand gently on the black stuff of my arm, 'She's right. I didn't think of it at the time, but of course I saw her. I followed her in.' He hesitated. 'It looked to me for a moment as if she'd come back to fix something, maybe; but she did come from the other direction. If she was right up the corridor as she says, she couldn't have done it unheard.' And on my arm, his grip tightened. I did not look at him. He was giving me something more precious than diamonds, and I did not want to see him fling his triumph at Kenneth. But Kenneth, surely, had no hopes of me now.

For a moment, again, there was silence. The others, standing behind in the doorway, had not spoken. Behind us, in this island of light, the whole Castle with its impedimenta lay lightless and empty, its trees tossing blackly about it, the rain beating on the parkland, the hills and the bay.

Somewhere out there, the four boats were rocking: Victoria, asleep in her bunk, the tearstains still on her face; Lenny, impassive, frying the mackerel he had caught and wondering why we were so long. *Binkie* was empty. On *Symphonetta*, the three lads would have exhausted their hymn of hate and, ill-fed from Hennessy's sparse larder, would have curled up to sleep. While out in the loch, by now

Sioras would have made her routine trip to the ferry, and laden with mail and parcels and maybe one or two passengers, the ferry would have turned and made for the mainland.

Without Michael. He would not have wished to die on an island. There is no status in that.

I was tired. I had had some sleep, but the others – the Buchanans, Kenneth and Rupert, Hennessy and Johnson and Ogden – had had very little, sailing watch by watch through the night and then driven by their various natures ashore here on Rum.

I looked at Johnson and wondered how much he believed Hennessy: how much, now, he would trouble to protect me over that other murder, in Rose Street. Day by day, I realized, too late now, Johnson's grip on my life had been growing. Already, I was in his power far more than I had been in Michael's. I wondered now, not for the first time, what reward Johnson meant to exact. Or if this was his reward. The pleasure of seeing me wronged.

Then Johnson said, 'All right. I accept that. But if Madame Rossi didn't kill Twiss while the organ was playing, we reach the next question: who did?'

This time the silence was absolute. After a moment Johnson continued. 'Food for thought, I observe. Suppose we all move downstairs to the Hall, and consider the question in comfort.' And as Hennessy, lingering, gave a glance at the ungainly lumber which sprawled still in the bath – 'Put the light out and leave it. Mr Twiss will not mind.'

It was cold downstairs. The lights, now switched on everywhere, merely emphasized the scale and emptiness of this museum set in a wilderness. The two ranks of oriel windows, yellow on black, transmitted to us tinnily the onslaught of rain. It would be stormy, outside.

We were seated, at Johnson's request, on chairs drawn over the shining parquet in a semi-circle before the great fireplace in the galleried hall. On the hearth, a heap of wet logs, resurrected from the caretaker's premises, had been lit and was greasily smoking. We sat uneasily; Hennessy and I next to the fireplace and facing the windows; Nancy and Bob together, facing the fireplace, their crêpe soles flat on the floor; and completing the circle, back to the window, Cecil Ogden and Kenneth, his face lined with strain and with weariness.

Behind us, in the centre spaces of the room, Rupert was roving. And before us, gazing abstractedly into the stark yellow stare of the lion, was Johnson, who had so suddenly taken command, and whom not even Hennessy had questioned. He stood and waited, the new smoke circling round his Navy-issue trousered legs, his reefer open, over a thick, high-necked jersey. In our hands, awkwardly, each of us held a tin cup from the three thermos flasks the Buchanans had produced, with tidy forethought, from the damp satchel at Bob's foursquare feet. The tea in it was hot, and stewed, and without milk and sugar, but we all sat nursing and drinking it, to remedy our coldness and misery. All except Johnson and Rupert, who had become so imperceptibly alien. There was thus enough to go around. For there were eight of us only, now.

We felt, I suppose, that you cannot merely walk out of a house in which there has been a murder. I do not know what we expected. In any case, Johnson did not waste time. He said, suddenly decisive, 'I make no apology for keeping you. If you are concerned about the race, the running order will not be affected. In fact, something much more serious has intervened. A man has been killed in this house tonight, and the murderer is one of you six.'

For the third time, Hennessy's temper broke through. 'Why the hell don't you phone the police then, and cut out all this poppycock? If there's a murderer here, I'd feel a damned sight safer, and so would the women, if he were under good strong lock and key… And I'd remind you there are eight, not six of us here. If you're fool enough to count in the women, then you and Glasscock are as suspect as any of us. Or what about outsiders, while you're at it? There are forty odd people on this damned island, not to mention your man, and the girl on *Seawolf,* and my three examples of modern youth out there. Couldn't they equally well have sneaked in?'

'No. This house is surrounded,' said Johnson. 'It was sealed when the last of us entered, and it will remain sealed for as long as I say. I should introduce myself. As well as taking part in your cruise, and painting Madame Rossi, I have some responsibility for the submarine *Lysander*. Under my special brief, I am the law at this moment, and in this particular case.'

I could feel the blood in my brain: a peculiar phenomenon. For a moment it deafened me, and I could not think at all. When I forced my mind to its duty, I found Bob Buchanan was speaking. 'Is that why—?'

He broke off, and flushed. It was why, of course, he and Nancy had been handled with that hurtful indifference by those in authority. Hennessy scowled. And Ogden, lying back loose-jointed in his chair, drumming his tin cup on its fine rosewood carving, pointed at Johnson and said, 'That's how they let Holmes leave South Rona! The rumour all over Skye was that he'd been a bad boy with his blueprints, and the Official Secrets Act was going to knock him into next week.'

'Is that so?' Hennessy's voice came sharply and quick. 'He's been your decoy, has he, flushing out allies? Is that what the Twiss affair is all about?'

'Nearly. Michael,' said Johnson, taking out his pipe without looking at anybody, 'was a blackmailer. And blackmailers can get into an awful lot of trouble without necessarily, of course, being spies.' He struck a match and held it to the tobacco. 'Who, for example among us here – and you can take it, Hennessy, that Rupert and I may quite properly be excluded – who among you six might be a profitable victim of blackmail? And who, besides Madame Rossi, had the opportunity to kill Michael Twiss?'

Bob Buchanan suddenly shifted on his sofa. 'I don't know what you mean, you have a responsibility for the *Lysander*. You've been a good friend to the RHCC, Mr Johnson, any time you've come north, but I never knew about this. Still, men have had under-cover jobs I suppose, before now… I just want to say, I'm with Mr Hennessy. I think before we go any further we should call in the police. There's someone been shot already, and to my mind the whole thing's too risky. And in case you think me and Nancy have some vested interest in stopping you, I may say that anyone trying to blackmail me would have pretty poor pickings. After *Binkie*'s kept running and paid for, there's nothing much left in our kitty. And there's nothing we've done we're ashamed of. I've got strong views on a number of subjects, I don't mind saying, but that's what's wrong with the world today: no one willing to stand up and say what they think about serious matters. I do. Just you ask any of the committees I'm on and they'll tell you. My life's an open book, and so's Nancy's. The thing we did last night on South Rona harmed nobody but ourselves. We're getting on, Nancy and I, for that kind of publicity stunt, but sometimes a gesture is needed. You have to give a lead – the young ones aren't used to it.'

He looked up at Johnson, nervous but firm. 'I shouldn't like a worthy cause to be affected, Mr Johnson, because of some mud that gets mistakenly thrown here tonight. I had nothing to do with the Twiss fellow, and neither had Nancy.'

'And yet you had the best opportunity of all. For you were both in the dark here with Michael, long before the rest of us arrived on shore at all... And there's something else. Don't you remember, Tina? Hennessy? Don't you remember hearing the sound of a shot when we were all in the Chief Warden's house? We put it down to a stalker, or I did. But think. *No one shoots on a Sunday in Scotland.*'

Buchanan's mouth opened. He was so palpably stupid and honest: I wondered why Johnson wasted time on him. Could he be foolish enough to expect another scapegoat like me? Nancy said, her hands shaking a little as she held a half-empty thermos, 'Cecil was here too. He came back with a torch. But we hardly saw Mr Twiss. Once we were inside he took one wing and we took the other.'

'You didn't hear a shot, then?' said Johnson.

Bob answered slowly. 'No. But it's a big house, you know. Though, come to think of it, we did hear a bit of banging about at the top there. Where Dr Holmes's room is.'

'That would be Twiss. He almost certainly caused the destruction in the lab,' said Johnson mildly. 'And I think, in fact, that big as the house is, you would have heard something as loud as a shot. There was no silencer. We should, of course, need to experiment. Later, none of us was so far away from that bedroom that we would not have heard shooting, except in the one period when the organ was on. Then you, Bob, came out of the library with Madame Rossi and joined us. Ogden, Nancy and Hennessy here were with me at the organ already. Dr Holmes was upstairs – you were worried,

Tina, weren't you, about that? There was no need. Rupert took over watching him from the moment I wanted to leave off.

'We know Dr Holmes didn't kill Michael. Michael was killed either soon after he entered Kinloch Castle, when the party inside the house was small and widely scattered, and might not have noticed the shot; or he was killed in the moments between our all meeting upstairs when Holmes called for us, and the switching off of the organ just after. Incidentally, who switched it off?'

Cecil Ogden had sunk back in his chair, his empty cup capping one bony dungareed knee. 'I did. Can't stand Mascagni anyway, and Mascagni with bronchitis seemed altogether too much. I had a job finding the switch. Thought I'd got it, behind a pillar, and the light came on instead.'

'I saw the light over the gallery. Saw you leave Dr Holmes's room too,' said Rupert briefly. He had stopped his roving and had come to rest on the lionskin, his fingers between the white, dusty teeth. 'You must have gone straight downstairs: there was no time to do anything else. Ogden exculpated. Who else left the lab. before the organ stopped?'

'Tina,' said Johnson. 'And Hennessy. That was all.' He gazed at the mess in his pipe, and finding it cold, bent to knock it out on the logs, which were burning, reluctantly, with a great deal of spitting and smoke. 'Both have motives. A wealthy singer is fair game for any blackmailer, particularly one in intimate touch with her daily life. And I don't suppose, when we look into it, that Mr Hennessy's past has been blameless. There was a business in Uruguay which had them all rather bothered at headquarters a year or two back. He is also meat for blackmail, and has money.

'On the other hand, he had no need to perjure himself, as he did, to improve Madame Rossi's alibi. A murderer would not have done that. It gives him no advantage, other than the obvious gratitude of Madame Rossi, and might jeopardize all his other activities if it were disproved. Then, of course, far from being the golden goose of her manager, Madame Rossi has been the victim during the cruise of his hysterical desire to get rid of her. You could say, of course, that blackmailers take fright and kill when their victims threaten exposure, and that in self-defence, the victim sometimes strikes back. But I am happy to say that we know for certain that this is not the case this time. Madame Rossi was in fact followed by Rupert from the moment she went out of the lab, and her account of her movements in the bedrooms is unequivocally correct.'

My thudding heart died. It was not Kenneth. And now, this. I said weakly, 'Then what made you...' and it clashed with Hennessy's rich, angry voice. 'I heard you accuse her, you bastard! You accused her, up there, of shooting the fellow. And now you try to say you knew it wasn't Tina at all? Do you know what you're doing, any of you? Because it doesn't sound like it.' He got up, a big man, confused and short of sleep, his head aching from the pain of his ear I expect, and a little fear in him, somewhere, on account of all those things Johnson had mentioned. 'If you won't phone the police, I'll do it myself.'

Johnson did not even move. 'When the lab was wrecked, the phone was put out of commission. It doesn't matter. You forget – the nearest policeman is at Mallaig, a nasty sixteen-mile journey by sea. I should think the wind is too strong now for a helicopter. If you contacted the coastguards, you might get a fishery cruiser, but not before well into tomorrow; and a naval launch would take almost as long. This is an island, my dear man. A douce research-station for the exercise of pure science among the birds and the bees. The Warden looks after the birds and the bees. I say it again. As far as we are concerned, *I am the law.*'

Rupert, after a glance, was more informative. 'We have a walkie-talkie here, sir. We've been in touch with the police. Weather permitting, they'll be here tomorrow. It's only a case of keeping the murderer safe here all night.'

The murderer. I forced my tired mind to work. Whom had he eliminated? Kenneth, of course, Stanley Hennessy, if Rupert followed him. Ogden...? I had got so far when Johnson said, as if I had spoken aloud, 'Yes: Ogden now. You left Twiss and the Buchanans at the door of the Castle the first time, and came back to *Seawolf* for your torch. We spoke to you from *Dolly.* Then after you'd unloaded your boat, you rowed back to the nearer, big jetty, and went straight to the Castle. Bob and Nancy and Michael Twiss were already exploring inside. Where did you go then?'

Ogden had not stirred. The long, knuckle-bone chin sunk on his chest, hands clasped on his stomach, he said, 'Up the first stairs I came to. I flashed the torch around, to let them all find me, but the first person I came across was Twiss. He was wrecking Dr Holmes's workroom.'

I know I gasped. Johnson looked up. 'You came across him! You didn't say anything later?'

Ogden raised his untidy eyebrows. 'Lovers' tiff, I assumed. Venting his spite on the third party. Far be it from me to drag in Madame Rossi.'

'Did he tell you it was personal spite against Dr Holmes?' Johnson was pressing.

Ogden grinned. 'You should have heard the names he was calling him. I told him he ought to have his backside slapped; but it'd cost those bastards in Whitehall a packet to replace all that bloody tat, so I wouldn't give him away. Then he's found dead. It seemed a dirty trick to give him up after.'

'Only common sense, I should have thought,' said Johnson thoughtfully. 'And after your encounter with Twiss in the doctor's laboratory, you went your two ways?'

'Uh-huh.'

'Did you see him again before or after the rest of us arrived?'

'No. I found the Buchanans eventually, along by the bedrooms, and we shared the big torch until we got to the library, and Bob began to fool about with that filthy eagle's red eyes. He had a small torch he was experimenting with, and Nancy was helping him. I went up and looked at the birds.'

'Did you hear a shot, then or beforehand?'

'No.'

'You're sure?'

'Yes. And I would have. The house was like a sounding-board with all that bare parquet. You could hear Nancy's cough all over, like the bloody finale of *La Traviata*, and thank God the organ didn't play that.'

But Johnson was staring into space, the sullen red of the fire flickering behind him, and an expression of irritation on his face. 'What a pity,' he observed. 'What a pity. For it really seems that you and Nancy and Bob Buchanan are the only people with the time and the opportunity to have knocked the chap off. And without an obvious motive, it seems a little invidious to pick any one of you. I suppose we'd better shut all three of you up. Unless –' ignoring Nancy Buchanan's squeal of protest – 'unless we conduct an experiment. Here –' he slipped his hand inside the reefer jacket and came out with something silvery and heavy. 'Here is a gun – a real one, Tina. It was careless of me to drop it on Staffa. The other, as you know, is just a dummy lighter. Let us take this one, which is about the calibre of Michael's and fire it off in that bedroom, while we make a few tests. It seems to me, for example, that a turret alcove surrounded by windows, especially windows with wildly tossing trees outside them, would not make very much of a listening post. While you were planning shocks with your eagle, Bob, do you really think a single shot would have reached you?'

It wouldn't. I was suddenly sure of it. I remembered the outspread wings in the dark, the red glare on the picture, the tinkle of glass. I remembered too the burst of sound from the organ, and then the increase in volume, met quite shockingly when the heavy door was swung open. For it was a swing door. I had forgotten that, too.

My eyes met Bob Buchanan's. He was picturing it too. And slowly, as all of us watched him, he shook his bonneted head.

'Well, well,' said Johnson mildly. 'Thank goodness for that. For an awkward moment back there I thought, Ogden, you were going to evade me.'

15

He had accused Ogden. *Ogden,* with the long, lugubrious face? Ogden, with his engine stuck at full speed ahead, tumbling head over ears in his dinghy? Ogden with his plugless basins and his lights tied on with string!

And what of Victoria? Surely no one watching her and her hopeless crusade could link her with murder and treachery? Surely no one engaged on secret and dangerous work would conceivably choose a Victoria to crew for him?

I looked at the others. There were Nancy and Bob, tired, muddled and hopelessly confused with all the evening's events, the shuttling of question and accusation. Nancy, bending, suddenly put the cork in the last thermos and shoved it into the rucksack: decks cleared for action. Kenneth, now very still, was giving all his attention, not to Ogden, but to Johnson's businesslike face. Beside me, as I turned, I found Hennessy also looking at Johnson and frowning. His mouth, that aggressive, muscular mouth, was a little open.

'I expect you thought you'd got away with it as well,' continued Johnson to Ogden, quite pleasantly. 'If Michael Twiss hadn't decided to blackmail you today.'

For a long moment Cecil Ogden himself was perfectly still. Then, disarmingly, his discontented, straitened face under the pixie cap split into a grin.

'God,' he said. 'If that's where you get with conjecture, I'm glad I got ploughed in my bloody prep-school certificate.' The bony wrists shot out of his frayed cuffs as he stretched, but the cultured voice was peeved, all the same. 'You don't pick on the big boys do you, you fellows? It's always the same. Find the man with the bottom

176

out of his trousers and shove the blame on to him. What's Twiss supposed to blackmail me about? Victoria?' His grin was not very nice. 'And what am I supposed to pay him with? Buttons?'

'Oh, come,' said Johnson. 'What did they pay you for damaging the *Lysander* and destroying our trust in Holmes, in one beautiful bang? What about all that dishy equipment hidden on *Seawolf*? To hear Lenny describe it on Barra, your fo'c'sle's like Santa's grotto.

'You see, Kenneth: Michael Twiss was just a blackmailer, that and nothing besides. Going round with Tina here, he had access to all kinds of dirt – no offence, Tina, but you know better than I do the social circles he was moving in. He sensed that Madame Rossi had realized pretty nearly all her ambitions; he perhaps guessed that one day his job would be done. Particularly he was afraid she would form a permanent attachment which would end his opportunities just the same, both for blackmail and for the kind of life he was used to as her manager. So he tried to dissuade her by every possible means from her proposed meeting with Dr Holmes for this and another very good reason: he was blackmailing Dr Holmes over his past connection with Madame Rossi, and he did not want Madame Rossi to find out... Fascinating, isn't it?' he added mildly, and the glasses winked as he turned, surveying us all.

'A moment ago you made a serious accusation against Ogden,' said Hennessy abruptly. 'I think before you go any further you ought to substantiate.'

Ogden's voice answered. Crossing his long legs, he found the lion's head in his way and flipped it over to spread itself, heavily, on Nancy's trim shoes. Nancy gasped. Ogden said, 'There's no hurry. Let him go on. I'm going to take a packet off him for slander anyway, at the end of all this.'

I had seen for some moments that Kenneth wanted to speak. He hesitated again, and then said to Johnson, 'But how do you know? Or is this all guesswork, about Twiss?'

Johnson grinned. He had hitched himself beside us, on the arm of Hennessy's chair and appeared perfectly at ease, smoking and swinging one foot. 'We knew. The same way that Cecil Ogden knew. We all searched the chap's luggage. Great people for fancy luggage, Tina, you and your manager. Michael's, you'll remember, came aboard at Rhu before he did. It was locked, and with such a particularly fine lock that even Lenny got suspicious. I'm afraid he got over-inquisitive and opened it. Tina's letters to Kenneth Holmes were inside. Or prints of them, anyway. Then, when we were all having our sing-song on *Evergreen*, I thought it would do Lenny good to have a long look at *Dolly* that evening through the spyglass. *Dolly* was quite empty, except for Ogden, who boarded her to borrow some oars.

'You were on board a hell of a long time, Ogden. We thought it might be simple curiosity – or even simpler plain pilfering. But we found when we came back that we had underestimated you. *Dolly* had been very thoroughly searched, including your cases Tina, and mine. And Michael Twiss's fine lock had been disturbed yet again. That was when we began to be quite definitely interested in Ogden.'

Unexpectedly, Ogden made no effort to refute this. His face, losing its defiant grin, wore the sullen expression with which we were all familiar. 'It isn't a crime – yet – to read other people's drivelling love letters. I was just having a look round. But I suppose you'll try and pin something on me, now, to protect your white-headed boy, Dr Holmes. I suppose you'll say I dismantled the crutch next, so that she got hit overboard.'

'*She*' – with a jerk of the head towards me. He hated women. It was because Victoria was sexless that he tolerated her. Johnson said, 'Don't be silly. We've affirmed with no reservations that the crutch was in perfect order both after you'd gone, and when Twiss and Tina and Rupert and Lenny all came back on board from *Evergreen*. The crutch accident was arranged by someone on board, and it had to be Twiss. How did he get you to come out of your cabin, Tina, incidentally? By talking like Holmes?'

I nodded. 'I thought so. There were some obvious gaps in your account of it. But that aroused our suspicions a little further, Ogden. For having read Twiss's letters, you might quite well deduce that this forthcoming meeting between Tina and Holmes was not to her manager's liking, and that he might be afraid of it. In which case, even an irresponsible blighter like yourself might have been expected to tip us off after the accident, however indirectly. There were one or two other things. You'd been hanging around the islands a lot this past season or two, scrounging stuff for the boat from the lighthouse men and the trawlers and the coastguards: everyone knows you and humours you. But this time you weren't keen to have anyone on board but Victoria, who knows better than to go into the fo'c'sle: you put an embargo on that, didn't you? What did you make her believe? That you'd actually pinched something valuable and hidden it there? She'd be unhappy, but she'd stick by you through that kind of trouble. Then at Crinan, Tom McIver reported a very interesting conversation.'

'*Reported?*' I could not help myself. It was Tom McIver, the big man from the puffer, who brought the first message from Kenneth to me. I couldn't look at Kenneth. All along, we had been betrayed and exposed; our letters read, our messages intercepted, our meetings spied upon. How could Kenneth have known, sending his chivalrous message, his warning to me to stay away, that McIver was Johnson's man?

'Tom's a good chap,' said Johnson now. He had relit his pipe and through the smoke he was looking, I saw, straight at Kenneth. 'In the Navy during the war, and did a bit of work for us, then and later. He doesn't like it much, but he understands what's important, and he's discreet. He passed on a message from you, Kenneth, which we took the liberty of editing slightly. And he reported to me, first that Hennessy had shown an interest in it; and secondly that Ogden had come aboard with some extremely inquisitive questions about Dr Holmes and *Lysander*. McIver had been told what to do if this happened. He informed Ogden, in strict confidence, of Holmes's message. He also gave the impression that although treachery had been nearly proven, suspicion was shifting away from Dr Holmes.

'That was when, Ogden, it occurred to you that Michael Twiss would make a nice victim. Not only blackmailer, but spy. And dead, so that he could no longer defend himself… You must tell us, some time, whom you got to plant the mine in the cave under Staffa. No wonder you didn't want to go ashore. And how annoyed you must have been when Lenny turned up and prevented you from completing the explosion. You had already quarrelled with Victoria to get her out of the way… and that wasn't difficult to do either, because you hadn't been keeping to the rules of the race, had you?

By Portree you were the only boat with electric lights on from end to end, because you were the only boat which has continuously been using her engine, whenever you thought you could get away with it. And Victoria wouldn't give you away, although I'd guess she has begged you to admit it.'

He paused. The fire had burned up now, although the wood-smoke lingered, hazily, in the darkness above. Behind us, arms folded, Rupert stood watching. Away from the ruddy glow of the fire the old-fashioned light was wan and barely picked out the dust-covered furniture. Above us, the gallery seemed empty, but one could not be sure. No one from the village could get in, Johnson had said. And no one from the boats. But how could one guard a house of this size? I remembered, belatedly, the tent by the shore, the small moving figures on the hillside, half-obscured by the mist. Glasgow students, Johnson then said. Culling the deer. And then I remembered Johnson's voice saying again, and more recently than that: 'Do you remember hearing that shot? We put it down to a stalker. But no one shoots on a Sunday in Scotland.'

No one shoots anything on a Sunday in Scotland. But people.

Sitting on the far arm of Hennessy's chair, Johnson had cut off from us all the warmth of the fire. Fear, I suppose, makes one cold. As I shivered, Hennessy put one arm round my shoulders, and I found it hard not to flinch. How did we know which was the murderer? Whom did we trust? Even before Ogden said, jeering, 'Christ, what a crime! So that's what's at the bottom of this farrago, is it? The deadliest sin in the book. First I read someone's letters, and now I've been cheating and using my engine... That makes me a murderer. And I'll tell you something else, too. I don't lower my bloody ensign at sundown. A bounder, fellows. Debag him, chaps. Run him out of the regiment!' The mimicry was angrily exact, and Rupert flushed.

'About that fo'c'sle,' Johnson said, undisturbed. 'You were claim-ing a moment ago to be among the great under-privileged. We had a good look at *Seawolf,* and *Binkie* too, when you were all on shore at Barra. You'd need more than a few tins of Navy Brasso to pay for a shortwave transmission set like the one you've got concealed in the fo'c'sle, Ogden...'

Nancy Buchanan said slowly, 'You were on *Binkie*? Then you saw...'

'The banner? Yes, of course; we knew all about it. I'm sorry, Nancy.' There was a thread of regret, ludicrously, in Johnson's voice. 'But lives were at stake. We had to find out where you and Bob fitted in. Then it was quite plain. On South Rona, you harmed no one and you made no move out of character. You even helped us, unwittingly, to explain the general alert and the multiplicity of security men, so that the real culprit didn't take fright and run. The choice at that time,' said Johnson placidly, 'lay between you and Hennessy, with the odds largely on you. There were various risks. One was that Michael Twiss, or even Dr Holmes himself, should have an accident or appear to commit suicide. Or even that Holmes and Tina should die, killed by Twiss. We took what precautions we could, but Hennessy didn't help by knocking out Tom McIver after we had planned that he should take Tina safely across to South Rona and protect her until she and Holmes met.

'We had planned,' said Johnson, glancing at me, 'for McIver to take you to the lighthouse harbour, where we would have arranged for you to meet Kenneth under safe supervision, so to speak. Instead, Hennessy took you to the far end, which meant a long and dangerous walk, and then insisted on coming with you. We had already sent Dr Holmes – sorry, Kenneth – a fake message from Tom McIver, altering the rendezvous to the Land Rover. We didn't want him roving all over South Rona in the dark – it was like King's Cross Station as it was. In fact, we had to take so many damned precautions that we almost inhibited anything from happening. Only Twiss, kindly transported by Ogden, took a pot shot at Tina and hit Hennessy – it was a difficult shot in the dark and he was basically a coward.

'He didn't know that, far from being suspicious, Ogden back at the lighthouse was giving him all the rope he needed to hang himself. He didn't know that Ogden left the lighthouse almost immediately after he did, but neither of them went back to *Seawolf*. Twiss took his little Spanish .45 automatic and fired at Tina, damaging Hennessy's ear. In the furore that followed, with Hennessy and the Buchanans and the Navy all tumbling over each other, Twiss lost his nerve and ran, dropping the gun. Ogden picked it up, we assume, and followed us. Remember, he had expected Holmes to be with Madame Rossi: he didn't know about the Land Rover scheme. I think in fact he lost her for a while. In any case the chap I had ready to follow her saw nothing of him. What seems likely is that he did eventually try the Land Rover either up on the road or after I had driven down to the jetty, and heard enough to realize that suspicion had indeed shifted now from Kenneth to Michael Twiss. If Kenneth wasn't going to be his scapegoat, as he hoped, in order to keep Madame Rossi out of it, then Michael would make an excellent substitute. Except that we must never be able to question Michael and to discover that he was really only a dirty little blackmailer after all.

'Unfortunately for Michael,' continued Johnson, with no regret in his voice at all, *'chacun à son métier,* he sealed his own immediate fate with great dispatch by ferreting out all Ogden's highly secret and highly expensive equipment in the fo'c'sle. Ogden, after all, had had to sail the yacht, with very little help, on that misty passage from Portree. He couldn't be below all the time. And Twiss was emphatically not bound by any ties of loyalty as Victoria was. In fact, his business was to pry. So on arrival at Rum, I should judge, he was ready when Ogden interrupted him playing merry hell in the lab, with an immediate counter proposal; pay me what I ask, or I tell the authorities there is something very funny going on in *Seawolf.* So that Ogden had, quite simply, to kill him – as soon as possible, and with his own gun. If he were lucky, we'd all think it suicide. If he were fearfully lucky, we should find it was murder and accuse Dr Holmes. In any case, everyone would assume Michael Twiss was the man who organized the accident in the *Lysander.* If he could steal letters from Holmes, he could microfilm blueprints.'

Suddenly Kenneth spoke. 'What makes you all so sure that he didn't? He had the opportunities, after all, and Ogden couldn't have come within a thousand miles of seeing that device. He might have arranged for it to be planted on *Lysander* – what you've told us isn't proof, but it adds up to a very strong possibility – but he couldn't have stolen or filmed it. Someone else must have done that: Michael Twiss. Of course they were in cahoots. Why otherwise would Ogden have taken Michael to South Rona and back?'

The wind, blustering against the windows, drove another squall of rain over the art nouveau acorns: water hissed into the hearth. Slowly Johnson got up from the chair arm, bearing his pipe, and knocked it out into the fireside and pocketed it. 'No. Ogden didn't take it,' he said; and clasping soft hands stood surveying us. Bob and Nancy, drawn and big-eyed, followed every flash of his glasses; Hennessy beside me breathed slowly and deeply; Kenneth's pale face was full of thin, frowning lines; Ogden, who had listened motionless, sulkily sprawling, to the last part of this recital, brought up his long fingers and tented them, pursing at Johnson his pale, fleshy lips. At length, reflectively, Johnson resumed.

'Michael Twiss might have pinched your little contraption and put it back later. Equally, Holmes, you might have staged the whole thing yourself.' And as Kenneth, flushing, grunted and sat up: 'I want to go into that in a minute. But meanwhile,' added Johnson, 'you're wrong about one other thing. We *have* proof that Ogden is guilty... Glasscock?'

Rupert stepped into the firelight. Johnson took from him a small, heavy object and set it on the lion-skin before us.

It was a tape-recorder. 'A small precaution,' Johnson was saying. 'I radioed here just after we left Skye this morning, and had Dr Holmes's room wired for sound. If I am right, you are about to hear the voices of Cecil Ogden and the late blackmailing Michael Twiss.' He pressed the button.

Ogden jumped. Ogden, the inefficient, the lethargic, his long face contorted, hurled himself on the lion-skin and scrabbled at the circling tape. For a moment, his pixie cap bobbed below us; then he had the reel wrenched from its socket and was back on his feet.

Johnson spoke. 'Stand still, Ogden,' he said. 'Or I shoot.' And in his fist was the gun which was not a cigarette lighter.

His back to Kenneth, one hand with the tape in his pocket, the other on the Buchanans' sofa, half thrusting past, Ogden stopped, and the fire gleamed on his eyeball as he turned.

'That's a good chap,' said Johnson. 'Handcuffs, Rupert.' And Rupert, fishing in his pocket, began to move forward. Without warning, every light in the house went out.

For an instant, there was perfect silence. Then, as the shouting began, the hall rang and resounded, unspeakably, with the deep voices of bronchial trolls, beating in despair against curtains and panelling: to be free, to reach Trallval and Hallival in the wind and the rainstorms outside. Induced by God knew what fiendish short-circuit, the organ was playing *Cavalleria Rusticana* all over again.

Johnson fired.

I saw the stab of the flame. Then as my pupils widened, the familiar faces about me, dusky in the firelight, jerked apart by the shock. In the place where Ogden had stood, there was nothing. Then from beyond our chairs, the sound of feet running: Rupert, with Johnson vaulting, gun in hand, after him.

Beside me, Hennessy suddenly said, 'You stay here. They've got guns. It's dangerous,' and thrusting me to one side, followed, too. Bob and Nancy had both risen. Bob I saw made a movement to go, then stopped, Nancy's arm in his own. Then her hoarse voice exhorted him. 'We'll need to give them a hand, Bob. Come on. Stay together.' And the darkness swallowed them up.

Then I shouted to Kenneth, above the clash of cymbals and the roll of the small wooden drumsticks and the stuttering roar of the music. 'He'll get out somehow. There's no sense in following him. There's only one place he can go, and that's *Seawolf*.'

For a moment, I sensed Kenneth's pale face staring at me in the gloom. Then he, too, understood. 'Quickly. The boats.'

The great front door was locked, and the key absent. In the end, it was the caretaker's entrance which we used. As we stepped out and the wind caught our breath a torch blazed, blinding us both, and a man's voice, interrupting Kenneth's curse, said, 'Sorry, sir. Orders. Mr Johnson said if he made a break for it, everyone else was to make for the boats. We're not to let a rat through, tonight.'

There was a rifle, I saw, in his hands. In Scotland no one shoots on a Sunday. Kenneth took my hand, and leaving the arcades for the path, we ran round Kinloch Castle and over the grass to the woodland road to the shore.

The wind had risen, but not enough to vanquish the rain. Under the giddy, turbulent trees the road was full of pebbles and mud: the little river, as we rushed over it, was jumping in hummocks and craters and spread dimly with foam. Behind the tossing rhododendrons an army could be marching in safety. We had to shout to each other to be heard.

Once, veering off the path, we found ourselves in a clutter of poultry. A moment later, shockingly, we broke through the dark undergrowth and something flung itself screaming against the blowing coils of my hair. A light shone, and I saw Kenneth's face, perfectly white, the eye sockets turned on me wild with shock and fatigue. There was another scream and I saw him fling up an arm as something frantically beating and dark began to thresh at his shoulders. The screeching, in odd, barking whoops, tore at the ear, mixed with a confused guttural muttering. Then I remembered the shearwaters, and lowering my head, I seized Kenneth's hand and ran past the Warden's back door. No one came out.

On the shore something moved: there was a deer in the water, its dark coat staring with damp underneath.

Here, in the last of the afterlight, the hills behind us were black on the sky, which was charcoal grey to the east, with slate storm clouds massing low over it. Behind us in the west all was dark except on the horizon. There the day had left a wash of green-blue, with a dash of storm-russet low in the saddle of hills, where the black castellated tower of Kinloch Castle rose like an obelisk above the terraced mass of the building. No lights showed. Kenneth slowed up, and I found we had come to the pier.

Sioras was locked: no one could take her out that night. And *Seawolf*'s pram which had been there, had transported an upset Victoria back to her cabin and was neatly stowed now, where, dark on the light waters, *Seawolf* herself swung and jolted to her anchor. Down below, the portholes of the main saloon were lit.

From *Binkie*, moving uneasily close by, there were no lights; nor were there any but riding lights on the lovely *Symphonetta*. Hennessy's boys, clearly, had dropped off to sleep. We looked in silence; then Kenneth said, 'Right. The other jetty,' and running, led the way on. For with his own dinghy gone, Ogden had those of *Binkie, Symphonetta* and *Dolly* to choose from, all tied up at the small pier further round the shore of the loch. It was then, as we stumbled over the shale-layered stone slabs and lichenous boulders and sand patches pale among the black rocks of the shore, that we saw, far ahead against the dim, moving sea, a black figure running.

'Ogden,' said Kenneth shortly; and releasing my hand, began to run in real earnest, towards the boats and the sea.

16

Even a scientist can be illogical when wrought-up and tired. In the tape Ogden was carrying there was proof, I supposed, in the counter-accusations between Michael and Ogden, confronting each other in that wrecked laboratory, that Ogden and not Kenneth was responsible for what happened to the *Lysander*. That there was proof of anything more, in spite of all that Johnson had said, I tried not to believe. But to get that tape, Kenneth was there with me, unarmed, outdistancing all our supporters, without considering that, surely, Johnson by now would have radioed news of Ogden's escape to his colleagues, and he would be intercepted long before he reached the mainland.

In so far as it was incriminating, of course, Ogden might well have thrown the tape away or concealed it already. But in so far as it was also an instrument of power he might be keeping it at all costs. With it, he could bargain. With it, perhaps, he could also blackmail. But I should not think of that. Kenneth had intelligence as well as principles: that kind of man does not change. He was by my side now. I wanted him to be at my side when this was all over.

There was a moment, as we approached the dark jetty and heard the slap of the waves, when behind us there broke out a faint outburst of what sounded like shouting, and I tried to look back. But the wind was blowing hard in our faces, and the noise, whatever it was, had been snatched clean away. Then suddenly, all other sound was lost in the roar of a motor launch engine.

As we ran down the jetty, *Symphonetta*'s speedboat cast off and, picking up revs, charged out into the loch. Ogden, black against the small running waves, was sitting crouched at the wheel.

We stopped. And there, in the blowing darkness, Kenneth confronted me. 'I'm going after him. Tell Johnson I'm sorry I had to borrow his boat.'

'I'm coming with you.'

For a moment he stood, staring at me, and I wondered what he was thinking. He said, 'It'll be dangerous.'

'I know. I want to be with you, Kenneth.' For a second, his hands touched my shoulders and his cheek, wet with rain, was pressed hard against mine. Then he was in *Dolly*'s dory, handing me down, and the outboard was ripped on and the painter inboard and we were off, bouncing through disturbed sea, with the iron triangle of wake following rigid behind and the salt water clattering over us unheeded and soaking us through.

Symphonetta's boat was faster than ours. As we stared at the remote, rocking discs of *Seawolf*'s portholes, we could see Ogden for a moment, dark against her green topsides as he climbed up the companionway, and a shape which must be Victoria, roused by the noise of the speedboat. Then he was on board, and *Symphonetta*'s launch had been cast off to drift, and after standing for a moment, no doubt in startled inquiry, Victoria slipped forward to get up the anchor while Ogden disappeared below.

Soon, the engine would start, and Ogden would help Victoria get the anchor aboard, and then running back to the cockpit, would put the engine in gear and away. I wondered what story he had told to Victoria. And I thought, we can't catch them now. Then the stutter of a starting motor, stammering again and again, came faintly over the beat of our outboard and I remembered, with a cold excitement and nausea combined, that Lenny had been on board *Seawolf* that night, ostensibly to look at the battery. Whatever you thought of Johnson and his friends, they were efficient. Of course *Seawolf*'s engine wouldn't work.

Kenneth had realized it, too. He said, 'They'll have to raise sail. That means he'll have to get rid of us first. Can you manage this outboard?'

'Yes. I think so.'

'Good. Look, we'll have to divide forces. I'm going to steer over to Hennessy's speedboat and get myself aboard. Then while I have his attention, I want you to get on his blind side and somehow get on board *Seawolf*. Once she sees what's happening, Victoria will help you. He may realize what we're doing, but he's only one man. He can't be in two places at once.'

There were many things one could say: sensible things. He can't get far, under sail. Why not wait for the others? There was still *Binkie*'s boat, there on the pier, and along the shore now, a twinkling of torches, jerking and streaming. The Buchanans, Hennessy, Johnson and Rupert were all coming. Then I looked at Kenneth's face, and I thought of the tape and all that it might contain; and I said only, 'Be careful. He'll have a gun now.'

Then we had reached the rocking black shape of *Symphonetta*'s smart speedboat: there was a lurch, and I was alone, the helm in my hand. On *Seawolf*, something light flapped near her bows – Victoria had untied the jib and was trying to raise it while Ogden cranked up the anchor.

But he had left it too late. As *Symphonetta*'s speedboat, hissing, curved and made straight for his gangway, I saw Ogden drop what he was doing and run back along deck. As he passed the skylight something silver glinted in his hand, and I drew a long, shallow breath. Then I put the helm down and made for *Seawolf*'s opposite side. A moment later, and I was tied up to her rail.

It was as I was standing there seesawing in the dinghy, staring upwards, that someone let off a revolver on the other side of the boat. I counted three shots. Then Victoria screamed.

I had drawn breath to call her when I heard running feet, and she came. 'Tina?' Either she had seen me sail round, or Kenneth had managed to tell her. Silhouetted against the dim glow from the hatches her face was staring and white, half-hidden by her rough flying hair. Poor Victoria, who thought she could treat men as ponies. She saw me and said, 'Cecil's gone crazy, I think. They were fighting… Dr Holmes had an oar… Cecil's flung him back in the water and taken the companionway up…'

'Victoria. Listen. Get the companionway, if you can without Ogden noticing. And bring it here.'

She stared at me, hardly listening. 'He's got a gun! He's shooting! Tina, we have to get help.'

'Victoria! *Get the companionway.*'

She obeyed orders. That is why she does so well, on a boat. In two quiet steps she had it lifted over the coachhouse roof, and let down beside me. A moment later, I was on deck beside her. 'Now listen. Is Kenneth hurt?'

'I don't know. I don't think so. He dived, and Cecil went on shooting into the water. Then Cecil left it and jumped into the cockpit. I think he's trying to find out what's wrong with the engine... Listen!' She looked distraught. 'He's calling. He'll want help with the anchor. Tina, let's get back in the boat.'

'No... Wait! Go forward and do what he wants,' I said quickly. 'He won't harm you. He can't, he needs you to help him sail. The engine won't start: Lenny fixed it – never mind why. It's a long story. The others will come and help soon – look, there's *Binkie*'s boat putting off from the jetty now. We only need to delay him a little, and try not to let him see the companionway is down on this side. If Kenneth's all right, he'll swim round to it, and then we're three against one. But if he sees you trying to leave he'll shoot, Victoria. Pretend to help. That's safest and best.'

She said, 'All right,' although she was shaking. 'But you—'

'Never mind me. You go and get the anchor in and the jib up, and take your time about it.' And as she ran forward, in answer to another command in Ogden's sharp voice, I slid into the cockpit, and found my way down a small flight of steps to the wide four-berth saloon down below. Here the motion was violent – the anchor must be tripping and the jib either down still, or up and not yet trimmed. A book Victoria had been reading slid backwards and forwards on the floor, and unwashed tea things rattled in the steel sink. She had been feeling very low, Victoria, it was clear. At the far end of the fo'c'sle, a door opened and shut slackly with every roll. Running below for his revolver, Ogden had left the fo'c'sle unlocked. In a moment, I was inside.

At first, I despaired. It was a mess of patched clothing and old tumbled blankets mixed up with capstan handles and tarred twine and cakes of marine glue and old boathook heads, all tipped out on the floor when the starboard bunk had pulled away from its fixing. Then I saw that it was made to pull out, and that the old

190

lining boards which formed the curving walls of the fo'c'sle were also partly dismantled, showing behind a gleam of something neat in plastic, with cables and dials. I pulled aside the rest of the lining then, but there was no sign of the tape. Instead, I found Ogden's two other guns. I pocketed them while on the deck above me there was a confused trampling of feet, the sound of Ogden's voice, giving orders, and thinly, Victoria's breathless replies.

I realized that the running rattle of the anchor chain through the hawse-hole had stopped, and what I was hearing now was the creak of blocks and the clink and shuffle as the mainsail leapfrogged up. As *Seawolf* caught the wind I saw, across the dark fo'c'sle where I stood and beyond the galley and the lit oasis of the deserted saloon, a stir as Ogden entered the cockpit to take his place at the helm. I saw his arm reach behind him and sheet in the mainsail. Then the deck below me threw me off balance, and suddenly I was on my side in a tangle of bedding, the two revolvers digging hard in my flesh.

We were sailing. Victoria and I were alone on *Seawolf* with this mad and desperate man.

There was a hatch above me, locked on the inside. I glanced just once through the fo'c'sle door, to see his bulk, tethered now to the tiller. I wondered if he had seen *Dolly*'s empty dinghy, which I cast off as I scrambled aboard, and if he was wondering where I had got to. Kenneth, he must suppose, was swimming somewhere out there, or wounded, or drowned. It was possible. But with luck, he might reach one of the boats safely, and the Buchanans' launch, now heading for *Dolly*, would find him and take him on board.

I hoped so, for Kenneth was not really a practical person. And to get what you want in this life, you cannot always play a clean game. I closed the door and began, gently, to unlock the hatch. I had a job to do. And on the whole, I should be better off doing it on my own.

It was dark on deck, and slippery, and very wet. At first I lay full length quite still where I was, between the brass handrail which ran along the side of the coachhouse roof and the ridge of the gunwale. It was not a very happy position. I was against the lee rail of a hard-sailing ship, and if I released my grip of this icy brass rail, I should be hard put to it not to slip sideways between those wide manropes and thence into the sea. As it was, the sea was coming to me. Ogden was aiming for speed, not finesse, and there was a good-going wind blowing up from the south-east. Every now and then, she put her head down and dug into a good one, and then a cold body of water streamed down my left side. A little earlier I had zipped up my hood and my pockets, and I was grateful: there was no famous hair blowing to obscure my sight or give me away. I wondered fleetingly what the management of the Colón, where I ought to be performing, would say if they were watching me now. Lying there, I breathed deeply and easily. Even against the blustering pressure of wind, my chest muscles were supple and strong. I could have lifted up my voice then and quelled the sea and the wind: I could have sung Brünnhilde and Isolde. I could deal with Ogden. I knew it.

First, where was Victoria? The sails were set and drawing, their sheets roughly belayed, with no sign of a change of course to come. There had been little effort at tidying: the rope ends, uncoiled, were slithering tangled together and an empty paint tin, left on deck with its brush in calmer, sunnier days, was rolling clanking between anchor and hatch. Victoria's work was done there: Ogden would have called her back to the cockpit.

And then I thought, he would need her, of course, at the tiller. He had work to do, hadn't he, below? He had the fo'c'sle door to secure and the mess inside to clear up. Most urgent of all, he must have messages to send. Tape or no tape, Ogden wouldn't stay to be caught now. He'd make for the mainland, at Mallaig, Morar or Arisaig, and a fast car to a small airfield. Or perhaps in some bay a foreign crab boat was waiting, innocently riding out the bad weather, and ready to take Ogden on board while a blindfolded Victoria, perhaps, was ferried conveniently ashore.

That was the help he would ask for and what he would have been told to expect. I wondered, myself, if they would trouble with him. Those who arrange boats and planes and fast cars have to take considerable risks, and Johnson's alarm call would be all over the country by now. Ogden's employers, with an amused and irritated smile, like the members of the Royal Highland Cruising Club, might well have written off Cecil Ogden for good... Unless

Gold-tooth would help him, as he had done at Staffa. I wondered very much if Gold-tooth were still at the other end of a radio telegraph on Duke Buzzy's yacht. And I tried not to wonder whether or not Ogden knew that his ally Gold-tooth had been given diamonds by me to defect. I lifted my head, and slowly moved back along the narrow, wet strip of deck.

It *was* Victoria at the helm. Abaft her head, appearing and disappearing in the dark tumble of waves a long way behind us, were the riding lights of at least two other yachts, one sailing up to the wind, and one paid off and well reefed away from it. The red port light to the south of us looked like *Dolly*'s; the green starboard light was undoubtedly Bob Buchanan's. I wondered briefly where Hennessy was, and if *Symphonetta* still swayed by herself dark and asleep on the loch. I was surprised that Johnson had taken time even to ferry the Buchanans to *Binkie*, when every moment took Ogden further away. I was surprised also that either yacht was troubling with sail, until I raised my head further to look in the cockpit, and felt the force of the wind. Nothing could have driven them faster than that, or kept them as steady.

Victoria was in the cockpit, alone, and the door leading down to the saloon had been firmly shut. I slid down beside her, unzipped a pocket, and handed her one of Ogden's two guns.

She was very frightened, her hands almost boneless with cold; and as she spoke to me, her nervous attention was distracted again and again by the heavy steering, and the pull of the waves. The wind was backing a bit and still strengthening: ahead the tide and the wind and the swirling quarrel of currents would chop the waves for us round the long, black spit of Sleat, with its lighthouse winking, steady and white at the end.

Beyond, faintly, other lights glimmered and blanked as the intervening waves jumped; and sometimes, mothlike, grey in the night, a seabird passed silently, close. Beside us, the foam minced back from our flanks, rosy-gold in the light from the portholes, and Victoria said, 'He's below. I'm not to go down. What is it? *What's happened?* He isn't well, you know: that's why he's got this boat. Why did you make me come back on board? *I can't hold this damned thing!*'

But she *was* holding it, although she was crying, and I knew that if I bullied her, she would go on holding it as long as she lived. I said, 'If you sheet her in hard and then bring her up to the wind, what will happen?'

'She'll rattle herself to bits. In time,' said Victoria, chattering.

'But she'll stop sailing?'

'She'll do that: yes.'

'Right. Victoria, I'm going below. Keep her steady. It isn't easy, I know, but I don't want to be thrown off balance if I can help it. Then when I yell, bring her round.'

'What are you going to do?' Her eyes in her dim face were staring at me with a kind of horrified fascination.

'Look out!' I waited while she swung *Seawolf*'s bows round, and the water we had taken over the nose came streaming down and into the scuppers. The self-draining cockpit was having a hell of a time. I said, 'I'm going to lock Ogden into the fo'c'sle, that's all. Then all we have to do is wait until *Dolly* and *Binkie* come up. Simple.'

Simple. Ogden was now in the fo'c'sle, doing God knew what, but believing that he and Victoria, stuck at the tiller, were the only two on board the boat. I had locked the fo'c'sle hatch from the top. All I had to do, in order to make Ogden a prisoner, was to open the cockpit door, step quietly down through the saloon and the galley, and turn the key in the door to the fo'c'sle... Except that I wanted something else too. The recording tape.

The door down from the cockpit creaked badly – all the doors on Ogden's boat did. I might have worried, as I opened it gently now and closed it as gently behind me, so that the light from within should not distract Victoria... I might have worried if I had not once already heard the noise in the fo'c'sle, where the wind reverberated and buzzed like hornets, rising a half-tone and then another, dying to nothing before starting all over again. Ogden would not hear me coming.

I picked my way softly through the litter on the saloon deck, where the fallen book had been reinforced by a newspaper, a scatter of cushions and a torch, its bulb broken. Just ahead of me was the vital door, the key left logically and confidently on the outside.

I had only to turn it to be safe. Except that, Kenneth – Kenneth, are you all right? – except that I meant to find that spool of tape and destroy it because of what it might say. Because it might reveal how Kenneth's top secret leaked, in the first place, from that locked lab in Nevada. For there were only two keys. Mine was one – and although Michael Twiss might have used it, Johnson said Twiss didn't poach the device. Johnson was convinced, and for my money, knowing Michael, that was quite true. So whom did that leave?

Now, Ogden had to be dealt with. It did no good to hang about waiting. I put my hand on the tarnished brass knob of the fo'c'sle, turned it slowly, and flung it wide open. The man sitting at the transmitter inside jumped up turning, the gun bright in his hand. Then I fired.

I fired – and he fell. But I saw long before he dropped at my feet that it wasn't Cecil Ogden at all. It was Kenneth Holmes I had shot.

Electrified, I forgot my own prearranged signal. I cried out, and Victoria, obeying instructions, brought the yacht head up to wind.

The effect in sound is roughly as if a teashop had been picked up quickly and dropped again. Physically, it means a violent shifting of gravity for every object animate and inanimate within reach. The deck jerked from my feet. Shelves, bunk-edge, door-handles attacked my sides like pitchforks; cupboard doors clapped and thudded, grazing my head. And as I smashed like an escaped roller skate into one corner, Ogden, who had been pinned in that corner by Kenneth holding Ogden's own gun – Ogden now kicked the gun from my grasp, sending me sprawling, pocketed it and got up, his own automatic safely back in his hand, pointing straight at my heart.

He was grinning. 'Well done, sweetheart. Tosca could hardly do better. But I don't trust you, all the same. Now, stay just where you are while I investigate…' But I was already looking at Kenneth.

He wasn't moving. What a fool I was! What a bungling idiot! Of course, Kenneth came up the companionway while I was below and Ogden busy with the anchor and the jib. Where could he have hidden? Then I had it. Of course. *Seawolf*'s own wooden pram, lying lashed upside down by the skylight would cover a single man easily. And then later, when Ogden was busy below, Kenneth would merely unlock the fo'c'sle hatch from above and drop down on his head.

'He'll do,' said Ogden now, rising, and I saw that he had Kenneth's hands and feet lashed tightly together. I could only see the side of his face and a lot of blood just below. For a moment I remembered Hennessy's ear, and had to bury an impulse towards insane laughter. Kenneth was alive, and not in danger: I accepted Ogden's word for that. But if ever I needed to live on my wits, it was then. For they were all I had to live on, I and my voice at that moment: my common sense and my will to succeed.

Then Ogden said in his colourless, sulky voice, 'Then Victoria's got the other gun out there, has she? We'll have to get this damned boat turned round and running, won't we, sweetheart? Never do for our friend Johnson to catch us. The trouble is,' and the straggling eyebrows rose, and the fleshy lips parted in a grimace above the long, knobbly chin: 'The trouble is, we'll need to go about soon, and I'm a trifle short-handed. In fact, I could do with a little help. I pay well, you know. Generously, in fact. Would you give me a little help, Madame Rossi,' said Ogden, while below me, damn, damn, Kenneth stirred and opened his eyes – 'Would you give me a little help to sail where I want to go, if in return I promise you *this*?'

It was Johnson's small spool of rust-coloured tape. I looked at it in his dirty big palm, while Kenneth, pale-faced, shouldered himself up to a sitting position, and said, 'No. She won't.'

We stared at each other, Kenneth and I. At length I said, 'Do you know what is on that tape?' And Kenneth replied instantly, with violence. 'I don't know. I don't care. But neither you nor I is going to do a hand's turn to sail this damned boat.'

'He'll throw it into the sea.'

'Let him.'

'But it exonerates you. It's bound to show that Ogden and not you got the bomb on to *Lysander*.'

'There's enough evidence here and with what Johnson's dug up to show that already. You can't suppose either he'll stand up to questioning. Valentina' – the blood was filling in with glistening purple all the stitches of his navy blue jersey – 'if you help him now, I'll never forgive you.'

'Then we'll have to use other persuasions, won't we?' And slowly, the little black mouth of the automatic shifted to cover Kenneth as he half-sat at our feet. 'Go and tell Victoria to fling her gun overboard where I can see it, and bring the boat round back on course. Or lover-boy gets a shot in the heart.'

Kenneth couldn't blame me now. I didn't look at his upturned, agonized face, but ran through, leaving the fo'c'sle and saloon doors wide ajar, as Ogden had ordered, and did as he asked. But when Victoria had thrown her gun in the sea, and she and I had tried in vain to bring *Seawolf* round on her helm; and when Ogden, abandoning Kenneth, had come blundering through from below, shouting orders, and had wrenched the helm from us – by the time all that had happened, we were no longer sailing *Seawolf* for Cecil Ogden under duress. We were sailing her under a thick sky, in spewing, ravenous seas whose spindrift filled the night with grey mist, and a wind blowing westerly in what was now a full gale. We were sailing, unpractised fools that we were, for our lives.

On *Dolly*, they would have noticed that the barometer had dropped to 29.5 and was still falling, while the wind had veered from south-east to south-west. *Dolly* would have three or four reefs already in her mainsail, and canvas covering her skylights and hatches. The storm jib would be out of the sail locker, the lifeline shackled ready to the jackstay, the pumps checked, and everything loose below made secure.

But we were on *Seawolf*, where everything was old and borrowed and held together with string. Ogden's face as he felt the weight of the helm betrayed an alarm he had not shown before Johnson or any of us up to now. His other hand, which had been holding the mainsheet, altered its grip and instead pulled the sail again taut, while the boat, jumping crazily, veered back again, and up into the wind. Barely clearing our heads as we crouched, lurching, in the cockpit, the great wooden boom jumped and rattled, the mainsail kicked, the jib and staysail snapped, distressed, in front of the mast. Ogden shoved the helm into my hand and, shouting at Victoria, climbed on to the razor-edge deck.

They had two things to do: to take down the staysail, which would reduce the canvas in front of the mast; and lower the mainsail and put a reefed storm trysail in its place. From the light striking out of the saloon, I could see the whites of Victoria's eyeballs as she turned to follow Ogden out of the cockpit. Up to now, her code had driven her to obey his every command, but this clapper-bell of shuddering timber, with the spray falling like gravel into the cockpit and the wind screaming through the high rigging, was frightening her out of her wits. Her face white, her hair in soaking rat-tails about her, Victoria carried out her primary orders and adjusted the set of the jib.

But there was no question of handing the staysail, for with a series of cracking explosions the elderly stuff of the staysail had blown itself apart into ribbons, and like some jeering mace of buffoonery, fluttered its ghostly bunting at the bows. I saw her look up, as the staysail tore, and I saw her knuckles whiten where they gripped the brass storm rail at her side. Then the competent Victoria was sick.

There was through the extraordinary confusion of noise, a shattering crash as *Seawolf* tipped sharply from one side to the other and the ill-stowed contents of the crockery shelves hurled themselves in the air. I could see Ogden, braced against the mast, with the mainsail halyard in his grasp, shouting at Victoria, who was hanging on without looking at him, clearly incapable of anything but continuing to be sick. I thought, briefly, of Kenneth, bound hand and foot, crashing helplessly to and fro in the fo'c'sle, and of Johnson's tape, thrust into Ogden's pocket. While we were hove-to like this, the motion would be at its worst. On the other hand, we had stopped actually sailing, and the distance between *Seawolf* and *Dolly* and the Buchanans in *Binkie* behind her must be lessening every moment. Except that once his spread of main canvas was reduced, Ogden would almost certainly set *Seawolf* sailing again. And whether he did or not, it was rapidly becoming a question whether, sailing or rescued, we could hold together long enough to survive.

Then I realized Ogden was calling me. The next moment, he came crashing down beside me in the cockpit, improvised a hasty lashing to steady the tiller, and seizing me by the arm, pulled me up on deck in the roaring, rain-spattered darkness. The deck nudged, slid and contracted under my feet: the mainsail canvas shuddered and leaned on me, reducing my standing space to a sliver. And beyond that sliver, the sea revealed itself darkly in tall escalators and rockets of foam and on the slate and indigo horizon as a running tumble of changing black peaks. There was no sign, between range and range of these liquid mountains, of the lights of either *Binkie* or *Dolly*. There was only the dim yellow glow from the skylight under my feet, showing Ogden's long, unshaven face, half intent, half nervously distraught, as he wrestled to lower the wet, wrangling canvas, and the bent shoulders of Victoria, clinging retching and choking to the faltering deck. Half my mind was occupied with compelling, immediate dangers; with controlling the great, shiny boom as the fabric towering high above all our heads lowered into a ruckle of wet leaden folds; with gripping these during the pause of Ogden's brief indecision; and then the dizzy, nailbreaking horror of balancing oneself against sea, squalls and the juddering boom, while with Ogden I moved from end to end of the mainsail, knotting the reefpoints and thus binding and shortening the canvas. Half my mind was on this. The other half told me that no one sailing a yacht in the Inner Hebrides this night would find it a matter of either blame or surprise if Cecil Ogden and his reel of standard play tape were both lost overboard.

Perhaps, as we faced one another over the boom, he read something of this in my face. In any event, his thick lips formed a sudden contortion, and as his fingers ceaselessly worked, he observed, 'That's right. Be a good girl. After all, Ogden's the only one of us who knows how to sail. *And* he keeps his word. You help me get to the mainland, Tina my sweetheart, and what's in my pocket is yours.' Then the reefing was done, and the peak and throat halyards set up; and with the sails set and the tiller unlashed and in Ogden's big, dirty hand, *Seawolf* paid off and, lying flat on her port rail, headed into the storm.

After a single slithering crash, indicating that everything below decks had shifted in turn to the lee side, *Seawolf* settled down to a kind of bucketing rhythm on her new tack and Victoria, her face greenish-white behind the strands of her hair, stopped being sick and lay limp in the cold, swilling cockpit, her head on her arms. I took a step down towards the saloon.

'No. Oh, no, you don't.' Ogden's arm pulled me back and held me, roughly, against the bench seat beside him and I stayed still, for the moment's inattention had its price. *Seawolf* instead of sliding up and round the next foaming mountain dug her bows in, and shuddered as if stopped by a mudbank, while creaming water shot down the scuppers towards us and joined the slapping tide in the cockpit. 'It's self-draining,' said Ogden with malice. 'Unless we get too much water, too fast.'

The wind rose half a tone, then another, and *Seawolf,* leaning over, plunged down into a chasm and began its curling climb up. In the half-hour since I looked at the barometer, it had dropped by .03 and was still going down. I said to Ogden, 'Where are we going?'

He didn't take his eyes off the blackness ahead, but I saw his broken teeth flash dimly, in a kind of grin. 'Never mind. The mainland.'

'Haven't we got too much canvas? What if it gets worse?'

'That's all right. We'll take down the mainsail.'

Victoria, lifting her head, was looking at the weather, too, for the first time. 'Cecil. We should be hove-to.'

No reply. He wouldn't stop now. He had nothing to lose. We were plunging south on the last of the ebb, with a cross-sea driving towards us, pushed before an Atlantic south-westerly gale. There might come a point at which there would be less risk in our ignorance, Victoria's, Kenneth's and mine, than in his obsessive need to press on. And then, with help or without it, somehow, Ogden must go.

We were wet through. Victoria was shivering, and I could feel my fingers and feet growing numb with the beating cold of the water, the solid force of the wind, the great spilling spaces of icy air contained in the mainsail above us.

Victoria said, 'Cecil. We must get warm and have something to eat, or we'll be no good. Let me try to heat some soup in the galley. We can go down one by one, and get our dry clothes and oilskins on maybe. You probably haven't eaten all day.'

It was a brave offer, as well as a sensible one. To anyone who had been as sick as Victoria, the prospect of entering the reeling shambles below, far less finding and heating some food, was a terrible one. I wondered, for one light-headed moment, how she meant to locate soup among all these sopping, label-less cans and then realized that she couldn't in any case. The last thing Ogden had done before taking the helm was to switch off the saloon and riding lights. There was no glimmer now aboard *Seawolf* except for the swimming green glow of the compass. And he would not let Victoria go below. As she stood, hesitating, gripping the side boards of the cockpit, Ogden said perfectly calmly, 'If you move one step from there, I shall let go the tiller.'

She stood her ground and one remembered how well, in some ways, she must know him. 'That's silly. She'll be swamped, and you'll simply drown with us. Look, I'm not going near Dr Holmes: what good will it do? He can't sail either. He's hurt. He's probably knocked out by now.'

'Nobody's going down,' said Ogden, grinning again. He would drown with us, I thought, perfectly happily. Everything else had gone wrong but he still had this power of life and death in his own boat. This crazy tub of a boat, where the water swilled over our ankles and the engine would not work and the ropes were rotten and the lights were tied on with string. I thought: the lights are off. What if we meet a trawler, a drifter running for shelter? We have no lights and no engine. *Dolly* won't see us. And neither would they.

I said, pitching my voice over the distraction of noise, 'She's right. Soon we'll be too cold to handle ropes: you'll have no crew. If it's Kenneth you're worried about, give Victoria the tiller and go down and lock up the fo'c'sle yourself.' He had my gun and his own in his pocket but I didn't want to remind him of that. He knew anyway that he couldn't do without us. Not in this weather, at least.

He hesitated. Years of muddling about in these waters must have taught him the maxim Lenny was fondest of repeating: in a storm it is seldom the boat that gives in – it's the crew. But I had given him no easy way for his pride. It was Victoria who laid her glistening hand on the tiller and said, 'I think I can do it, if you show me how. As you rise, you pay off a little. Then you bring her round as you fall down the trough.'

'Not quite.' She listened as he instructed her. Then, her face grave, she took the tiller, and Ogden staggered below.

17

We were novices. Even Victoria, who had been Ogden's nurse and charwoman and cook and whipping boy half the season knew little but how to obey orders blindly. Or we should have kept quiet about our cold and our hunger and have seen that Ogden was putting off doing the one thing that before all else should be done. Before wind and seas of tumultuous strength, *Seawolf* was being heeled and tossed and wrung by her sail. The reefed mainsail was no longer small enough to be safe. *Seawolf* needed to ride on bare poles.

But Ogden had gone below.

I did not know what detained him, striding through to lock up his prisoner, but I could perhaps guess. The saloon floor would be nearly impassable. Everything from those ill-fitting cupboards and ramshackle shelves would have fallen, choking what little floor space there was. The flex festooning the deckhead would be dragged down, the Tilley lamps smashed, the cushions littered with broken bottles, and a soaking of meths and water and paraffin. I wondered how Kenneth was faring, injured and tied in that hell down below, and how he would feel when the door slammed and he knew that whatever the fate of *Seawolf* he could not escape. And all the time I was wondering, Victoria was struggling with the helm, until suddenly, on a little whimper, she cried out my name. And I stopped peering down into the blackness in *Seawolf*'s turgid belly, and looked round and saw.

It was fifteen feet high; the mountain that had risen behind us, and was rising still, blocking out the dark, curdled sky. Ogden, warned by some sixth sense maybe, moved down in the saloon and at the edge of my consciousness I saw his bonneted head, preparing to climb. Then my hands were on Victoria's as she pulled and pulled at the helm.

It was the wrong thing to do. For a moment we stared into the dense, palpitating blackness of the thing growing above us. The top had blown off its crest. The howling air, the peeling coach-work, the sails were all grey with spinning mares' tails of foam as the crust was shorn clear off the sea. We watched it reach the height of its arc, far above us, with a gravely pondered precision. For a moment it lingered. Then, slowly, it over-reached, curved, destroyed its glistening retainers of tension and balance, and fell, as a chimney might topple, on *Seawolf*'s starboard quarter.

The crash when it came was brain-numbing: it had the quality, raucous, unexpected, of exploding TNT in a quarry. With it came a slabbed ceiling of water that, falling interminably, hit rigging, cockpit, inclined sail and too-sloping deck, flinging Victoria and myself on our faces, tumbling Ogden back into the cabin, pouring boiling and choking over tiller, benches and instruments, and then leaping like a glistening animal to fill the shattered saloon.

Battered, retching, thrown back and forth by the unending sluice, as I got to my feet three times to be hurled back and back, I felt *Seawolf* had stopped. I felt the long, dying shiver with which the old, insecure timbers received their belabouring. And as the water fell in blackness and the sea crashed and the wind squealed and whooped, I felt *Seawolf* roll, where the slope of her decks and her sea-filled, pathetic reefed mainsail had already half carried her – rolling to port, to lay her mast in the sea.

I remember lying half drowned in the cockpit, my fingers cramped in some kind of grating, my feet encountering something supine and soft which must be Victoria, lying unconscious or drowned on the lee side of our water-logged coffin. I remember seeing the glint of foam spots floating well above waist-height in the saloon, and wondering where Ogden was, and if he had managed to lock the fo'c'sle door. I remember the deck heeling more and more until, do what I would, I slid on top of Victoria and the water poured up and over our heads and I seized her by the back of her collar and tried to stand upright, on the lee side of the cockpit.

There were no lifebelts. There was no dinghy – I had seen that burst free and slide over. There were no lights to attract help and no help to attract: in all this waste how could our pursuers find us, even supposing they had continued to sail?

A more worthy ship would have floundered. On *Seawolf,* in the midst of her dying roll, there came a single musical note, then another, plain through the crashing hiss of plunging timber and water. I looked up.

The wind and spume-ridden spaces above us were filling slowly, noiselessly, with a forest dropped from the skies. A ghostly, tumbling mosaic of wood and wire and hemp and torn, cloudy fabric which came closer and closer to clothe all the deck and slither, ballooning into the sea. The mainmast had gone.

For a moment, her deck nearly upright above us, *Seawolf* trembled, ready to follow her sails and her spars. Then slowly, sluggishly, washing, creaking, gurgling like a soft, groaning sponge, she started to right herself, levelled, turned head to wind, and lay finally still to her drogue. There was absolute silence – and stillness – and peace.

I looked at Victoria. In the cockpit, the water was ebbing although I could hear the sound of it slapping heavily in the cabin below. Around us, the deck and coachhouse lay darkly shining, swept clean on their weather side of every vestige of tackle. Forward, beyond the broken stump of the mast, the forehatch had been wrenched half free of its moorings, and the short seas that caught and streamed over us as we gently curtseyed and dipped must be spilling partly at least into the fo'c'sle. I drew a deep breath. Kenneth. Ogden. Pumps, somehow, if we could find them: Victoria would know. *We were going to live.*

Victoria knew. We needed to cut away the shrouds from the chain plates and free ourselves from the heavy spars which were already beginning to stir and jolt against our fraying, unvaleted sides. But for that we needed tools, and a brute strength that between us, cold and trembling with the weakness of reaction, we did not possess. The first step therefore for both instinct and reason, was to feel our way down the cockpit steps and into the watery darkness beyond.

It was a nightmare, but compared with the nightmare we had gone through, a matter only of cold perseverance. The motion was less than it had been, but it was still violent enough to make progress almost impossible in this lightless and waterlogged junkshop. I thought later that Ogden must have stumbled so far and then struck his head against the bulkhead or the mast, for we had hardly entered the saloon when we heard his voice, slow and soggy like the boat, just beside us. He said, as a statement, not a question, 'The mast's gone!' and I thought suddenly that for him, we might as well have gone down, for now, without sails or engine, he was a sitting duck. Victoria said quickly, 'Are you all right?'

His voice was sneering and rough. 'No. But what the hell do you care?'

'I do.' Her voice, in return, was thin but steady. 'We're all human beings, Cecil.'

He said, 'That's what's wrong with us. We ought to be spots in a computer. Or apes.'

The conversation seemed to have come to a dead stop. I said tentatively, against the dead, whacking sound that had begun to echo on the port side, 'Victoria thought you would want us to help clear the wreckage. It's beginning to bump. If you can show me, I can maybe help with the pumping as well.'

Now, dimly, I could see the white blur of his face. He was hanging simian-like on to the bulkhead, the water washing greasily about his long shanks. He seemed uninjured. After a moment he said, 'The pumps, yes. Or she'll settle. There's an up-and-down stuck in the...' He paused, and then finished with a grunt, '...in the fo'c'sle.' Kenneth...

There was not even a torch. All the shelves above the bunks were swept clean, and even the shelves themselves were hanging drunkenly by their insufficient nails. It was pitch black, except for the square of indigo behind us marking the door to the cockpit, and the low green sparkle that outlined our movements as we waded aft.

Ogden had not reached the fo'c'sle to lock it, but it made little difference. The door had jammed, and took all our power to open it against a force of water that poured out, spectral with phosphorescence, darkly sparkling round our thighs. The flood level in the fo'c'sle with its broken hatch had been higher than here. A man tied and unconscious on the floor would have had no chance at all.

Ogden, pressing through against the onrush of water, was intent on only one thing. Feeling above his head, we heard him exclaim with satisfaction, and when he stepped back, he had a lift-pump in his hand. 'Victoria, you've done this before…'

I let them wade past me, and then I stepped through to the small, triangular nook in the old bows of the boat where Kenneth had been left. The water, knee-high now, was full of rippling dark shapes. I stepped on a soft resilience made up of tumbled cushions and bedding, and I recoiled and stood on the raised metal threshold, holding tight to the doorway. Outside, the impact of the broken masthead and boom against the flanks of the ship had settled down to a steady rhythm, shivering the water below as it rolled to the pitching and swaying. Inside the saloon I heard the voices of Ogden and Victoria, talking quite normally together as they fixed up the lift pump and its discharge pipe, somewhere near the steps to the cockpit, I judged. In a moment I heard the sawing sigh of the pump starting; and the minor sound of trickling water, fluctuating in volume and tone as the seas rose and fell beneath it, came tinnily through the orchestration of water sounds in my ears.

If only I could see. For the third time I said, 'Kenneth?' and when there was still no answer I bent and sank my hands below the cold slopping water. Then, abruptly, I stood up. For there ought to be light, a little light, at least, from the broken hatch cover above.

I looked up. Blackness. More than that: a dragging noise that had nothing to do with the gear lying tangled the length of *Seawolf*'s port gunwales. These were hands working, dragging something – a tarpaulin, perhaps, over the hatch. And footsteps moving cautiously to and fro. Then inside the saloon, the voices and the sound of pumping suddenly faltered, and Victoria, her voice high, said loudly, 'Listen!'

But already I was listening. For low voices, footsteps, pumping cannot be heard in a storm which wraps you, as we had been wrapped all the night, in a blizzard of sound.

I listened, and I heard nothing but water-filled silence. For the wind had totally stopped.

Our hearts beat, and we were silent too a moment with our different thoughts. Then Ogden said, with deliberation, 'Get on with the pumping. It won't last. It's the centre of the depression. It'll give us time to get rid of the water and that clutter on deck: that's all.' He paused a moment and then said, 'That must be Holmes, up there. It's just as well. We'll need him.'

I don't know what I thought: that Kenneth, with total surprise on his side, should have come flying down the steps from the cockpit, brandishing some invincible weapon, and forced Ogden at gunpoint to sail straight for *Dolly*. I realized I was tired, and daydreaming. The only guns on board were in Ogden's big pockets. We could not sail anywhere: our mast and mainsail had gone. And if we were to stay alive, merely, we needed all the working help we could muster. Ogden, poor thing that he was, represented our only source of knack and experience. Kenneth, with whatever strength he had left, our only other male help. Friends, lovers, allies, enemies on dry land, we were all now only ciphers, in a derelict boat. I followed Ogden on deck.

It *was* Kenneth. He was kneeling on deck, swiping one-handed at the tangle of wreckage with a small half-blunted axe. I wondered fleetingly what department of government contributed it. I dropped beside him – 'All right?'

'I'll live. My left shoulder.' He looked up at Ogden. 'You shouldn't leave open clasp knives in your lockers. I've cut the lee shrouds. The weather ones and the backstay have gone. There's no point in trying to save any of it unless you want a sea anchor. How long before the wind starts again?'

Ogden, on his knees too, was examining the mess. Water slopped over the gunwales and ran out through the scuppers as we leaned over to the weight of the wreckage. The seas were silent and huge, lifting the billowing mass and swaying it down all the time in front of our eyes. Ogden said, 'Oh, we have maybe twenty minutes, half an hour. The sail can go, but I want to save a good spar. We could mount a staysail maybe on that.'

I said, 'Call me when you want me. I'll go below and give Victoria a rest.' As I went, I heard Ogden answer, in reply to some query of Kenneth's, 'It'll veer, probably: my guess would be from the

207

north-west maybe. And harder. We'll have sea-room down nearly to Ardnamurchan. But then, the tide'll be against us. We'll not run so hard, but we'll have some fine, dirty seas.' He was, in a queer way, enjoying it.

I have never worked harder than I did in these twenty minutes; and in a way, like Ogden, I found it almost enjoyable. Victoria was satisfactory to work with, willing, quick and sparing herself nothing. We made short work between us of the pumping, although her face in a little while went very pale: it is hard on the midriff. Some of the water we should never get out. Both the deckhead and the bulkhead were leaking: probably they always did; maybe the extra stress had now sprung them further. But I had discovered and rigged up an Aldis, and in its light Victoria got the cooker going and we found and opened a tin or two of something sloppy, which did in fact turn out to be soup. There was a tin mug in one of the bunks which we should all have to share: the rest seemed to be shattered. Nothing came out of the sink pump, and there was no hope, now, of dry clothing. But we should do.

Up on deck, the worst of the wreckage had gone, and the staysail was up, on a temporary boom. It looked like a teacloth after *Seawolf*'s great spread of sail. But this, with a scrap of jib, was going to steady us. Victoria, the last to have her soup, came up to see. 'We're going to make it.'

Ogden looked round. Crouched in the cockpit, he was working on his knee with ballpoint and charts, trying to calculate our where-abouts and possible drift. 'We ought to. I should be there before daylight,' he said; and the little smugness in the tone lingered and died in the ensuing silence. 'Where?' said Kenneth: then, sharply, 'You're not proposing seriously, surely, to try and sail on?'

Ogden didn't trouble to look up. 'We're bound to drift south anyway. There's quite a chance I can reach the right spot on the shore. Victory out of defeat, eh?' He looked up then, and grinned into our staring faces. 'Oh, there's a risk. But there's a risk in staying hove-to. I'm going, anyway. And you haven't much choice, have you?'

'Single-handed?' said Kenneth. I shut my mouth, and so did Victoria. 'Won't you need help with the sails? And relief from the tiller? You don't suppose any of us is going to help you?' And after a moment he added, 'We don't need you now, you know, Ogden. There are enough of us to keep her afloat until help arrives. Head to wind, we can handle her as well as you can. If you sail, you'll have to sail her alone.'

There was a long silence. In the quiet, it seemed to me I could hear above the constant movement and splash of the seas an odd and remote murmuring, like the growl of a hungry animal on a hot summer's day. Then I dismissed it, for Ogden was saying, 'Not alone. Tina will help me.' He added amiably, catching Kenneth's eyes on his ballpoint, 'Like it? It isn't in the shops yet. You could call it a travellers' sample. Tina, sing to us.'

'*What?*' I, too, lifted my blank gaze from the pen to Ogden's cynical face. 'You're mad.' It *was* a growling, a low, distant murmur.

'I'm not mad. I just feel like a tune. What about something good and high? The Bell Song. The Doll Song. The Jewel Song. Something with a really nice sharp *cadenza*, with a top note to finish.'

The growl had become a very soft roar. 'You *are* crazy.'

'Maybe.' Ogden was still smiling, but one hand was slipping into his pocket and when it reappeared it was holding an automatic, pointing straight this time at Victoria's heart. 'Maybe. Mad enough to tell you to sing, dear. Sing one phrase. One note, even. Sing your party piece, dear. The last *cadenza* in *Lakmé*, with that famous G sharp in alt. Or Rupert's young dollybird will meet a sad end.'

'Why? No!' And as his fingers tightened on the trigger and Victoria's white, eye-filled face went rigid with horror: 'No!' I added more rationally. 'No. All right. But I don't know if I can strike it. Not after all this. And in any case, I can't guarantee it exactly: I haven't got perfect pitch.'

'That's all right,' said Ogden. 'I have. Sing.'

Every coloratura from the beginning of time has recorded the Bell Song from *Lakmé:* I did it in Rome. That was when I first caused a sensation by altering the top *cadenza* from E to G sharp in alt. All the same, it was a good piece of work.

Now, I looked at Kenneth, and at Ogden's hand hard on the trigger. I drew a long, deep, quelling breath, and I prayed to the gods of ambition and hard work and justice and I felt in all the spaces of my head the high, pure note I had chosen. I opened my lips, shaped to the sound of the bell, and I sang the last pointed phrases and the rising notes of the final *cadenza* – and at the top note, I held it.

I sang into silence, and I finished in silence: a long, spreading moment of infinite quiet. Then Kenneth said, his voice unaccustomed and hoarse, '*The note isn't true?*'

Ogden was smiling. 'The pariah's daughter has a rather flat bell, sweetie. Sing it again.'

I could not move.

The cultured, bodiless voice blandly continued. 'You can't simply let Victoria die? You have the note there, all right. All you must do is produce it. A single tone higher. And if you don't get it this time, you can try it again. I'll tell you when you hit it. Or you'll know when you hit it, won't you? Won't you, *cara, carissima diva?*'

'Valentina!' It was Kenneth's harsh voice again. 'Sing. For God's sake sing as he asks you.'

And I could not. Even if that dirty hand tightened and the automatic went off and Victoria lost her life, I would do nothing about it. For I knew, and Kenneth now knew that I knew, that the pen lying so innocently on the bench at Ogden's far side had much more than solid ink in its case. It was a piece of concentrated, high-power explosive triggered off by a sonic device. It was, in fact, the twin of the pen which last week had exploded inside the *Lysander*. And another copy of Kenneth's own prototype, which I, Tina Rossi, had abstracted from his locked Nevada laboratory for my principals to photograph and return.

I have never had such a reception in my life for my singing, as I had that night for my silence. Ogden did not shoot Victoria. He waited, the insufferable, interfering fool, until my refusal was established, and all my refusal implied; and then he laughed and dropped the gun in his pocket, and said, 'No, Madame Rossi won't sing. She doesn't want to explode in mid-ocean. She is hoping to glide homewards soon to those cosy bank accounts and those cinnamon diamonds; to the applause and the adoration and the comforting arms of Dr Holmes... I underestimated your ambition, Tina. I apologize. I made sure you were going to betray us: I was convinced you were flying to Rum to confide all to your loving friend Kenneth.

'What a loss to the world of music, if our attempt with the mine had succeeded! What a loss to the world of science if Dr Holmes had killed himself, there in Rose Street, a self-confessed traitor.' His voice was jibing and thin. 'You could have continued to work for us then, with no risk of suspicion. If my colleague hadn't taken Chigwell for Holmes, and killed the wrong man...

'Your assignation was ill-chosen, Tina. We didn't mean you to be involved in that killing. We didn't mean you to meet Johnson. Especially we didn't mean you to meet Johnson...'

I said, through my excellent capped teeth, 'Why didn't you tell me about him? Why didn't you make yourself known?' and saw that he was smiling. He was truly crazy.

'Haven't I told you? We didn't trust you, my dear,' Ogden said. 'But it's all gone now, Tina, hasn't it? There's nothing left for you now back on *Dolly* but handcuffs. So you and I had better make for the mainland, hadn't we? You see, Dr Holmes, how I have a helper after all? Ogden's mate!'

We are kept, we agents, we amateur contact people, as a rule quite separate from each other. In the chain stretching from me to the man who finally passed the ballpoint pen bomb, innocently, as a present, to one of the crew of the fated *Lysander,* I do not know what part Ogden played, and I did not know until Johnson exposed him that Ogden was one of us. On the other hand Ogden it seemed, had all along guessed my identity. I suppose since he found me on board, he had known that he had only to expose me to make of me an ally of necessity. I wondered, a little, why he had held his hand up till now. Either to earn kudos, since I could then continue to operate. Or for blackmail.

It did not now matter. Behind us the roaring was now quite distinct: it was near, and growing second by second louder. 'We don't need this,' continued Ogden, picking up the ballpoint pen between finger and thumb. 'Do we? It served its purpose. Let's confide it to the ocean. Then even if someone ever comes and sings a G sharp in alt over it, Tina, it still will not explode.' And he rose, turning, to fling it as Victoria screamed.

It is a sickening sight, to see rolling out of the dark a long, black glistening wave, streaming dully with foam, which is advancing steadily along all its length towards you with the whole ocean in storm drawn behind it. I watched it quite without feeling, as if a bad film had intruded on some deep personal grief. Kenneth, I thought, felt the same. He sat limply across the well of the cockpit, his hands loose between his knees, and his gaze resting, almost blank, on my face. He was not seeing me. He was seeing, probably his precious, world-famous *diva* with the candid heart, who rose, unspoiled from her humble beginnings. I am sorry, Kenneth. That was me, too. But Michael was expensive, and although I was against the blackmailing at the beginning, it did permit him to live perfectly happily on his ten per cent. And having seen how easily Michael did it, I found it child's play, myself, to toy with the grown-up, deeper, better paying end of the game... My God, I have never handled money like it. I was richer than my voice alone could ever have made me. But Michael didn't know that.

We were sitting there, staring at each other still, when the renewed storm overtook us.

It was Ogden and Victoria who saved *Seawolf* in that first terrible impact when four hands on the helm were hardly enough; and we bucked and rolled in spite of our shorn pole and our sea anchor, with the seas pouring black on our shoulders and sheering down the worn decks in response to our tilt. Then we lifted our heads from the first onslaught of water, and Ogden swung the helm to the new compass point of the wind, while Kenneth began to lurch about cautiously, trimming the remaining scraps of sails, and I went below and restarted pumping. Victoria stayed, taking her orders from Ogden.

I remembered that she knew nothing, even what Ogden was accused of. And what had happened just now was a total mystery to her – except that Ogden somehow was about to shoot her, and that, asked to save her, I refused.

In everything, Victoria was solitary. Slave to the drunks, the leper colonies, the children's missions, the jobs where no one cares if you have talent or beauty or intelligence or anything but a capacity for unremitting, unsavoury work, she got her satisfaction perhaps from our horrified alarm at her abasement. From that, and the power she wielded. We were very alike. She was calming to work with.

We took turns at the pump, Victoria and I, for a long time. It was not a matter of sailing anywhere: it was a matter once again of staying alive. The Aldis, safely lashed, had been switched off to save electricity and all the ship was quite dark. Kenneth and Ogden in the freezing cockpit spoke very little. One had to shout, against the violence of the new wind. Against its freezing impact, we had no protection. I did not care, at that moment, where Ogden took me.

After a long time, Kenneth came below. I was pumping and retching, for I who was never sick had found that there comes a time when willpower and good physique together can do nothing more. He had to touch my arm to make me look up. 'You can stop pumping now. It's moderating a little. We're sailing.'

It was foolish to hope. I knew Kenneth. But something must have communicated itself to him, for he shook his head sharply. 'North. With the tide, towards *Dolly*. The transmitter was working well until just before the mast went, and radio is one of my things. Johnson knows just about where we are... I've come for the Aldis.'

My voice did not work very well. I said, 'Ogden?' And Kenneth answered, 'Ogden is dead.'

He talked, and I listened, but I didn't take in much of it. The temporary boom, it seemed, had broken apart, and since there was almost nothing now on deck to give a handgrip, Kenneth had made Ogden fit on a lifeline before crawling along the side deck to fix it. The motion had been pretty bad, and the lifeline was an old one, rust-eaten at each end by the splices. They had found this out, he and Victoria, after the line broke and Ogden, without even a cry, had tumbled sideways like a large bony doll into the sea, the pixie cap fixed on the long, melancholy cranium. The tape had gone with him. The tape, with the conversation between Ogden and Michael Twiss, in which Michael accused Ogden of spying and Ogden had said – what? about me.

Now we should never know what was recorded. For not even Johnson had heard it. I thought, standing in silence beside Kenneth: now the concrete evidence clearing Kenneth and fixing the guilt for *Lysander* on Ogden has gone. All the other evidence against him and against me, was so far circumstantial. And the only real proof – the trick Ogden played on me with the pen and what followed – was seen only by Kenneth and Victoria.

Victoria even yet did not understand it. Victoria was always, in any case, for the underdog. I drew breath and Kenneth said, in an abominable voice, 'Don't. I can't bear it.'

So long as there was the faintest chance that I might not be guilty, Kenneth would have loved and protected me: would even, perhaps, against all his own interest, have destroyed Johnson's tape if he got it from Ogden, unheard.

But not now. He was a man, hell, of Victorian principles.

I didn't try to dissuade him.

Soon after that, the lights of another boat appeared far away and approached dancing, blinkered by the intervening seas. It was a largish boat, a motor cruiser, and coming from the south, not the north where one would expect *Dolly* or *Binkie* to be. Kenneth, roped round the waist, knelt on the coachhouse roof with the Aldis, and after a moment, their signal replied.

Soon they were alongside; a tow rope passed, and a man in yellow oilskins jumped nimbly aboard to belay it. Then one by one we were guided over the rail and on to the other smooth manicured deck, shining like a well-kept street with its wash of storm spray; its windows glistening and spreading the warm golden light from its plate-glass over the heaving, watery wastes.

Rotund in oilskins, the owner trotted out to greet us. 'Madame Rossi! Victoria, my dear! Come in, come in. What an ordeal. What an experience! My, you'll have something to terrify the old folks back home with! Come along. Hot baths. Hot drinks. Then straight to bed with a bottle. Not that kind of bottle, ha! ha! Though I'd say you deserve it. Come along, sir. We've room for you all. Come along; May is waiting inside.'

It was the floating Wimpy Bar. May and Bill Bird with their power yacht *Evergreen*.

18

I lay for a long time after waking in my warm bunk, watching the sunlight from the porthole casting a golden disc, seamed with watery light, on the panelled walls of my room.

It was very still; and only the remotest swaying beneath me betrayed that we were on water, in some Highland harbour no doubt. I felt, as one must feel after childbirth, peaceful and empty and numb. My recollections of arriving the night before were hazed over with heady fantasies of whisky and steam and the warm anaesthetic of bed. I remembered watching Kenneth talking low to Billy Bird and thinking, I was right. He is giving me up, in all the senses there are. That is the kind of man Kenneth is. With another, I might have persuaded this queer pair to help me. I might have got to the mainland and safely away.

At the time, it did not matter because I knew that bodily I could go nowhere. Now, I was sorry; but only a little. In Kenneth, I had found an honest man, who had been my undoing. In Johnson – I face facts; I admit it – I had found a master. I spit. Oh, I spit.

I lay dreaming, until my dreams were dispersed by a voice I knew: Rupert's. Speaking very close, perhaps in the next room, with a porthole open near to mine, it said, 'We played fair.'

And Kenneth's tired and roughened by exposure and shouting replied, 'You call that playing fair?'

Rupert said patiently, 'You must see our side of it, sir. A hell of a lot of people depend on your work. There were other leaks, small ones we did know about. Not your fault, we were convinced, but we never felt we had your full confidence. So, we put you on unscheduled work, and took certain other precautions. And candidly, sir—'

'What?' said Kenneth's voice sharply.

'You didn't make it too easy.'

He hadn't. He had protected me all along; and it had led to the *Lysander*. No wonder, poor Kenneth, you vanished from Rose Street when you found the flat had been bugged by your own people. Kenneth said now, curtly, 'You didn't make it easy for her, either. Hounding her... Spying on her... The only rules she knows are the hard ones she's been made to live by. Now what chance has she got?'

Rupert said quietly, 'You told us the truth about her yourself, sir. First thing this morning.'

'I know. Of course I did. I had to – once I knew what the truth was for certain.'

'It may reassure you to know that we gambled on that.' That was Johnson's voice, rougher too than I remembered it. Of course *Dolly* had also been sailing all night, with Hennessy and Rupert and Johnson on board. Johnson went on. 'You and Tina both wanted the tape for your various reasons. It seemed likely that, having got you together, Ogden would exorcize his anger by telling you all about Tina. Obviously, his powers of persuasion would be greater than mine.'

Kenneth said slowly, 'So you meant us to join Ogden on *Seawolf*?'

'Which would fall apart, in the classic phrase, if the termites stopped holding hands. Yes, it was intended. For the risks I made you run, I apologize. But Christ, Holmes! The risks moral and ethical you were running made tonight's big thrills look pretty small beer... What got into you? Oh, no need to answer. Tina Rossi got into you. And despite this rugged exterior of poor-quality talc, I assure you that after a week of her company, I can quite understand.'

I said aloud, 'Thank you, Master.' The efficient, dispassionate voice ran straight on.

'It took them a long time to dig Tina Rossi out of your private life; and having dug her, they flung her at me...' There was a pause. Then Johnson went on. 'I said I was responsible for the *Lysander*. In fact, I'm responsible for you. I'm the unofficial witch doctor in this bloody outfit. I've no commitments and no boss and no office. But if a key man, somewhere, develops unsavoury habits and starts throwing off stress signs like a Catherine wheel, I'm the bloke they ask to cruise around, painting, before the gunmen have to start moving in. Then, sometimes, the gunmen never need to move in... As when you told us the truth about Tina, of your own accord now.'

'And if I hadn't told you?' asked Kenneth. The tidy, scientific mind.

'Use your imagination,' said Johnson shortly. 'In any case, we had our own evidence long before then. There's a fellow in Stornoway lit up like a Christmas tree with gold teeth and diamonds who's told us all we wanted to know about Tina Rossi... I knew her history, of course: she made it her trademark. The rich little poor girl who can't cry, who feels nothing, who has worked hard and earned her rewards without treading on anyone's toes.

'I know that, left alone, you feel you could have given her the heart she has lost. I wonder in fact, if you could. You said something just now to Rupert about not making it easy for Tina. But that isn't the best way for Tina. The best way is to make it hard; and that is what we did, Rupert and I, through all that voyage with *Dolly*. Innocently or not, she was your main worry, we thought. So we set out to discover what she was like; and then to teach her a little about herself. It sounds damned presumptuous. It nearly succeeded. If it *had* succeeded, she would have confessed to clear and save you. But there wasn't quite enough time, or I hadn't quite got what it takes... or *she* hadn't quite got what it takes. It flopped, anyway.'

Rupert's voice, defending the prestige of his master, broke in against the almost tangible barrier of Johnson's intention. 'She was hard as bloody nails and you know it,' said Rupert, my god-like golden friend Rupert. 'As it was, we were afraid, sir, she'd make you her scapegoat. By eavesdropping in the Land Rover, Johnson put paid to that. But that's not all. She'd have killed Michael Twiss before Ogden did, if she had got to him first, that night on Rum.'

'Michael Twiss? Why Michael Twiss?' Kenneth's voice was distracted.

'Michael and she were in the blackmail thing together.' Johnson had stepped in, quietly, to break the news to the patient. Dear Johnson. 'Selling and photographing papers was her racket solely, however. Twiss didn't know about it, but she felt it would be convenient to land the blame on his corpse. She had a certain amount of justification in that Twiss had shown distinct signs of wanting to do the same thing to her. She didn't see the logic of amassing a small fortune to have Michael Twiss walk away with it.'

'She could have had police protection. She could stop him stealing, by law.'

'She could. She tried to safeguard her life, actually, by closing her deposits against him. But the final outcome of any legal case might not have sustained her.'

He paused. He did not, unfortunately, drop dead. He said, 'You know the story of how she met Michael Twiss and he became her musical manager? She never told all of it, and neither did he: it would have destroyed the *diva*'s elegant image. But he made one condition, the far-sighted Michael Twiss, when he first became this young, untried girl's impresario. In the greatest possible secrecy, he married her. Michael Twiss and Tina Rossi were husband and wife.'

There was a long silence. I listened, but Kenneth made no response I could hear. He was probably, like Rupert, rolling over the name on his tongue. Tina Twiss. Damn them. *Damn them to hell.*

I had one other visitor that morning, as I lay sipping my coffee: Victoria. Slipping round the door, dressed in some unsuitable pink chiffon thing of May Bird's, her hair still uncombed, her feet bare, she stood asking silent permission and then curled up on the chair by my bunk, her hands childishly folded, her gaze childishly direct. She had been crying. 'I'm sorry,' she said.

'I'm sorry too. I knew Ogden wouldn't kill you. It was just a test.'

She said, 'He was sick, you know. His people were rotten to him. They set him up with the bare ribs of *Seawolf,* and just dared him to get on with it. He hated them – and all the people with money to spend… He loved his boat,' added Victoria, her voice thickening. 'That was the really good part for him. And he got on well with everybody round the coast. They laughed at him, but they liked him. He always had a girl around you know, but he wasn't interested in us. Just someone he could order around, who would wash his socks and rub his chest when he got his bronchitis… He was getting a lot better with me, I thought. You can't blame him. I don't blame anyone… What are you going to do?' asked Victoria.

I don't know what I should have answered. No, that is not true. I do. But I didn't get the chance. For the door opened and Rupert appeared, and said briskly and formally, 'Good morning. Victoria, Dr Holmes wants you. Madame Rossi—'

'Rupert?' I said. 'Tell me, *is* there a proper bulkhead between this cabin and the next?'

He looked much older than he had done, sailing *Dolly*. He said, still formally, 'No. It's just a partition. Johnson thought…'

'I know just what Johnson thought. And did you think I was as hard as bloody nails, darling Rupert,' I continued sweetly, 'when holding my hand back on *Dolly*? I'm beginning to think Johnson's the only ethical person among you— Don't go. There's one thing I must ask you.'

'Ask Johnson.' He already had one foot out of the door.

'No, I want to ask you. Who won?'

He was careful. 'Who won what?'

'Who won the race. The race, you idiot. You had a five thousand bet on with Hennessy.'

'Oh.' He had totally forgotten. 'I don't know. Didn't we abandon it? *Seawolf*'s out of it anyway, using her motor and being towed in the end. *Dolly* didn't use her engine, except for the bits outside the race at Lochgair and South Rona. It was too damned rough last night: we got way off her, not on – and I don't think *Binkie* did. Or *Symphonetta*.'

'*Symphonetta*? But we left her at anchor off Rum. Surely you brought Hennessy back with you on *Dolly*!'

'Yes, we did. But the three boys evidently thought they ought to keep up with the old man. They sailed *Symphonetta* hell for leather after us, and came in damned nearly…'

A curious expression had overspread Captain Glasscock's tanned face. I said encouragingly, 'Yes? You came in this morning, after daybreak? By the way, where are we?'

'Tobermory. On the island of Mull. Yes. We came in, all sort of together. We'd all stayed hove-to more or less during the storm, and then *Evergreen* had radioed that she'd pick you up—'

'*Evergreen?* Had she got Dr Holmes's SOS?'

'Yes, of course,' said Rupert with some praiseworthy reluctance. 'The Birds are colleagues of Johnson's – did nobody tell you? We'll be taking you off in about an hour – a boat's coming from Oban. Anyway...' He returned to his decimating thought. 'So when the storm moderated, we went on rather together. *Dolly* sailed well: we got in just ahead of *Binkie,* and *Symphonetta* a little behind. And...

'And I've just remembered,' said Rupert simply. 'There was a bang as we came into harbour. I thought someone had tripped over a nail in the pier.'

'It was the winning gun,' I offered.

'It must have been,' said the good captain blankly. And a haze of dim, innocent pleasure surrounding him, he went out the door.

I can do this so simply with boys. But then, Johnson wasn't a boy.

An hour later, dressed in my Ricci suit and sheared beaver jacket sent over from *Dolly,* I stepped out on deck. Below me was *Evergreen*'s speedboat, with two discreet plain clothes men in her, waiting. And over there the ship which would take me to Oban and then to the south for public exhibition and trial.

It need not worry me now, the *Suor Angelisa* I was to do in November with Tolliati, who will not believe his leading oboe is sharp. I did not have to concern myself about the mosquitoes at the Caracalla baths or the long flight to Sydney next year.

Equally, I should not hear from my audiences that year, or the following year, or perhaps ever again, that silence after the *Aushaltung,* when I have finished singing and for seconds, worshipping, they withhold the intrusion of their applause.

I should now be famous as any gutter-child might contrive to be famous. I had made a fatal mistake.

I looked around me. It was high noon and beautiful; the trees and hills all washed green by the storm. From a blue, empty arch the sun blazed down on the bay, and like a flock of silver-toed birds left its track on it. A small class of yachts, at first a thicket of slivers against the deep trees, turned, and became a scatter of slit triangles as they made for their mark. A big steam yacht lay still closed and asleep, with a solitary seaman in overalls swabbing the deck.

There was *Symphonetta*, with her speedboat gone. Hennessy and the rest would be on shore. The boys had shown their mettle and would be proud of it: he might even be proud, with reluctance, of them. Some of his misconduct he had paid for, in diamonds.

And there was *Binkie*. Evidence of the Buchanans' stormy passage was all about: bunk cushions and mattresses drying lay lashed and neatly ranged from back to front of her decking, and strange flags of teacloth and towel flew from her rigging. Her bowspit was broken and I saw a tangle of wire still to be mended on deck. She had not got off lightly after all on her self-imposed mission. No one need ever know, I supposed, how tamely the Navy had considered it. Her scars would speak for themselves.

I stirred, and the single man standing waiting for me by the companionway, far down *Evergreen*'s spotless bow, stirred and straightened as well. I had left this to the last, this encounter with Johnson. He had told me indirectly that morning most of what I wanted to know.

It was a morning, I thought, for Sortilège. I had put my hair up in the way Michael had taught me, when I could not have the help of Janine. It was bleached and sticky with salt, but good enough against the tan of my skin. On my suit was a doctor bird in uncut stones and enamel: I had a pearl and enamel dome ring to match. I wondered, as I walked slowly towards him, if Johnson had begun yet to realize what he had done.

He did not seem to have changed. The black hair, the eyebrows, the thick woolly pullover and the glassed-in verandah of his face, on which the sun shone in two baffling discs of white light: these were the same. I pinned down, fleetingly, my abomination of these ungainly, mirror-like glasses. They were ungentlemanly. As I came up to him, he said, 'What is your real name?'

'It is Valentina Lakowski. Or Twiss,' I said, to deny him the pleasure of adding it. 'For the charge sheet?'

'For the charge sheet. Don't hope, Tina,' said Johnson. 'There's too much now piled up against you. Between us, I'm afraid we have silenced your voice.'

'I shall still have my voice. Other people won't be able to hear it, that's all,' I said. 'It was a Judas kiss, then, that night in Edinburgh?'

He appeared, damn him, to rake his memory. Then, 'No,' he said. 'That was pure sex and champagne bubbles. I didn't know you were in the opposite team – not for certain – at least until we got to Lochgair.'

'Why Lochgair?'

'I wirelessed headquarters from *Evergreen*. They told me a man had been seen leaving the flat just about the time Chigwell's murderer bolted in Rose Street. They gave me his description. And it didn't tally with your description at all.'

'So that's how you traced Gold-tooth to *Vallida*?' I said. I'd wondered. But of course, someone would have been watching the Rose Street flat all the time. Poor, stupid Kenneth. 'I suppose Chigwell was one of your people too?' I said. 'I always wondered why that body never appeared in the headlines.'

'He was, but Gold-tooth, as you called him, didn't know it until he'd killed him, in pure mistake for Holmes, who had left shortly before. It was only while he was tidying up and preparing to fake suicide that Gold-tooth found Chigwell's papers and photograph, which made it pretty clear who he was. And then, Kenneth's note pointed pretty clearly to an imminent visit by you.

'Gold-tooth hadn't meant to compromise you. As soon as you'd gone, he came back and got rid of the body. The hanger, I must admit, I took to Rhu all by myself. I underrated your nerve. And I salute your nerve, Tina. You might have pulled your chestnuts out of the fire right from the start if your husband had been just a little less greedy. If he had restrained himself from blackmailing Dr Holmes without telling you. It was a damned nuisance to me, I may mention. For while Michael was breaking his neck to prevent you and Holmes from getting together, I was breaking mine to bring it about. We had to know whether Holmes was mixed up with you in the spying or not.'

The glasses flashed. 'In the event, of course, it was all very clear. What I overheard in the Land Rover settled it, even without the tape recording in Rum.'

'Poor Kenneth,' I said automatically. Through the D's of his bifocals he was watching not me, but the gulls. 'I really tried not to hurt him. I did my best to get hold of that tape.'

'I know you did,' said Johnson mildly. 'And you'll be relieved to know that it's safe. I loaded the machine at Kinloch Castle that night with a dummy one, in case someone quixotic or criminal made a snatch for it. So the evidence exonerating Kenneth is quite intact. Also the evidence against yourself... But it was pretty clear long before that, that you didn't want Gold-tooth caught, for example, because he was on the same side as yourself. Otherwise you'd have told both Kenneth and me what happened that night on the *Vallida*. It would have touched Kenneth to know how much you valued him; and we could have had Gold-tooth chased and your diamonds recovered in one piggish stroke. He had another pen-bomb and a revolver on board, by the way, as well as his little mine crate, tucked away in the stores. He was a professional, that one.'

'I noticed,' I snapped, 'that you didn't risk touching Kenneth too much by telling him I had tried to buy off his life.'

'No,' Johnson admitted. 'It puzzles me yet why you did. After all, your own principals wanted Holmes out of the way, both to take the blame for all the security leakages and to stop his advanced work. Yet you didn't want him murdered, did you? I wonder why? Because he still had your letters, perhaps. Or because, if you could shift all the blame on to Twiss, and also disperse any of Holmes's own misgivings, you might contrive to continue your career, with his love and his secrets as well? It was obviously vital to get to him. One fine day he might come to his senses, and think it important to tell someone to whom he gave the second lab key in Nevada.'

I liked Johnson. 'Go on,' I invited.

He was looking straight at me, through the long and short focus. 'You are enjoying it. I'm not.'

'Why not?' I said. 'Another success for you. I don't want your pity. If I've made a mistake, I can pay.' I paused. 'Find a nice girl for Kenneth,' I said.

Slowly, Johnson lifted one hand and took off his glasses. Underneath was a tired human face. 'Poor Kenneth. But the instinct was right. The instinct that brought you together. He was the fire you needed to warm your hands at. But he was the one who got burnt.'

It was tiresome to have Kenneth talked of as if he were in knickerbockers, but there was no time to wrangle. I said, 'We should have had longer on *Dolly*.'

'Yes. I tend to think so, too,' said Johnson. 'For a number of reasons. This among them.' He had replaced his glasses.

'This' was something square, wrapped in brown paper. He slipped the coverings off, and extended it.

It was my portrait, now vividly finished. It was my head and shoulders and clasped hands as I reclined on the tweed cushions of *Dolly*, a rum and lemon provided by Lenny to hand, while the blue sky and still bluer sea were racing behind. My hair was unpinned and stirred in pale shining folds on my shoulders, my dress was chiffon, my emeralds glowed in the sun.

But it was the face that arrested you. The young bones, the supple sweetness of Gilda had changed with the crisp strokes of paint upon paint. The nose, so deliciously shortened, had gained a shadow hinting at its true length; the eyes were not misty, but liquid and cool; the mouth, beautifully drawn, was the trained mouth of a singer.

It was my own face, the face I was born with. The face I cannot escape.

I looked up at the flashing bifocals, and I smiled, a wide, pretty smile; and I thanked him for his help and his care and his beautiful painting and then, packed, I set off downstairs. I set off downstairs as I had done, over and over in childhood. To the nameless persons waiting below.

Also available

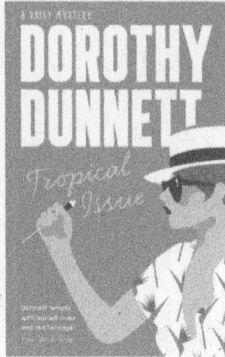

Tropical Issue
(A Dolly Mystery, Book 1)

Rita, a small, tough Scottish make-up artist, is on Madeira trying to find out who killed Kim-Jim, an American make-up supremo. Also anchored off the island is *Dolly*, the yacht of Johnson Johnson, with whom she teams up.

Rita's fighting spirits are aroused despite her danger. She is not one for quitting, even when she learns she is caught up in an international drug-smuggling ring.

But she also discovers that dealing with the maddeningly enigmatic Johnson Johnson is, by no stretch of the imagination, plain sailing.

OUT NOW!

Preview

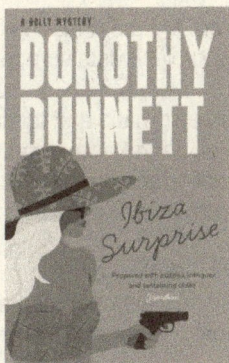

Ibiza Surprise
(A Dolly Mystery, Book 3)

When Sarah Cassells, a young British woman who has just completed her training as a chef, hears of her father's violent death on Ibiza, she refuses to believe it is suicide.

She goes to Ibiza to investigate and becomes involved with an art dealer; with two beautiful jetsetters; with her brother's strange predicament; with a remarkable American woman who is not all that she seems – and with Johnson Johnson, the mysterious portrait painter who shows up on his yacht, *Dolly*.

As Ibiza prepares to celebrate Holy Week with the traditional processions, events become more and more macabre...

COMING SOON

About the Dolly mystery series

The Dolly mystery thrillers feature undaunted heroines in far-flung locations and plot twists sure to surprise.

In the background is the enigmatic and taciturn Johnson Johnson – famous portrait painter, secret agent and fixer of people's lives. Also an accomplished yachtsman, he's never far from his gaff-rigged ketch, *Dolly*, where much of the action takes place.

Yet the real focus of each adventure is the female narrator and protagonist. Singer, chef, doctor, astronomer, nanny or make-up artist, each is self-assured, independent, and whip-smart.

Dorothy Dunnett wrote the Dolly novels between 1968 and 1992, in non-chronological order of the story. The series is now re-published in chronological order of the story.

The full series –
Tropical Issue
Rum Affair
Ibiza Surprise
Operation Nassau
Roman Nights
Split Code
Moroccan Traffic

About the author

Dorothy Dunnett (1923–2001) gained an international reputation as a writer of historical fiction. She moved genres and turned to crime writing with the acclaimed Dolly books, also known as the Johnson Johnson series. She was a trustee of the National Library of Scotland, and a board member of the Edinburgh International Book Festival. In 1992 she was awarded an OBE for her services to literature. A leading light in the Scottish arts world and a renaissance woman, Dunnett was also a professional portrait painter and exhibited at the Royal Scottish Academy on many occasions.

Note from the Publisher

To receive background material and updates on further titles in the
Dolly mystery series, sign up at farragobooks.com/dolly-signup